Pins & Needles

Laurinda Wallace

Cover Design and Photo by Annie Moril

Author Photo by Reign Photography

ALL RIGHTS RESERVED

This is a work of fiction. Any references to real events, businesses, organizations, and locales are intended only to give the fiction a sense of reality and authenticity. Any resemblance to actual persons, living or dead is coincidental.

God wrought for us this scene beyond compare
But one man's loving hand protected it
And gave to his fellow man to share.

Sara Evans Letchworth
Plaque at Letchworth State Park

CHAPTER 1

Cars jammed the Clarks' driveway, and ladies in jeans and T-shirts tromped up the front steps of the home. Theresa Clark stood ready to open the door, allowing the female horde into her living room. Her husband, Bob was in the process of slipping out the back door. He'd announced a drive to Letchworth Park after receiving notification of the impending executive summit. Now he was off to enjoy "the burgeoning display of arboreal splendor only revealed in October." Theresa sighed at his dramatic exit. He was reading John Greenleaf Whittier of late and had started spouting colorful, poetic descriptions in the last week, which she found puzzling.

"Girls, come on in," Theresa said, herding the friends into the kitchen, while watching her husband's car disappear under the red-and-yellow maple canopy overhanging the street.

Coffee was ready, as were apple-cinnamon muffins fresh from the oven. Their irresistible fragrance drew the women to the counter, a couple wasting no time slathering butter on the warm muffins.

"I have some pictures you all need to see before we go over to Lulu's." Theresa placed her phone on the kitchen table. "You won't believe how bad it is now. Why, six months ago, you could still sit in the kitchen. I'd be surprised if a cat could make it through the mess. I was afraid of falling into something, never to be found again."

She swiped the screen and pointed to a photo.

"Oh my stars!" Suzie Richardson exclaimed.

"I told you," Theresa said. "Look at the next two."

The women groaned in concert, and Gloria Minders shook her head sadly.

"Poor Lulu. She's really out of control. Where does she find all the money to keep buying fabric and sewing machines?"

"I think she's buying stuff on eBay and other online sites," Suzie replied, brushing muffin crumbs from her fingers.

"She'll run through all of Ed's money if she keeps on. Remember, she retired from her accounting position too," remarked Margaret Mason. "Theresa, have you called her brother?"

"I did yesterday. He's not in good health, and neither is his wife. He can't do anything—so he says. Plus, Lulu hasn't ever been very close to them. You know how she is. They're not going to help and don't want any part of it. It's up to us. We have to do an intervention."

Gloria nodded. "Lulu's burned bridges with her family and Ed's, such as it is, which is sad. When Ed died in April, she ran them all off after the funeral. She's got it into her head that they were only interested in her money. It's a shame she and Ed never had children. She's really all alone."

Murmurs of sympathy and more nodding heads bobbed over the photos.

"I'm surprised Lulu even let you in, Theresa," Margaret said, plunking herself into a chair.

"I am too. Especially the way she's been the last couple of months. She keeps the curtains drawn and hardly goes anywhere. So I took her an apple tart and asked her about donating a quilt for the Christmas bazaar next month. I took the pictures while asking her what colors she might use for the quilt. We wandered through the fabric canyons, looking at everything until she decided she wouldn't be able to finish it in time."

"How are we going to do this?" Suzie inquired, snatching another muffin from the plate.

"I think we need to tell her the truth," Gloria said firmly. "She's crowding herself out of her home—it's not safe anymore. She has to stop buying stuff, or Social Services will get involved."

"You mean we'll blow her in to them?" Margaret asked.

"That's exactly it," Theresa confirmed. "It's already a health hazard. If she fell, or one of those towers of cloth fell on her, she'd be trapped—maybe for days or worse."

"Does it smell?" Suzie wrinkled her nose.

"Well, not too bad." Theresa winced. "But it's not all that clean. And you know how Lulu kept that house while Ed was alive. You could eat off the floor. Now you can't find the floor."

"All right. If we're going to do this, we might as well get it over with." Margaret sighed and finished off the crumbly muffin with streusel topping. "I'm probably going to regret it, but we need to see if a little shock treatment will snap her out of this funk."

"It's worth a try before calling in outside help. I'd hate to have strangers take over without our at least trying," Gloria said.

"I know. That's what friends do—point out you're going crazy before they carry you off to the funny farm." Suzie laughed glumly.

"Since she's done this in the space of less than a year, we may have caught the problem in time," Theresa added, her expression hopeful.

The faces of the other women weren't quite as optimistic.

***

The convoy of sedans parked on Oak Street in front of Lulu's colonial, a green-shuttered, two-story house. The detached garage's door was halfway up, revealing tables piled with blankets, stacks of plastic storage containers, and a jumble of sewing machines. Dark garbage bags bulged under the tables. The women exited their cars, staring at the chaos. Theresa hadn't checked the garage on her previous visit. The door had been completely down, hadn't it? Now, it couldn't be shut all the way. What else lay in wait here?

Gloria, as the pastor's wife, took the lead and rapped on the door. The others huddled together, looking uncertainly at one another. No one answered. Gloria knocked again, calling for Lulu. After a polite space of time, and no Lulu, Gloria turned the doorknob.

"It's unlocked," she said, pushing through the mass of boxes. She was barely able to scrape back the clutter.

"Let me see if I can find her," Theresa said.

It had been at her urging that they were there. The least she could do was locate poor Lulu. The house smelled stale and a little rancid. It was hard to put a finger on what the odor was.

"Lulu, where are you? You've got company," she called out.

The faint sound of the TV led the women further into the maze of boxes, stacks of fabric, and cartons of scissors, thread, and all manner of sewing paraphernalia.

"Come on, Lulu, you've got company," Theresa yelled.

"What? Who's there?"

"It's Theresa. The girls and I came over to visit you."

Lulu, dressed in a blue chenille robe and matching scuffs, emerged from what was the living room area. Taller than the average woman, she had a thin, long nose, almost beak-like. Her straight brown hair had a streak of white on the left side and fell limply to her shoulders.

"What are you all doing here?" she demanded, hands on narrow hips.

"We've come to talk to you, Lulu," Gloria said, drawing up all of her five-foot-two as straight as she could. Every gray hair was in place, and her warm, friendly eyes focused on the disheveled woman.

"What if I don't want to talk with you?"

"We're your friends. We want to help you," Gloria said.

"What for? I don't need any help."

"Lulu! Of course, you need help. Look around you," Theresa exclaimed. "What's happened to you? This place is ... is ..."

"It's just the way I want it, so please go," Lulu Cook said coldly, pointing toward the door.

"Your problems have overwhelmed you, and we want to help you get back to normal," Margaret urged.

"Problems? You think I have problems? You'll have a few unless you leave, and now." Lulu's eyes blazed.

She stepped toward the women, who scrambled to locate the path that would lead them outside.

"I'm afraid we can't," Theresa said, holding up a hand to stop the others.

"If you were my friends, you'd leave me alone. Alone." The woman's face crumpled, tears forming in her eyes.

"Oh, Lulu. You've been through a bad time. We want to help you. You can't live like this. It's dangerous," Gloria commiserated. She edged her way through the mess and put an arm on Lulu's shoulder. "Let's talk about it. Come on, dear."

Gloria steered a sobbing Lulu toward the sound of the TV, with the rest of the group trailing after.

CHAPTER 2

Gracie threw a tennis ball for Haley and Max in her backyard. Marc ambled onto the patio, rubbing his hair, which tousled it quite attractively, she thought as she watched her soon-to-be-husband.

"Tire them out yet?" he asked.

"I think they could go all day," she answered, tossing the fuzzy yellow ball once more.

Haley, her black Lab, slid through slick leaves, edging out Max, Marc's German shepherd, by mere inches to grab the prize. Haley ran off, playfully chomping on the ball, daring Max to take it from her. Such a flirt!

"Any word on your clearance?" Gracie asked, tucking curly auburn hair behind her ears.

"Not yet. I'm not sure this will work out," he said glumly.

"They said it would take time, right?"

"Right. But it's been almost two months. I think there's a problem because of my half-brother."

"Ohhh."

"Any relative in a federal prison, especially on a domestic terrorism conviction, is a problem for a security clearance."

Gracie kicked at the multicolored leaves covering the lawn. "You told them up front though."

"Yeah. They knew the story the day they offered the job."

Gracie nodded, remembering that intense conversation. The job offer from the Defense Advantage Company or DACO, which was a Department of Defense contractor, had made her head spin at the time. The generous salary was surprising, but the prolonged time away from home and the possible danger of the job hadn't been what she'd expected when Marc had applied for a corporate security position. How could she stand in the way of such an exciting career move? She had covertly prayed for the sheriff's department to fix its budget woes and beg him to come back. At least he would be working in the same country, rather than constantly traveling to parts unknown—locations that she wouldn't be privy to. So far, the answer was negative on going back to being a deputy. Marc had been immediately concerned when he'd learned that a secret security clearance was necessary. His half-brother was sitting in federal prison in Terre Haute, Indiana. And would be for the rest of his natural life.

"Why don't you call them and find out what the status is?" It seemed like a reasonable course of action. Why stew about it?"

"Not today. I'll give it another week or so."

"All right then."

She wasn't going to push it. Besides, there were a few errands to run for their wedding, which was less than two weeks away.

"Don't forget. We have a counseling session with Pastor Minders at two, and we need to stop by the Glen Iris to pay the balance on the reception."

"Are you sure we can't elope?" Marc's puckered brow and lopsided smile made her laugh.

"Absolutely not. We'll only have about twenty-five people. It's a nice dinner at the Glen Iris. No fuss, no muss."

"You say that, but ..."

"Gracie! Gracie, are you home? Jim said you were up here!" an imperious, all-too-familiar voice bellowed.

Gracie cringed. What was her cousin, Isabelle the She-wolf of Deer Creek, doing here?

"Come through the gate. We're exercising the dogs," came Gracie's unenthusiastic response.

The squeaky gate latch announced Isabelle's entrance into the backyard. Max barked and ran toward Isabelle, who threw up her hands in an effort to protect herself.

"Max! *Pfui! Hier,*" Marc commanded the shepherd.

Max immediately stopped and trotted to Marc, who had the dog lie down. Haley greeted Isabelle with a slapping tail against her wheat-colored ensemble of a pencil skirt and blazer. An infinity scarf of navy blue encircled the svelte, blonde's neck.

"Haley, come over here," Gracie said, shaking her head. No doubt black hair would be all over Isabelle.

"Well, at least Marc's dog behaves. When are you going to do something about her?" Isabelle carped, pointing a French-manicured finger at the Lab.

"Good grief, she just wants to say hello. Did you need something?" Gracie strained the question through her teeth.

She could only hope that Isabelle was soliciting a donation for a charity or wanted her to help with some fundraiser. A quick writing of a check or a firm "no" should send her away.

"I'm here to help with the wedding, of course. You've been avoiding me for a month."

Marc's eyes widened. Gracie's mouth went dry.

"I haven't been avoiding you. It's been so busy. Uh ..."

What could she say? She *had* been avoiding her cousin and felt quite pleased with herself that she'd heretofore been successful. Gracie absolutely didn't want Isabelle's help with the wedding, her advice, or her sniffing disapproval of Gracie's plans.

Isabelle ignored her excuses, and raised an eyebrow and looked at the backyard, as if evaluating it. "But, as you know, people seek me out for these special occasions. The details of a wedding require expertise, a certain flair for a really elegant event. Even though my schedule is jammed, I have cleared my calendar for you. I'm ready to relieve you of what must be an overwhelming chore."

Gracie felt her jaw drop. What was Isabelle smoking? An anger, coming up from her toes, revealed itself on her face in what she sensed from the heat rushing to her face was an unflattering beet-red hue.

She took a deep breath and released it slowly. "Isabelle, I assure you," she began in a voice of barely controlled fury, "'your expertise,' as you call it, is *not* required. Honestly, everything is fine and under control. You just need to show up with What's-his-name and witness our vows."

"You're not thinking clearly, Gracie," Isabelle countered in that sing-song, patronizing tone that Gracie had known and loathed since childhood. "This yard is an embarrassment. How will it be ready in time? I can arrange for my gardener to come in and do something with this ... this ..." She waved her hand at the yard in a deprecating gesture.

Marc's phone rang, and with a look of a condemned man who'd been saved from the noose, he retreated into the house to take the call.

"This yard is perfectly fine," Gracie growled.

She looked around at the fencing that enclosed the space. The white picket fence was new last year. Multicolored mums and fountain grass filled the flowerbeds. Orange nasturtiums sprawled around the remnants of summer flowers, leaves brown and flowerless. The maples and white birches flamed with color. It was the perfect place for her nuptials. The yard needed raking, but nothing else. If it rained, they'd be married on the covered patio, darn it all.

Isabelle's eyes glittered with steely determination. "There's always room for improvement, and I'm sure you want Marc's mother and sister to be suitably impressed with everything. They are coming all the way from Indiana, after all."

Gracie closed her eyes, hoping against hope that when she opened them, Isabelle would have vanished. It was not to be, naturally. Isabelle strode down the edge of the flowerbeds, clucking and shaking her head.

"Indiana isn't exactly on the other side of the planet. Besides, I'm not trying to impress anyone. It's a casual, outdoor wedding, with close family and a few friends. Simple is what we both want, and that's what will happen. Really, Izzy, don't worry about any of this. It's all under control. *My* control."

"Well, if that's the way you feel. I was just trying to help," she bristled. "Oh, Haley! Leave me alone!" She pushed the sniffing Haley away from her skirt. "I have a house to show anyway. See you at the wedding."

Isabelle offered a royal wave and disappeared through the gate. Disaster averted momentarily. Gracie looked at her watch. It was almost time to leave for their counseling session, and she needed to change.

CHAPTER 3

Theresa carried a plastic container full of nicely cut quilt blocks to the overstuffed garage. Lulu had given permission to move a few things to make it easier to move from room to room in the house. She had tried to throw out a couple of dingy and threadbare pillows, but Lulu had refused. Her anxious friend watched the crew of women like a Doberman guarding her property. At least, they'd made it a little safer. Lulu was deep in grief, feeling abandoned by her late husband and her distant family. Ed, God rest his soul, had plunged over the bank of a remote road in the Adirondacks on an early spring fishing trip. The car had burned up. The intense fire had incinerated all of poor Ed, except for a dental bridge that had been discovered a few feet away from the vehicle. That had been the only bit of Ed that could be identified. To make it worse, the accident hadn't been found for several days. A horrible thing!

Theresa sighed and plopped the container on top of three other bins filled with what looked like finished quilts. Maybe, if they were in good condition, Lulu could be talked into donating them to the shelter in Batavia or to the Red Cross. Just getting rid of one container would feel like success today. Lulu had always been a generous person, happily making quilts or cute baby hats. Thank God she didn't knit too!

Theresa brushed a strand of gray hair from her eyes, bending to make a quick count of the handmade quilts. She'd have to wash them though. Who knew the last time Lulu had washed anything? There were four beautiful patchwork quilts encased safely in the tub. The smell of lavender rushed to greet her nose as she opened the lid. The quilts were in perfect condition—clean and smelling wonderful. Now to see if Lulu would part with any of them.

"These are so nice, Lulu. Wouldn't you like to donate them to the bazaar or Red Cross?"

Lulu studied the patchwork color explosions Theresa laid out in front of her. She stood on the side steps of the house, pulling her robe tightly around her body.

"Those are some of my best work. I plan to enter one or two of them in a quilt competition."

"Are you sure? The bazaar needs really good items if we're going to make this year's goal," Theresa wheedled.

The look of doubt in Lulu's eyes didn't bode well for a donation.

"I don't think so. Just put them back in the garage," Lulu said firmly and trudged up the steps, disappearing inside.

Gloria appeared immediately with a worried look.

"I think we'd better call it a day," she said. "Lulu is pretty agitated. I'm afraid she'll just pile things up again and trap herself in the living room."

"You're probably right. Did Margaret or Suzie talk her into getting dressed and going out to eat?"

"They're working on it now," Gloria answered. "I don't think she will though. It's going to have to be baby steps with her."

"Bob said we'd end up calling Social Services, but I hate to have them involved after only one try."

"I agree. There's food in the fridge, and the bathroom is okay. Her bedroom is a sight; she can only get in the bed from one side. But I was expecting worse. Here, let me help you put that tub back in the garage."

Gloria lifted one end, while Theresa grasped the other handle. They shoved the containers back a few more inches to gain clearance to shut the door the entire way. Theresa pulled the rope to close the door, both women watching it squeak past the plastic towers.

"Aha! Made it!" Gloria said, smiling.

Theresa breathed a sigh of relief. That was quite enough lifting, pushing, and pulling for one day. She was sure to feel it tomorrow morning.

"Look! Here comes Franny Walczak," Theresa said, spotting a rather fast-moving white-haired woman coming across the street.

Gloria brushed dust, lint, and fabric bits from her Deer Creek Community Church long-sleeved T-shirt and glanced up.

"She doesn't look happy," she said.

Franny wasn't happy in the least. Her cheeks were red, and her mouth was determined.

"I'm glad I caught you," she said breathlessly. "You need to know what's really going on here. I'm ready to call the police."

"What do you mean?" Theresa asked.

"It's Lulu. She's stolen my heirloom quilt." The dumpling-shaped Franny pointed to the garage. "I'm pretty sure she put it in there."

"Really?" Gloria asked. "I can't believe she'd do anything like that."

"Believe it, Gloria. She's been skulking around my yard for months. When I asked her what in the H-E-double hockey sticks she was doing about a month ago, she just ran home without a word."

"Ran? Lulu *ran*? You must be joking!" Theresa shot back, incredulity overwhelming her manners.

She found this beyond hard to believe. In the fifty years she'd known Lulu Cook, running anywhere, even if there was a tornado bearing down on her, wasn't ever a thought in the woman's head.

"Well, it's true. My quilt is gone, and I'll bet you my Social Security check that she's got it hidden in this mess."

"That's a serious accusation," Gloria said. "When did you notice it was missing?"

"After I went to Geneseo today. I keep it in the cedar chest at the foot of the bed. I was putting away the sheets in the chest after I got back, and the quilt was gone." Franny glared at the two women, daring them to challenge her further.

In for a penny, in for a pound, Theresa decided. "Was the house locked?"

"Yes. I always lock it when I go to Geneseo. I don't think the neighborhood's what it used to be."

"Is the extra key still under that rock by the front steps?"

"Well, yes. And Lulu knows where it is. I just want to look in that garage."

Gloria shrugged, and Theresa nodded.

"Sure," she said, yanking the handle to pull the door up.

"Good night nurse!" Franny squeaked, taking in the stacks that filled the space. "She's a loon! I didn't realize it was *this* bad. It'll take weeks to see if my quilt's here."

"She has tons of stuff crammed in here. There's lots of fabric," Theresa said. "I don't know about what's in the back, but she'd never be able to get to those tubs anyway. I did find one full of quilts though."

With a grunt of effort, she eased the tub once again from the stack. Gloria unsnapped the lid for Franny's inspection. The pudgy woman eagerly sorted through the quilts.

"No. It's not here. This is an old quilt that she stole. It's signed by my great-great-great-great-great-grandmother. She made it in 1803. That's the year Deer Creek was incorporated, you know. It's worth a lot of money, plus the sentimental value."

"What are *you* doing here?" a voice demanded angrily from the side steps.

Lulu stood with hands on hips, Margaret and Suzie behind her.

"I came for my quilt, you thief!" Franny snarled, stalking toward the house. "I want it back."

"I don't know what you're talking about," Lulu declared.

Shoving Suzie and Margaret away from the door, she slammed it shut behind them and vanished inside her chaotic lair.

Margaret and Suzie looked quizzically at the trio below.

"I guess I'll have to call the police," Franny muttered, smoothing the sleeves of her pumpkin-colored sweatshirt.

"Give us a chance to look inside," Gloria pleaded. "She's really not herself, and it may be that it's in plain sight."

"Huh? Are you kidding? She's a schemer if I ever saw one. She has it hidden somewhere. If she doesn't fork it over, I can't be held responsible for my actions," Franny declared, looking alternately angry and hurt. "You think you know a person after thirty years of being neighbors."

"But ..." Gloria trotted after Franny, who was making short work of the distance between the houses.

"Never mind," Franny muttered, crossing the street. "I'll take care of it."

Her front door slammed. Gloria stood on the sidewalk, looking between the two houses.

Suzie and Margaret joined Theresa, walking side-by-side across the shaggy lawn to meet Gloria on the sidewalk.

"That went well," Margaret muttered, rolling her eyes.

"No kidding," Suzie retorted. "And Lulu locked her doors. I heard her throw the deadbolt when she went in."

"Fabulous," Theresa said, suddenly feeling quite weary. She looked at her watch. They'd already been there more than two hours. "Want to call it a day? We can try again tomorrow. Gracie and Marc are coming over for supper. I should already be cooking."

"I second that motion," Margaret said, looking back at the garage. "Oh rats! That door is still open."

"I'll get it," Suzie piped up. She scurried to the garage, pulling the door down to meet the ground.

The convoy of sedans moved out, leaving Lulu Cook peering from her front window, while Franny Walczak observed the activity from across the street.

CHAPTER 4

Gracie and Marc stepped into the sunshine of the church's parking lot after an hour of premarital counseling with Reverend Minders. It was helpful, Gracie admitted, but they weren't teenagers or twenty-somethings. Her longtime pastor tended to think of her as one of his own kids who were in the same age bracket. It was their last session though and one more thing to check off the list.

"That wasn't too bad," Marc said, opening the door of his pickup for her.

"You've taken his admonition of 'manners still matter' to heart, I see," Gracie said as she climbed in.

"I wouldn't want to lose the parson's support, milady," he said with a sweeping bow.

He popped into the driver's seat. "Now where to?"

"The Glen Iris. We need to pay the balance on the reception."

"Your wish is my command."

"Oh boy. You may be overdoing it."

"You're so hard to please," he teased. "I'm in a quandary about what behavior is just right."

"Sheesh, Marc." Gracie feigned exasperation. "I'll have to sic my dog on you."

"My dog can take yours any day."

That was probably true. Haley was a lover, but she'd come to Gracie's rescue in a rather dangerous situation a while back and won the day. She didn't know what she'd do without the goofy Lab.

"All right, but you said before we left that you'd had an interesting phone call. That was the one that provided your nicely-timed escape during Isabelle's visit—right?"

"The timing was perfect. It was Investigator Hotchkiss with some sheriff's office news."

"What kind of news?"

"The union found out about the sheriff's decision to eliminate positions because the dispatcher and another deputy filed a complaint. The cutbacks are now under some sort of review."

Marc slowed the vehicle as they drove through Castile and turned onto Park Road East to Glen Iris Road.

"Interesting. Does that mean you'll get a call back then?"

"She wasn't sure right now. But like I said before, the work environment hasn't been the best for a while. We're staying in touch." He slowed again as a tractor chugged up a hill and turned into a barn driveway. "And you'll like this, she's thinking about running for sheriff herself."

"Hey, that *is* interesting."

In Gracie's head, the wheels were spinning out-of-control about the employment possibilities. Even though the investigator and Gracie weren't always on the best of terms, the no-nonsense policewoman thought highly of Marc and had kept in touch with him over the last two months.

"Does that mean you're interested in going back, if they offer you a position?"

"I'm really nervous about not hearing about the clearance from DACO. I know it takes time, but if Jeremy screws it up for me, I don't have any other offers right now."

Gracie nodded. Marc's half-brother, Jeremy, wasn't ever supposed to see the light of day for his part in blowing up a church and a section of a courthouse in Missouri. She had no idea what impact that would have on a government security clearance for Marc and what Defense Advantage would think of this evil man. She shivered, hoping they'd never know him.

After paying the park fee at the Castile entrance, they were caught in the predictable stream of leaf peepers, most of them driving in no particular hurry. With the leaves almost at peak, the park would be even more jammed by the weekend when the annual October Arts and Crafts show began its three-day run. Gracie glanced at her watch. She hoped the manager was available so they could go over the guest list one more time. Finally, they wound their way down the steep hill to the Inn's parking area. The pool with its fountain spouted prettily as groups stood around, taking shots with their cameras and phones.

The manager was on site, which made Gracie's errand easier. She pulled the credit card from her wallet and handed it to the black-haired woman, whose reading glasses rested on the tip of her nose. Marc paced the small room, looking out the windows.

"No other changes then?" the manager asked.

"None, Connie. Everyone has responded. There'll be sixteen prime rib dinners and ten Chicken Florentines."

"That's excellent."

"And my special request? Is that taken care of?" Marc interjected.

The manager looked up and smiled. "Yes. As a matter of fact. You are one very lucky man, in more ways than one," she said, laughing. "Shall I or would you ...?"

"I'll tell her," Marc said, sitting in the chair next to Gracie.

"Tell me what?"

"I know that we agreed to honeymoon at the house, because of everything going on, but Connie just gave me good news. The Cherry Suite with the Jacuzzi and falls view is available for our wedding night. We've been trying to work out an arrangement with the couple who reserved it earlier. I guess the negotiation was successful."

"Oh, Marc! That's wonderful!" Gracie leaned over to meet his lips. "I've always wanted to stay here, but we lived just down the road." She stopped, remembering her late husband, Michael nixing a weekend at the inn.

"It's only the one night," Connie confirmed. "The cancellation for the Beech suite sealed the deal this afternoon. I'm so glad it all worked out, Mr. Stevens."

"Me too. I was sweating bullets on it. There wasn't a plan B. So we're good to go, then."

"We are," the manager said, rising. "I'll see you on your wedding day—just ten days away."

Gracie grabbed Marc's hand. "It's really happening. It's almost like a dream."

"Hopefully not a nightmare," Marc said, leading her toward the door.

***

"You're sure that everything is all set?" Theresa asked her daughter with a soul-piercing look that made grown men cringe.

"Absolutely, Mom. The Glen Iris is taken care of, with a bonus, courtesy of my beloved," Gracie said, giving Marc a meaningful smile.

"You know your mother," Bob Clark chimed in. "She's really unhappy you've handled all of the details yourself. She's not feeling needed at the moment."

"Bob! That's not true. A wedding day should be perfect, and that means details. It's easy to overlook something crucial." Theresa shot her husband a reproving look.

"I get it. Even Isabelle can't handle that she's not involved," Gracie started.

"Poor Isabelle. She really does mean well. If you can, you should let her help with something."

"Really, Mom? Like carry around a guestbook, make some favors? No. We want simple. It is simple. No one is stressed. I myself am quite relaxed." She brushed back a strand of hair nonchalantly to make her point.

"Speaking of stressed, I had an awful afternoon trying to help Lulu Cook with her hoarding problem." Theresa plunked herself on a dining room chair and began dishing out Dutch apple pie.

"Lulu? What's she hoarding?" Gracie asked, eagerly putting a fork in the pie.

"You know she's been a quilter and seamstress for years, but since Ed was killed, she's gone over the edge. She's collecting fabric and quilts, sewing machines, thread, patterns. Good grief! The girls and I were on overload just looking at the stuff stacked in the house and garage."

"Sounds like you need the family involved," Marc said, appreciatively eyeing the large slice of pie Theresa handed him.

"She only has one brother and a sister-in-law, who has a bunch of health issues. They can't help," Bob said. "I say Lulu has a serious mental problem that needs professional help, but your mother is trying to solve everything via the Holy Meddlers Squad."

"Oh," groaned Gracie. "So Margaret, Suzie, and Gloria are in the posse?"

"We're not a squad or a posse, thank you very much. We're her friends and we care about her," Theresa insisted. "But she might be a thief too. Franny Walczak accused her of stealing an heirloom quilt from her today."

"Drama on Oak Street, huh? I'd call Social Services if there's no one to help her," Gracie said. "She might have some serious issues—beyond your capabilities." Gracie lifted the crusty brown sugar topping with her fork, ready to enjoy the treat.

"You never know what will put someone over the edge. I'd recommend getting them involved," Marc added.

"I know," Theresa conceded. "But we decided to give it another go tomorrow. If we don't make progress, we'll have to call somebody."

CHAPTER 5

Oak Street was quiet when Theresa pulled her car to the curb. She stepped to the sidewalk, inhaling the crisp air, which smelled of drying leaves. The sun was shining brightly in a cornflower-blue sky. That early taste of Indian summer made her wonder when snow would make its first appearance. She unzipped the garter stitch cardigan, steeling herself for another round with the stubborn Lulu. She saw Gloria's silver Honda Accent around the corner. At least she wouldn't go it alone. Suzie and Margaret should arrive at any time too.

"Have you been to the door, Theresa?" Gloria asked, slinging her red-patterned Vera Bradley bag onto her shoulder.

"No. I was waiting for reinforcements."

Gloria smoothed her hair and smiled grimly. "We might as well see if she'll let us in."

The sound of a loud male voice caught the women's attention. It was coming from Franny Walczak's Victorian home directly across the street.

"I'll be back tomorrow," the gruff voice stated. "You'd better have it ready when I get here. Make her give it back, or I'll take care of it myself. You know what it means."

A short, stocky man, with a dirty red ball cap stuck on a shock of brown hair, appeared from Franny's backyard and clambered into a road-weary pickup parked in the long driveway.

The women watched the truck loaded with an assortment of lawn equipment back out into the street. "Is that Art?" Gloria asked.

"It must be. I haven't seen him for ages in Deer Creek. I heard he was living in Perry."

The truck made some clunking noises, and the muffler rattled loudly when the man drove down the street. He kept his gaze directly ahead, not acknowledging the women on the sidewalk. Theresa recognized the profile of the man. Art Walczak had broken his nose umping a Little League game years ago, and the crooked contour still testified to the old injury.

"That's Artie," she confirmed.

"The last time I saw him was at least three years ago. I think it was at a fund raiser for the fire department," Gloria remarked. She turned to walk toward Lulu's.

"Could be. He's been under the radar for quite some time. I didn't know Franny and Artie even spoke. Sounds like there's some trouble brewing."

Gloria nodded, looking at the Walczak house and back to Lulu's front sidewalk. Theresa joined her friend. Her churning stomach confirmed the dread she felt anticipating another confrontation with Lulu.

"And here comes Suzie and Margaret," Gloria said lightly. "Strength in numbers."

Lulu answered the door on the first knock, fully dressed in an outfit of brown polyester slacks and a flowered sweatshirt. Her hair was combed and neatly pulled back with barrettes. She appeared to be more like her old self.

"You look nice, Lulu," Gloria commented, accepting the invitation to enter the house.

"Thank you, Gloria," Lulu said, her mouth set resolutely. "You girls all come in here. I want to talk with you."

The group looked at each other, apprehension written on their faces. The path they'd managed to widen yesterday was even wider today. When they reached the living room, Lulu had done some heavy lifting to open up the seating area. The couch and two chairs were cleared of yesterday's junk. The tubs were precariously stacked on the edges of the room and in front of the windows.

"Take a seat. I don't want to waste a lot of time," Lulu said brusquely.

"We're in no hurry," Theresa assured her.

"But I am. I have things to do," Lulu retorted, her eyebrows arched.

"Oh. Of course," Gloria said meekly.

They bunched together on the couch, with Suzie ending up perched on the arm.

"I know you mean well, but I'm doing just fine. I don't need help or people nosing through my things. I happen to enjoy my sewing materials being around. They make me feel good, and for that matter, safe too. Please, don't bother yourselves anymore. It's my house, my life, and if I need help, I'll ask."

The four women stared at their friend, who'd transformed from the pathetic, depressed wretch of the day before to an almost normal Lulu. Theresa stood, and the others followed suit. Lulu's little speech was crystal clear. Margaret was the first to speak.

"Why, we never wanted to butt into your business. We only meant to help you. We were worried about you. I hope you know that."

"Sure. I understand. But just because I want to live a little differently from you doesn't mean you can come in here and mess up things." Lulu sniffed and looked toward the doorway.

"I'm sorry if we've offended you," Gloria began, her face rosy with embarrassment.

"It's okay," Lulu said. "Like I said, I've got things to do."

"Right. Sure," Theresa jumped in. "If there's anything you need, let us know."

Lulu nodded, and the quartet filed out, weaving through the piles to the front door.

Once at the curb, they looked back at the house, and without further conversation, slipped to their cars. Theresa decided that Bob would not need to know about this particular encounter. It would only feed his ego. Why did he have to be right all the time? Just as she opened the car door, Franny hurried down the front porch steps.

"Theresa, wait a minute!" she called.

Failing to catch Gloria before she drove away, Theresa hoped Franny wasn't going to go on about her stolen quilt.

"What's the matter?" she asked, seeing Franny's worried expression.

"Did she throw you out?" Franny was eager for information.

"I think she's making progress on her own."

"Right," she stated skeptically. "Well, she's still a thief. I'm going to call the police on her."

"Are you sure you didn't put the quilt somewhere else?"

"Absolutely not. I've always kept it in the cedar chest at the foot of my bed. It has a lock, and I keep it locked."

Theresa had seen the Stederman family quilt a handful of times over the years. It had been featured in antique quilt exhibitions at the Arts Council in Perry, probably twice if her memory served. The quilt was a beauty, a rare example of *broderie perse*. The Stedermans had apparently been quite well off at the turn of the nineteenth century because only the wealthy had these types of quilts. She remembered a quilt expert explaining that *broderie perse* was a technique that used appliqued designs made from chintz and intricate embroidery. It was exquisite. Flowers and richly embroidered birds were arranged in an elaborate design over the fabric.

There was some delicate beading as well on Franny's one-of-a-kind work of art.

"Has anyone been in your house lately, or did you show the quilt to anyone?" Theresa asked, grasping at straws.

Franny's expression changed to a more pensive one, her brow wrinkled.

"No. No one's been around," she said.

"Oh." Theresa wondered if ex-husbands counted as visitors. "Are you sure?"

Security wasn't exceptionally high anywhere in Deer Creek. Spare keys and garage door codes were given out generously. Artie would certainly know how to enter his former residence if Franny wasn't home. Their relationship had always been contentious, and yesterday's little encounter confirmed it remained so.

Franny rubbed her temple. "There was a woman from the American Quilters Society that called me and then came out to see the quilt a couple of months ago. And some colonial history club was here and took pictures of the quilt about the same time. They had a top-notch photographer working with them on a special article. But groups come out two or three times a year. It's kind of a famous quilt in this area." Franny looked about to burst with pride. Her cheeks were rosy and brown eyes shining.

"How do these people know about the quilt?"

"I'm a member of the American Quilters Society, and the other women had some connection to the Society. AQS wants to display it at the annual show in January. It's one of the best examples of *broderie perse* in the country, you know."

Theresa nodded. "Who was the woman from AQS?"

"I've got her card in the house. Her name was Mildred something or other. I have the card from the colonial history organization too."

"Could I see them?" Theresa knew she was pushing it, but she might as well after the debacle across the street.

"I guess. It has nothing to do with Lulu stealing the quilt though, if that's what you're thinking."

"Maybe not, but they were in your house, right?" Theresa answered, quickly following Franny inside. She still couldn't believe that Lulu would actually break into someone's house to steal.

The house was comfortably shabby, and the smell of orange oil indicated that Franny had been dusting recently. The old woodwork and the hardwood floors gleamed with loving care.

"I put those cards by the phone," Franny said, snatching a pair of reading glasses from the kitchen table.

She sorted through a pile of business cards and drew out a colorful card that featured a patchwork quilt design and another creamy, rich-looking business card.

"Mildred Quested. That was her name. She's the event coordinator for the Society." She pointed to the large antique script on the card. "I really need to call her and tell her I can't show the quilt, maybe not ever."

Theresa looked at the card, turning it over, feeling the weight. It was a good quality cardstock and looked legit. But who knew anymore? The other card read, "Colonial History Guild," and the organization was located in Nunda.

"Well, I guess I'd call the police then. Lulu isn't inclined to let anyone go through her stuff, but if she really stole it, she has to face the consequences."

"I hate to do it, but she's been impossible the last few months. After Ed died, I helped her box up his clothes and things. What a terrible way to go, burning up in a truck." Franny shuddered. "That was hard, but Lulu seemed to be doing all right until June. Something happened, and she started collecting all kinds of sewing stuff. She hardly says 'boo' to me now. I can't figure out if I said something that made her mad. She won't say. But that's no reason to go off your rocker and steal from your neighbor."

Theresa had to agree. "You'd better call today and not let it go any longer. Now, you're sure it's not in the house?"

"No. I've looked all over. It's not here. That quilt is worth over fifty thousand. The last time I had it appraised anyway. I have to get it back."

Theresa's mouth gaped open and then closed quickly. "Fifty thousand? You absolutely have to call the sheriff's department." She had no idea the bedcovering was worth so much. Maybe three or four thousand, but fifty?

Franny's face went a little pale, and she pressed a hand against her heart. "I think I need a pill," she gasped.

"Where are they? Are you all right?" Theresa scanned the counter by the sink, trying to find a prescription bottle.

Franny sat down hard onto a wicker-bottomed chair, gulping in air. "It's the nitroglycerin."

Theresa knocked over an empty plastic tumbler on the counter and sorted through the collection of brown bottles. "Okay, I found it."

She handed the bottle to Franny and quickly filled the tumbler with water. Franny slipped the pill under her tongue, closing her eyes. Her breathing eased. After a moment, she opened her brown eyes and smiled weakly. "Sorry about that. This angina is a stinker."

"I hope I didn't upset you."

"No. It's not your fault. The quilt thing has me pretty upset, and I'm supposed to avoid stress. Hah! That'll happen when I'm dead."

"Oh, Franny, I'm so sorry about all this. If I can help ..." Theresa wasn't quite sure what that help would look like, and Bob's voice echoed in her head: "Don't get involved."

"Aww, don't worry about it." Franny rose slowly from the chair. "I need to call the sheriff and get somebody out here. Lulu's not going to cooperate, so I don't have any choice."

Theresa nodded, straightening up some papers on the table. She glanced at them again, taking in the red lettering on some of the envelopes that read "final notice."

"Do you want me to stay?"

Franny took the water glass to the sink and put the pill bottle back with the rest.

"No. I'll be all right."

"I saw Art here the other day. Is he or are you …" Theresa hesitated. Bringing up her marriage difficulties might not be wise.

Franny's face hardened. She licked her bottom lip. "He's put me into a terrible position, and, no, we're not going to reconcile. I'd rather not talk about him."

CHAPTER 6

Gracie smiled, listening to her business partner, Jim Taylor, whistle "Hound Dog" as he worked on a couple of kennel latches a few feet from her office. Haley scrambled from her cushy corner bed and trotted out to find him.

"He's irresistible, huh, girl?" Gracie said, laughing at the full chorus of howls and baying that ensued once he broke into song. "Oh my gosh! Can't you just fix the doors and not start a riot?" she called after him.

"Sorry," he called back and continued singing.

"All right then." She got up, shut the door, and went back to the computer to finish updating the website.

Jim appeared almost immediately with a boyish grin plastered on his handsome face. His short black hair and intense blue eyes made him real eye candy for the ladies, but Jim had not succumbed to anyone's charms yet.

"I'm just trying to keep everyone entertained and lighthearted until we move past the big event," he said, plopping himself into a decidedly ratty, green plaid recliner, which screamed 1970s.

"I'm as cool as a cucumber, sir." Gracie arched an eyebrow at Jim and then saved her changes on the Milky Way Kennels website.

"Marc doesn't seem to be so cool, if you ask me," Jim said, pushing his Yankees cap up, leaving it perched on his head.

"He's stressed about the job situation. Plus, his mother and sister will be here in a couple of days. He has to clean his house."

"Ah … Well, that'll keep you jumpy. Has he put the house on the market yet?" Jim took off his hat and placed it on the arm of the chair, fiddling with the bill of the cap.

"He's going to rent it through the winter and then try to sell it next spring. My fingers are crossed that life in general will be all smoothed out before then."

"No word yet on his security clearance?"

"No. The company was trying to expedite it, but it could take up to six months."

Jim shook his head. "Not what he wanted to hear, I'm sure."

"No. To add even more angst, Investigator Hotchkiss is trying to woo him back to the sheriff's department. Apparently, some people who lost their jobs complained, and the union is looking into it. It's possible he could get his old job back."

"So where do you want him to work?" Jim gave her a sly look.

"Oh no, you don't. Wherever he wants to work. He needs to be happy. Just like you, right?"

If she were honest though, Marc going back to the sheriff's office was her first choice. She'd committed to zipping her lip about any such opinion at the moment. Marc had spent hours filling out paperwork for DACO. They wanted to know everything, maybe even how many pieces of toilet paper he used. He'd be protecting company executives when they traveled, and that made her more jittery than the regular law enforcement job. There were a lot of crazy, bad people out there, no matter where you went though. He had a dangerous job either way.

"Nerves of steel, huh?"

"Maybe aluminum foil."

Jim laughed. "It'll all come out in the wash, as my grandmother used to say."

"I suppose it will. He needs to be working though."

"And so do I. Cheryl has all of her evening obedience classes filled now, and those heaters have to be operational in the training barn before we close."

"It's been pretty chilly at night, so I guess that's a good idea." She glanced at her watch. "I'll get the crew moving on feeding our guests their dinner."

The kennel helpers already had feeding time well under way when the bell jangled in the reception area. Gracie could hear Marc talking to Marian, the groomer. She hurried to greet him, and Marian made a swift exit, with a broad grin and wink to her boss.

"Hi, handsome," she said, giving him a quick kiss on the cheek.

"*Hola,* gorgeous," he responded, stepping away from her. His blue eyes were worried, eyebrows drawn together.

"Everything all right? You're looking a little ... uh ... odd."

"Let's go in your office," he said, pushing the Dutch door open to the corridor.

"What's going on?" Gracie asked, shutting the office door. Marc's expression remained unreadable.

"It's a rumor I heard about Kevin."

"Kevin? You mean Isabelle's live-in boy toy?"

"That's the one." Marc eased himself into Jim's recliner.

"What about him?"

"I understand from Midge that he's a player."

"I would think that's obvious. He's at least ten years younger than Isabelle."

"I don't think it's obvious just because he's younger," Marc said. "They seem well-suited. He's a bank executive and all about money. Isabelle's been successful in real estate since Tim—well, died."

"Of course, she's successful. Everything she does is successful. Except for choosing husbands and lovers." Gracie's temper surged just thinking about Isabelle's continual interference in her life, especially the earlier visit, and the attempts to make Gracie look incompetent.

Marc frowned and sighed. "Anyway, Kevin's been seen with quite a looker, at Isabelle's house of all places. Is there anyone who might give her a heads-up?"

"First of all, we don't know if it's true. Second, there's no way I'm throwing myself in front of a freight train for Izzy. Why are you so concerned?"

"I'd hate to see her end up with another Tim-like character."

Gracie had to agree. "Me too. But she wouldn't listen to anyone, especially me."

***

Franny opened the door to the nice-looking deputy who had responded to her call. He patiently took down the information and asked her to open the cedar chest. Of course, it wasn't there. Lulu had it.

"Do you have insurance on this quilt, ma'am?" the deputy asked.

"Yes, I do. My insurance agent is Howie Stroud, here in town."

"Have you filed a claim with him?"

"No. I need your help to make Lulu give it back. I don't want my rates to go up because she took it."

"But you didn't see Mrs. Cook in your house or actually with the quilt, right?"

"No. But Lulu's tried to get me to sell the quilt to her for years. She asked me a while back how much I wanted for it. I can't sell it. It's my family heirloom. It means nothing to her, except she's always wanted it for herself. Plus she couldn't afford to buy it anyway. I want you to tell her to give it back."

The deputy scratched his head and sighed.

"Can't you just go over and search her house? It's a real mess, but it's got to be in there somewhere."

"Not really. But I'll go talk to her about it."

Franny huffed indignantly.

"I pay my taxes. And the one time I need help, do I get it?"

"Let me talk to her and find out what she has to say. You said she's not been herself since her husband died. Maybe Mrs. Cook needs a little extra help from the county or something."

"She's going to need some help if I don't get my quilt back," Franny snapped, stamping her foot.

"Just take it easy, Mrs. Walczak. Give me a few minutes to talk to her, and I'll be right back."

Franny sat on the front porch swing, watching the deputy cross the street and ring Lulu's doorbell. She exhaled with relief when Lulu immediately ushered the man into the house. So far so good.

It wasn't more than ten minutes later that the deputy returned to inform her that Mrs. Cook was sure she didn't have the quilt in question. A few colorful phrases describing her longtime neighbor slipped from Franny's lips, and she signed the report confirming that the Stederman quilt had indeed been stolen. Then she drove herself to the Stroud Insurance Agency to make a claim. She'd never made an insurance claim in her whole life. Tearfully, she filled out more paperwork with the genial Howie Stroud, who gently informed her that someone from the insurance company would come out to talk to her. Her hand was actually shaking, and her stomach lurched when the reality hit her. They'd probably make use of some obscure clause in the policy and not pay her a dime. Crummy insurance companies.

Once back home, she punched in Lulu's number and held the harvest gold wall-phone to her ear. The call was answered on the second ring.

"I made the claim," she said grimly.

"Good. Let's cross our fingers that it will all work out."

"I know. I'm so sorry you had to talk to the police. It's made me a nervous wreck. What if they come back and ask more questions?" Her breathing was labored and she tried to steady her quivering voice.

"Franny, you need to pull it together. You wanted my help and the police report was necessary for the insurance company. It has to look legitimate. I can't tell you how many times Ed droned on about people who were caught in this sort of thing. It's really your only chance. Only a few weeks to go and you'll be home free."

"I know. What if the insurance company gives me problems? I need the money."

"Don't even think about it, Franny. You'll be over tonight at seven, right?

"Right," Franny replied, biting her lower lip.

She hung up the phone and popped a pill under her tongue, sitting heavily into the kitchen chair.

CHAPTER 7

Sirens screamed past the Clarks' house, making Theresa rush to look out her front window. Throwing on a sweater, she hurried down the front walk to see where a police car and ambulance were going. Lights flashed through the haze of leafy trees and the vehicles made a left onto Oak Street. A feeling of foreboding made her shiver, and she quickly returned inside. Had Franny suffered another angina attack, or had Lulu been crushed by her collection of junk?

Bob was watching a football game, which meant he was snoring in his recliner. He was blissfully unconcerned that there was an emergency up the street. Probably thanks to the second helping of chicken and dumplings he'd had for supper.

"Bob, wake up. Something's happening on Oak Street." She gently shook his shoulder.

"Huh? What?"

"An ambulance just went up Oak. Something could've happened to Lulu or Franny."

Bob brought the recliner upright. "We'll find out about it tomorrow, I guess. How do you know it's Lulu or Franny?"

"I have a bad feeling about it. I told you that Franny had an angina attack today. And Lulu lives in a debris field. If one of those container towers fell on her, it could … and then the quilt … What if they got into a fight?" Theresa twisted her hands, looking around for her handbag. "Do you know anyone with a scanner?"

Bob shook his head, scratching his silvery-white hair and then smoothing it. "They may have gone up another street from Oak."

A firetruck roared past the house, sirens full blast and red lights slicing through the darkness.

"See. It's bad. Let's go up there."

"We'll be in the way. It could be a car accident or something." Bob yawned and went to the front windows.

A sheriff's SUV sped past, scattering leaves in its wake.

"That's the second police vehicle. I'm going up to find out," Theresa declared, finally locating her handbag on the kitchen counter.

"I'll be here when you get back," Bob answered, resuming his seat in the brown leather chair. He stared at the TV, frowning. "The Bills were ahead when I dozed off. They're behind thirteen points now. I might as well go with you, I guess. This game isn't going to end well." He powered off the TV with the remote and sighed.

***

Most of Oak Street had vehicles, both law enforcement and emergency services, taking the prime parking. Bob and Theresa parked at the corner and walked down the uneven sidewalk in the chilly night air, their breath visible. The Harwood brothers, Emery and Ian, volunteer EMTs and the owners of the Harwood Funeral Home manned a gurney, hauling it across Lulu's lawn.

"Oh no," Theresa cried, clutching her husband's arm. "Something must have happened to Lulu. I knew it. I just knew that house was an accident waiting to happen."

Lulu's next-door neighbor, Butch Novak, was gawking at the scene from the middle of the sidewalk. He had on shorts and a T-shirt, which made Theresa feel like giving him her sweater.

"Is it Lulu?" she called out as they approached the heavily bearded man, who jiggled back and forth on his feet, rubbing his arms.

"It must be," Butch responded.

"What happened?" Bob asked.

"I'm not sure. There was some yelling. Sounded like a woman and guy to me. But then the cops showed up with the ambulance. Now there's a bunch of people." He rubbed his arms again. "Wow, it's cold out here. I need a jacket," he said, taking off for the house.

Bob and Theresa drew closer to Lulu's driveway where the ambulance crew was working over someone who was prone on the gurney. Theresa squinted to make out the person's shape. The side porch light provided weak illumination in the darkness, but Theresa knew. It was Franny.

Theresa was uncertain whether to approach Lulu or hang back. There was no doubt that Bob thought hanging back or going home was a better idea as he sidled away from her. Lulu stood by the deputy's SUV, not that far away. It would only take a minute or two. Glancing across the street, she saw a male form in the shadows near Franny's driveway. It looked like Art hugging himself, shuffling his feet while watching the scene in front of Lulu's garage. Why was he lurking in the darkness? He should at least do the decent thing and check on Franny. There was no time to confront him. Lulu was her immediate concern.

"Wait a minute, Bob. I need to talk to Lulu."

"All right, but they don't need your help tonight. There are plenty of folks to handle the situation."

Disregarding her husband's pointed comment, she hurried over the damp grass to Lulu's side.

"What happened? Is Franny all right?"

Lulu seemed to be in shock. She shivered, her eyes wide and staring. She wasn't wearing a jacket, just jeans and an old T-shirt.

"Lulu! Can you hear me?" Theresa touched her friend's arm.

Lulu jumped and goggled at her, as though seeing her for the first time.

"Theresa! What are you doing here?"

"I saw the ambulance come this way. Franny's hurt or sick. What happened? Maybe we'd better go inside," Theresa said. "You're freezing."

She put an arm around Lulu's shoulders and guided her toward the side entrance.

"Ma'am, where are you going?" A tall, gangly deputy stepped into the pool of meager light from the light near the door.

"I'm taking Mrs. Cook inside. She'll catch her death out here. Isn't that all right?"

"I need to ask Mrs. Cook a few more questions, ma'am. Don't go anywhere else."

"Of course, deputy."

Theresa hustled Lulu inside to the kitchen, hoping she could make some coffee or at least a cup of tea for the vacant-eyed Lulu.

"Sit down right here, while I make you something ..."

Theresa looked around the small kitchen, its limited counter space made even more limited by piles of plastic shopping bags. She pulled some of the bags away and unearthed a small microwave buried in back. Locating a mug in the cupboard, she searched the pantry cabinet for a teabag. Lulu sat silently at the round table made for two, seemingly unaware of Theresa's ministrations.

The microwave beeped, and Theresa handed the steaming tea to Lulu.

"Now, what happened to Franny?"

Lulu set the mug on the table and took a deep breath. "I killed her."

CHAPTER 8

"You killed her? What do you mean?" Theresa found herself grabbing the other chair at the table and quickly sitting down.

Lulu looked up, her mouth puckered as if she'd bitten into a lemon. "I killed her. She was in my garage. Nothing was supposed to happen."

"Why was Franny in the garage?"

Lulu's eyes were large and watery. She rubbed her hands together and shivered.

"I'm sure she was looking for the quilt."

Lulu hooked her finger into the handle of the mug, stood, and dumped it in the sink. She turned, facing Theresa, her face set in an almost haughty expression.

"What happened in the garage, Lulu? Please tell me." Theresa didn't like the detached way Lulu was behaving.

"I don't really know what happened. Boxes fell, and I called the ambulance."

Exasperated, Theresa rose, trying to decide if the woman needed a splash of water in the face to come to her senses. She almost bumped into the deputy, who unexpectedly entered the kitchen, a clipboard in hand.

"Mrs. Cook, I need to ask you a few more questions," he said.

"Should I stay, or do you need to talk to her alone?"

"Why don't you wait outside a minute? If we need you, I'll let you know. You are ...?"

"Theresa Clark. I'm a friend of Lulu and Franny. Is Franny ...?" Her throat was dry, and her eyes threatened to tear up.

"The EMTs are transporting Mrs. Walczak to Warsaw," the deputy answered officiously.

She quickly descended the short flight of steps to the lawn, looking for her husband. He was talking to Butch, and a deputy was just closing the back door of the ambulance. The Harwood brothers were already climbing into the front of the ambulance, which meant Cora Darling was in the back with Franny.

"Is she okay?" Theresa asked, tucking her hands back into the warmth of her sweater sleeve.

"Looks bad," Butch said, lighting a cigarette. "I'll get Kate, and we'll follow the ambulance over. She doesn't have any family around here—not since Art left." He jogged across the lawn to his driveway, jumped into his truck, and started up the ignition.

"Maybe we should go instead of Butch," Theresa offered.

Her husband shook his head. "Butch will take care of it tonight. He and Kate have been helping her with household repairs and other things for some time. He was telling me Franny's been thinking about selling the house."

"Really? She didn't say anything to me about that. Of course, she was focused on the quilt. Do you think Butch and Kate can handle things? Maybe we should still—"

"Theresa. Franny wasn't breathing. They finally got her back, but Emery was doubtful about a good outcome. Butch went and found Franny's purse, so they have her insurance cards and other things."

"What about Art?"

"Art? What's he got to do with this?" Bob asked.

"He's standing across the street, watching everything."

Bob looked where his wife pointed. "There's no one there."

Theresa looked again. Bob was right. Art was gone. Why would he leave?

She returned her gaze to the dimly lit garage, where men, with "SHERIFF" printed on the backs of their jackets, were combing through piles of plastic containers and black garbage bags.

"Lulu told me she killed Franny," Theresa said.

Bob looked at her in astonishment. "Killed her?" He turned a grim frown toward the garage. "Well, she may have, at that. Though, considering all the junk piled up in there, something could've just accidentally fallen on Franny." Bob shook his head, still marveling at the jam-packed garage. "And you thought *I* was a packrat. Boy!"

Theresa gave him a peevish look. "This is something way beyond being a packrat, Bob. But that's not the point," she said impatiently. "I know Lulu. She'd never harm Franny—not intentionally. This *had* to be an accident."

"I hope so. If Franny doesn't make it, Lulu has a lot of questions to answer," Bob said, moving away from the garage, as the crime scene technicians exited with a few evidence bags.

"I know. It's all over this quilt of Franny's. It's worth a bundle. Over fifty thousand dollars. I don't even know why she keeps it in her house. It should be in a museum or some place that has security."

"A quilt? How can a quilt be worth that much? It's cloth ... a bedspread, for heaven's sake."

"Don't you watch *Antiques Roadshow*? I've seen quilts valued at that and higher."

Bob huffed. "I guess. Are you ready to go? There's nothing more you can do tonight, is there?"

"I'd better check on Lulu. The deputy was questioning her."

Another sheriff's department SUV pulled to the curb.

"Oh boy. Look! It's Investigator Hotchkiss," she said, spotting the trim policewoman striding toward the house.

"Must be serious then," Bob remarked. "I think we'd better skedaddle. Lulu might be taking a trip to Warsaw herself, and it won't be to the hospital."

"I'd better …"

Theresa hesitated. Bob had probably assessed the situation correctly. Maybe once the police saw the mess in the house, they'd find help for Lulu. But if she'd intentionally clobbered Franny, then Lulu was in a heap of trouble.

"Let's skedaddle then, dear."

***

The sky was overcast when Theresa pulled into her daughter's driveway. She wanted to concentrate on the wedding and not think about Franny's untimely death in the clutter of Lulu's garage. Although Lulu hadn't been arrested, it looked inevitable. Lulu had easily confessed the deed to her before talking to the police. What had she told them? Bob insisted she stay out of it, so she'd make sure Gracie didn't say anything in front of her father.

She unlatched the gate into the backyard and looked around. Why didn't she have Marc raking leaves? The yard was looking a tad overgrown too.

A half-hearted woof from Haley greeted her at the kitchen door. She rapped her knuckles on the screen doorframe before entering. Gracie was stuffing a sandwich into her mouth at the kitchen bar. Haley slobbered on Theresa's brown houndstooth slacks, begging for attention.

"Hey, Mom. What's up?" Gracie asked.

"I've had some bad news this morning," she said, patting Haley and pushing her away.

"What happened?"

"It's Franny Walczak. That's one of the reasons why I stopped by."

"What happened to Franny?" Gracie dabbed at her mouth with a paper napkin. She slid off the bar stool, wadded up the napkin, and tossed it into the wastebasket.

"She died last night. Apparently, Lulu buried her in a pile of containers in the garage."

"She did *what*?" Gracie could hardly believe her ears.

Theresa sighed. "I need some coffee, and then I'll tell you."

"Use the Keurig," she said, pointing to the coffeemaker next to the stove. "Now, run that by me again, Mom. Lulu buried her, did you say?"

Theresa shook her head. "I don't understand what really happened yet. Lulu and Franny had been friends forever. Then Franny up and accused Lulu of stealing her heirloom quilt."

"Right. You told me that before."

"Oh. Sorry. I'm kind of wound up about this, I guess. Anyway, Franny snuck into Lulu's garage last night, trying to find her quilt in the towers of plastic that are crammed in there. Lulu heard some sort of commotion and went outside. She naturally thought she saw an intruder in the garage."

"What did she do? Knock over a pile of junk on Franny?"

"That appears to be what happened, yes. Franny had a heart problem, which probably contributed to her death." She stuck a K-cup in the coffeemaker and selected the largest cup size. The hot liquid steamed into the mug.

"That's terrible. What's Lulu got to say for herself?"

"She told me last night that she'd killed Franny." Theresa grimaced. "I'm sure it was accidental. It has to be."

"Let's hope. Come on, Mom. Sit down. You look beat."

Theresa took a seat at the breakfast bar, wrapping her hands around the warm cup.

"What happened to this quilt? Didn't Franny keep it in a safe place?" Gracie asked.

"She said she had it locked up in a cedar chest in her bedroom. I don't know who would've taken it. Why would anyone steal her quilt?"

"Didn't you say it was worth a lot of money?"

"Yes. But how does someone sell a well-known quilt? It's been shown at art shows, and a local magazine showed up to take pictures of it for an article."

"You've got me there. Maybe she's misplaced it or let someone borrow it."

"Not a chance." Theresa waved a hand as though trying to shoo away something unpleasant. "But enough about that. How are the wedding plans?"

The next few minutes were strained between mother and daughter. It seemed to Theresa that Gracie must have forgotten some vital detail for the perfect wedding day. The cake, the flowers, the dress—something must have fallen between the cracks.

"All taken care of, Mom. Honest."

Gracie's gaze was confident and no-nonsense. Her daughter's eyes sparkled with real joy, which Theresa hadn't seen since before Michael's death.

"The dress didn't need any alterations," Gracie elaborated. "It fits me with a little room to spare. I'm carrying a single rose. So is Kelly. We can buy them at the grocery store, if we have to."

"What? You can't do that," Theresa objected. "Esther will have a fit."

The owner of the Blooming Idiot, the best florist around and the only florist in Deer Creek, would be hurt beyond words.

Gracie laughed. "I thought that would warrant a rise from you. Esther has my order for everything, including boutonnieres for the men and corsages for the mothers. Kelly will pick them up."

"What about the ring? Is that ready?" This was certainly something that needed follow-up.

"Done and my ring is ready too." Gracie grabbed her sweatshirt jacket from the hook by the door. "We can continue this in the kennel. I have to go back to work."

Theresa silently conceded defeat. Gracie was on top of the details. She would call Isabelle to confirm that the wedding was under control.

"No. I'm going over to see Lulu," she declared. "I have to know, once and for all, if she has that quilt. Who knows what will happen now? She must be devastated."

"All right. But don't get too involved."

"You sound like your father," Theresa observed a little sourly. "Oh, what about Marc's family? Are they still coming in on Monday?"

Gracie opened the door, stopping to zip up her jacket. Haley pushed through and bounded down the steps.

Gracie's smile seemed a bit forced. There was a hint of fear. It would be the first time she'd meet Marc's mother and sister. Maybe she was nervous.

"They are. Marc's warned me that his sister, Miranda, is a bit—well, like Isabelle. Mom, I have to run," she hurriedly announced, suddenly anxious to end the interview. "Cheryl's leaving early today, and I need to finish up the playtimes for about fifteen dogs. I'll stop by later tonight, if you'll be home."

Theresa felt a bit queasy. A difficult sister? She sighed. That was nothing new to her, but Gracie didn't need the extra pressure.

"Sure. Dad and I'll be home tonight. Is Marc coming with you?"

"Maybe." Gracie hesitated. "Yeah. He'll be there too."

She jogged down the long driveway to the kennel, leaving Theresa standing in the doorway, organizing exactly what she'd say to Lulu.

CHAPTER 9

Marc found Investigator Hotchkiss seated at Midge's on the periphery of the dining room. He smiled and shook her hand when she rose to greet him.

"It's good to see you, Marc. Congratulations on your wedding."

"Thanks, Emily."

Marc took a seat across the table. Mugs of coffee and two pieces of apple pie awaited them.

"I wanted to bring you up to speed on the latest developments in the budget cut issue," she began.

"I hope you have some good news, because the security job may not work out."

The slender woman with short brown hair, flecked with silver, looked at him quizzically.

"Really?"

Marc nodded, fiddling with the package of napkin-wrapped flatware on the red-checked tablecloth. "My half-brother, who's in federal prison, seems to be holding up the security clearance I need for DACO. Hopefully, I can jump through this hoop. I don't have a relationship with him—never did."

"I didn't know about this half-brother of yours."

Marc frowned. "It's not something that comes up in casual conversation. The guy's messed up. Jeremy is the product of my father's affair with a bimbo. It broke up my parents' marriage."

"I'm sorry to hear that. If I can help, let me know."

"I appreciate the offer."

The investigator took a sip of coffee before continuing. "I wanted to talk to you about Sheriff Chamberlain. He was recently diagnosed with a serious heart issue. His wife is campaigning for him to take an immediate early retirement and not complete this second term."

Marc rubbed his cheek, the wheels of possibility turning.

"Will he resign then?"

Her lips drew into thin line. "I think he'll step down in the next couple of weeks. Even though he hasn't been the easiest guy to work for, he is a good cop, and he'll leave some big shoes to fill."

Marc had to agree. Sheriff Chamberlain had improved the technology and the vehicles for the department. His penny-pinching extremism that had frozen salaries and left several positions unfilled had earned Marc's ire. He'd spoken out against the budget cuts the last two years a bit more vocally than was probably wise, and he believed that candor had landed him in his present unemployed status. He'd definitely seen the relief in the sheriff's eyes when he'd signed off on the temporary duty, assigning Marc to the Sierra Vista Police Department in Arizona at the beginning of the year.

"That's true. Will the undersheriff take over if that happens?"

"He will. There will be a special election, and I do plan to run. The undersheriff has stated he doesn't want the big job, and I'd be happy to have his experience as second in command. That leads me to a proposal for you. There'll be an investigator position open if all those ducks line up, and you *are* qualified. Interested?"

Marc leaned against the chair, his fingers interlaced on the tabletop. The generous salary DACO offered still dangled like a diamond-studded carrot before him. The familiarity of returning to the sheriff's department and remaining in real law enforcement was just as enticing. Both were in the future somewhere—no certain hire date and no promises that could absolutely secure either position. It was all dependent on circumstances out of his control.

"I am interested. However, if my secret clearance comes in during the next month or so, I don't know how I can refuse DACO's offer. I would go back to the county in a heartbeat. Therein lies my dilemma. But no one's offering a job that starts next week. I'd like to be gainfully employed again and soon."

Midge, the wiry owner of the restaurant, unexpectedly appeared next to them, coffeepot in hand.

"How's the groom? Nervous? Cold feet yet?"

Marc laughed. "Not yet. I've got a few days though."

"You'd be crazy to back out on a woman like Gracie. You're a lucky man." Midge's sharp eyes were intense and little scary.

"I know that for sure. Don't worry. We're right on schedule."

"Good. It had better stay that way. Want more coffee?"

After declining, Marc and Emily sat silently, concentrating on the pie that was still untouched. The investigator toyed with her fork.

"I'm sorry I can't offer an immediate position. There are a lot of things up in the air. I'm just asking that you consider it, Marc. Your plate is plenty full at the moment. Why don't you enjoy your honeymoon, and let me know in a couple of weeks?"

"I'm not sure that's enough time given my clearance situation. I can say I'm definitely interested. Why don't we see how things progress with the sheriff first? If he doesn't resign, there's no position for me."

"I'm pretty confident he'll retire very soon. There doesn't seem to be any interest from any other party to run for sheriff. At least, that's what the political machine tells me. I expect to run unopposed. If my offer is on the table before DACO clears you, will you take the job?"

Marc almost said "yes" and stopped himself before giving an answer. "I'll need to talk to Gracie about it. I'll let you know. We need a little more time with so much happening in the next couple of weeks."

"I'll be waiting to hear from you."

Midge's pie couldn't be left to languish, and they quickly devoured the cinnamon-spiced apples packaged in flaky pastry before driving in opposite directions.

***

Lulu sat with a pair of binoculars behind a stack of cardboard boxes that gave her a good view of the Walczak house across the street without being observed herself. The folding chair was uncomfortable, and she was getting a crick in her neck from peering around the boxes. Perseverance paid off when Art's clunker pulled into the driveway. He slunk around to the rear of the house. It figured he'd try and break into his former residence. Franny's body wasn't even cold yet, and he was probably looting the place. The disheveled man reappeared a few minutes later. She scribbled the time down in a notebook. His hands were empty, which was a shocker. That was something anyway, but she'd keep watch over the house. It was the least she could do for her best friend. Tears spilled down her cheeks. How could she go on after this development? It was all her fault. But who else had been in the garage? The voices had been garbled. How many people had been in her yard?

Shuddering, the lanky woman padded back to the sewing room. The work would keep her on task. There was still plenty to do.

CHAPTER 10

Theresa pushed the doorbell twice and began knocking on the door when Lulu didn't answer. Finally, Lulu appeared, with bare feet and dressed in a worn, pink chenille robe. Theresa exhaled with relief, once she caught sight of her friend, who opened the door a mere crack.

"I'm glad you're here," Theresa exclaimed, noting the dark smudges under Lulu's eyes.

"I really don't feel like talking," Lulu said, pushing the door shut.

"Lulu. Please. I know you're hurting. I just want to talk for a minute."

Lulu's eyes closed and she scowled, opening the door.

"All right. Come in."

Theresa uncovered a kitchen chair, holding the newspapers on her lap, while she sat next to the despondent woman. After a few minutes of silence from Lulu, Theresa squirmed uneasily. Despite her best efforts to elicit any tidbits of what happened the night before, Lulu's reluctance stalled her attempt. Lulu gruffly thanked her for coming and announced she was going to bed. Theresa grappled with another information setback, but had to admit she wouldn't want to talk to anyone either under the circumstances. She had so many questions though. Lulu didn't return Theresa's parting hug either. It was like hugging a department store mannequin. Stepping out into the sunshine, she saw an unfamiliar white SUV pull into the Walczak house driveway.

Theresa sat in her car, debating if she should wait to see who was converging on the empty dwelling.

A heavyset, pleasant-looking woman, carrying a leather portfolio, climbed out of the vehicle, along with a raven-haired younger woman. The pair clambered up the front steps; the larger woman pressed the doorbell.

Theresa opened the car door. No sense in wondering what was happening.

"Are you looking for Mrs. Walczak?" Theresa called to them as she hustled across the street.

The women turned around quickly, looking confused.

"I hope we haven't come at a bad time. I'm Ann Gallagher from the American Quilters Society," the woman with the portfolio under her arm replied. "Are you Mrs. —?"

"Oh, no. I'm a friend of Franny's. Theresa Clark," she said, extending a hand as she reached the porch.

Impatience flashed in the eyes of the younger woman, who took a step back, keeping her hands in her coat pockets.

"I'm Lisa Stederman Kronk. Where's Mrs. Walczak?"

"I'm afraid I have bad news about Franny. She passed away last night."

"How awful!" Ann Gallagher exclaimed. "I had no idea."

"We had an appointment with her today," Lisa Kronk responded with annoyance.

"I'm sorry, but that's not possible *now*."

"I'm a cousin of Mrs. Walczak's," the dark-haired woman continued frostily. "I was supposed to see the Stederman quilt. She's stood me up on two other occasions."

Theresa hastily decided not to offer any extracurricular information about the missing quilt. She struggled to keep her composure, flabbergasted at the woman's rudeness.

"We should go," Ann said, shifting her feet. "As I said, we had no idea about Mrs. Walczak."

"What happened?" Lisa probed, arranging her expression into a look of concern.

"Well ... we're not quite sure yet. An accident or possible heart attack. I don't have any other information at the moment."

Lisa's brow wrinkled. "That's confusing. Which is it? What about next-of-kin? It's critical that I see the quilt. There is some question of ownership, and I'm here to clear it up."

Theresa stifled a gasp. An ownership dispute? Franny hadn't mentioned anything about that. Was that why she'd reported the quilt stolen? Some bad blood was simmering on the front porch. Lisa sure wasn't grieving over Franny's death. She was merely inconvenienced.

"I would recommend you contact Mrs. Walczak's attorney. I'm not sure who that might be, but if you call the Wyoming County Sheriff's office, they may have the information."

"The sheriff?"

Lisa swallowed hard. The women looked at one another. After a moment, Lisa seemed to regain some poise after a sharp look from Ann Gallagher.

"I see. She has no one else?" Lisa asked in a more subdued voice.

"Not really. No children, and Franny was divorced. She was the youngest in her family. There may be a sister who's still around, but I think she's in a nursing home. I really don't know. I'm sure you must know the family tree as a cousin."

Lisa shifted uncomfortably, not meeting Theresa's gaze.

"I'll have to check with my grandmother. That's really why I'm here anyway. She called Frances a few weeks ago and wanted to discuss the quilt's ownership, but it was a non-starter. My grandma isn't doing well health-wise, and I wanted to help straighten things out. It's been such a stressor for her. I've never seen the old rag myself."

"I think we'd better be on our way," Ann Gallagher murmured insistently. She smiled and adjusted the portfolio under her arm. "I'm so sorry to hear about Mrs. Walczak's passing. When Mrs. Kronk contacted me and mentioned her family's connection with the quilt, I was honored to try to help the families come together. I'd ... I'd worked with Mrs. Walczak several times before." The woman paused, as if unsure how to continue. She looked at Lisa and then back to Theresa. "We had no idea of what had happened." Ann reached into the pocket of her tweed blazer, drawing out a set of car keys.

"I'll be contacting her attorney," Lisa confirmed. "I'm sorry for the misunderstanding."

Before Theresa could respond, Ann and Lisa made a speedy retreat to the SUV.

***

Gracie shut off her computer, calling for Haley. The black Lab happily followed, her thick tail waving like a metronome. Jim met them in the reception area, a denim jacket slung over his shoulder. He removed his ball cap, running his fingers through his rumpled, black hair.

"Dessert at seven tonight?" he asked.

"That's right. S'mores and coffee by the bonfire," Gracie confirmed. "Oh, and mulled cider too. I hope Marc comes back soon to start getting the wood ready for that."

"Look. He's driving in now." Jim motioned toward the driveway to the house.

"Good. I also need him to pick up any land mines in the backyard that Haley and Max may have left. I didn't have time to take care of that little chore today."

"A marvelous idea. That could ruin the evening." Jim said, grinning.

Marc met them in the driveway. Max playfully plowed into Haley. The two dogs loped back to the house, waiting by the gate to the backyard, while the humans straggled behind.

"How did things go with Investigator Hotchkiss?" Gracie asked, reaching for Marc's hand.

"All right," Marc replied.

"More hurry up and wait?" Jim asked.

"Pretty much," Marc said. "I just can't win right now."

"Don't worry about it. You should enjoy the break, because once you do go back to work, it'll be crazy," Gracie advised.

Marc grunted.

"I'll see you two later," Jim said, stopping at his pickup. He pulled on his jacket and opened the truck door. "It's getting nippy. That bonfire will feel good."

"Bonfire! Shoot! That's right," Marc yipped. "I need to pick up the wood. Sorry! I'll be back." He released Gracie's hand and took off for his truck.

Jim burst into laughter. "The groom is a little absentminded."

"I knew it. I give him one job—the fire—and ..." Gracie giggled and snapped her fingers. "And I forgot the graham crackers for the s'mores. We're a fine pair."

"Well, I hope you have it together by the time everybody shows up tonight."

"Me too," Gracie answered, charging for the RAV4, the dogs running to meet her.

***

The bonfire was a success, even though Marc had struggled to keep it aflame in the beginning. Sparks crackled and flew up into the darkness, while Jim and the Clark family—which included Tom, Gracie's brother, his new wife, Kelly, Tom's daughter, Emma, and the elder Clarks—formed a circle of chairs to enjoy the evening. Haley and Max sniffed around the chairs and the card table laden with goodies, ready to capitalize on any food mishandling. Between the warm, gooey s'mores and ice cream sundaes, Gracie felt like she should have worn sweatpants to the gathering. "Has everyone overindulged sufficiently?" she asked, hauling herself from the nylon web chair.

Groans were the response.

"Take it away," Tom pleaded. "I have no will power."

"Yes. Put a fork in me. I am done," Marc added.

She lifted the tray of ice cream toppings from the table. Kelly quickly joined her, gathering up the box of graham crackers and a dish of chocolate bars.

"Come on, Emma. Help us take the rest of the stuff inside," Gracie said.

Emma wasted no time scooping up the bags of marshmallows with the dogs on her heels. Theresa followed up the rear with an armload of paper plates and napkins.

The men resettled themselves a bit further from the fire, which was now intensely hot. The yellow flames and the smoke rose straight up in the chilly night air.

"Gracie mentioned that you're still waiting to hear about the job in Batavia," Bob Clark said, pulling back a couple of empty chairs even with his own.

Marc nodded, stomping on a stray ember that had landed near his foot.

"It's gotten a bit complicated because of my family situation."

"How's that?" Tom asked.

Marc haltingly recounted Jeremy's violent history and the additional red tape. Not only was it uncomfortable to reveal this significant blemish on his family, but he was helpless to make any promises about its resolution.

"That stinks," Tom said, putting his hands out toward the fire. "They must realize you aren't connected to him though."

"I would think so. I was up front with them from the start when I knew a security clearance was required. They dig into every nook and cranny of your life. I'm going to call them in a couple days to see if things are moving again."

Jim stood and kicked a piece of wood that rolled out of the flames back into place.

"Be patient," Bob said, looking up at Marc. "Tom's been through the process a few times over the years. It always takes longer than you think, even if there aren't any worms in the apple. Right, son?"

"Yeah. It's always the same," Tom confirmed. "I was in the Army and the Reserves for twenty years. I had to have a clearance redone right before my last deployment to Afghanistan. Everything is complicated."

"That's why I enjoy the civilian life," Jim said. "I've got some control over things."

Tom looked at Jim with a wry grin. "Really? You *are* the guy who's in a partnership with my sister, right?"

The men roared with laughter.

CHAPTER 11

Theresa stood in front of the full-length mirror in her bedroom. She squirmed into the teal sheath, sucking in as much as she could stand. The brocade jacket lay on the bed. She'd bought the ensemble on sale in August. Bob had protested that both children remarrying within two months of each other didn't require two outfits. There was no way she was wearing the same outfit to two weddings so close together. Besides, such a sale shouldn't be ignored. She'd snatched it off the rack without thinking twice. Her confidence in the power of a good foundation garment made her bold enough to purchase it, although the dress was a touch snug. The jacket was longer and more forgiving, which was a good thing. She felt like a shape-shifter these days. Who knew where unwelcome lumps and bumps would appear next? The dress finally slid on the rest of the way, actually clearing her hips. Now to zip it up.

"Bob! I need your help," she called from the top of the winding staircase.

"What now? I'm just leaving to play golf. Last foursome of the season."

"I need you to zip up this dress."

"What are you all gussied up for? I thought you were going grocery shopping."

"I am. I needed to try on the dress for Gracie's wedding to make sure it still fits."

Bob clumped up the stairs, a putter and cleaning cloth in one hand.

"I'm sure it's perfect, my dear." He tossed the golf equipment on the bed.

"I need to be sure." She turned her back and felt the tug of the zipper. About halfway up her back, he stopped.

"The zipper's stuck," Bob said.

"What? It can't be."

"Well, it is. I can't budge it. I might wreck the dress."

"There's probably a bit of material stuck in it. Look at it and see. If there is, pull it out. Carefully." She tried looking over her shoulder without much success to assess the problem.

"All right." He fussed with it and finally corrected the zipper malfunction.

She felt the zipper reach the back of her neck. Turning around, she looked for her husband's approval.

"Nice dress. I'll see you later." He gave her peck on the cheek and hurried down the stairs. The front door slammed, and she heard his car start up.

Sighing, she went back into the bedroom to don the jacket. Looking at herself from every angle, it seemed satisfactory, especially with a little help from her good friend Spanx. She reached to unzip the dress, and the zipper stopped halfway down. It wouldn't go either direction.

"Are you kidding me?" she asked her reflection.

Taking a deep breath, she gave it a firm yank. It gave way, and then she felt it separate at the bottom.

"Oh no," she groaned.

Peeling off the dress, she gazed at the broken zipper. It had come apart with no possible repair. Now what? Her sewing skills were sub-par. It was something she hated.

Competently operating a sewing machine was questionable, and replacing a zipper was unattainable.

"Lulu. I'll beg for her help. She must have enough zippers for an army."

***

Lulu was dressed and seemed pleasant enough when the door opened. More organization had occurred, which gave Theresa hope for a recovery from the recent hoarding tendencies.

"Look at it. I won't be able to wear it unless the zipper's replaced."

Lulu adjusted her half-glasses, studying the damage.

"You're right. Everything is so cheaply made nowadays."

"It must have been on sale for a reason," Theresa agreed glumly. "Can you fix it?"

"I think so. The color's a little unusual, but let me check and see what I have."

Lulu drifted through the maze of containers, disappearing before Theresa could catch up.

"Hey, Theresa. Come here and see what you think of this match."

"Where are you?" She'd lost her bearings in the jumble. The place was still like a rabbit warren.

"In my sewing room."

Treading carefully between several plastic container turrets, she arrived safely in Lulu's surprisingly well-ordered sewing room. Shelves of fabric were neatly stacked. Two sewing machines were set up, along with an uncluttered worktable. A laptop sat on a small desk. She hadn't expected this. It looked perfectly normal.

"This is the closest color I have."

Lulu held out an almost exact match to the teal. It was even the right length.

"That's perfect! Can you replace it? I'm hopeless when it comes to sewing. You know that, of all people."

Lulu laughed. "I'll do it. The last time we sewed together, I ended up ripping out your seams at least twice."

"Which is why I only cut out the quilt squares for the sewing circle. My mother wasn't very good either. It must be hereditary."

"It's possible. I can have this ready probably by tomorrow."

"Wonderful! I can't tell you how much I appreciate this."

"Glad to assist the mother-of-the-bride."

Lulu laid the dress out on the worktable and opened a wooden sewing cabinet next to it. Several pieces of colored paper fell to floor when she pulled out a large pincushion.

"Here. Let me help," Theresa said, bending to pick up the paper. She was startled to see that it resembled some sort of foreign currency.

"I've got it," Lulu said, blocking Theresa. She gathered the mess quickly, stuffing it back into the cabinet. "I'll give you a call when the dress is done," she said.

Lulu had gone on the defensive, focused on the dress and not on Theresa. It was time to retreat and be grateful the dress would be repaired.

"I have to run anyway. Thanks, Lulu."

Threading her way back to the kitchen, Theresa slipped out the door, wishing she'd had a better look at whatever Lulu had stashed in the sewing cabinet. Gloria's Honda parked in front of Franny's caught her attention. She'd better find out why she was there.

***

Gloria Minders opened the front door for Theresa.

"Good timing. Come in. You can help me pick out an outfit for Franny," she said wearily.

"You got the assignment?" Theresa asked bleakly.

"Yes. We found out last night that Albert is the executor of the will. Can you believe it?"

"Really? Then he'll have to deal with the Stederman family. Franny's cousin was here yesterday trying to see the quilt. A Lisa Stederman Kronk had an appointment with Franny, along with a woman from some quilting society. That was interesting and awkward all at the same time."

Gloria rubbed her temples, closing her eyes.

"Oh yes. We've already had a call about her claim on the quilt. And Art has called to tell us he still has stuff in the house and that she owed him money. For some reason, Franny made out a new will about a month ago. It must be because of the divorce. Why she chose Albert as executor, I can't imagine. I wish he'd resign from the appointment."

"You know he won't. He'll do his duty."

Gloria exhaled. "I know. Well, help me find a dress for poor Franny."

The bedroom was gloomy. Gloria flipped on the wall switch, illuminating the small neat room. After sorting through the sparse wardrobe in the large closet, they agreed on a pleated navy blue skirt and matching long sleeve top.

"It's appropriate," Theresa said.

"It is. What about some jewelry?"

"Pearls would be nice, if she has any," Theresa said, opening an old blue leather box with a broken clasp, which sat on a small chest-of-drawers. "And here's a necklace."

She drew the short strand from the box, handing it to Gloria, who laid the clothing, pearls, and shoes on the brightly patterned quilt that served as Franny's bedspread.

"I'll take this to Emery at the funeral home," Gloria said. "They're releasing her body to them this afternoon."

"Was a cause of death determined?"

"It was a heart attack. She was badly bruised and had a broken wrist, but the boxes didn't kill her, although the incident probably triggered the heart attack."

"Lulu isn't going to be blamed is she?"

"I don't know. I can't believe there would be any charges. Nothing could be proved one way or the other. Franny had a bad heart. She was trespassing, and Lulu thought a stranger was in her garage."

Theresa wasn't so sure. Lawsuits over everything made the news daily.

"I hope that's all there is to it. Lulu is devastated. Has anyone told her about the autopsy results?"

"I'm not sure, but Albert plans to call on her this afternoon, and I'll go with him."

Gloria rummaged around in the closet, dragging out a small carry-on. She packed underwear and shoes, along with the navy outfit, into the suitcase.

"Can you think of anything else?"

"I think that covers it," Theresa said, running her hand over the quilt on the bed. "This is really a beautiful pattern. Looks like some of Lulu's work. Is it the Jacob's Ladder pattern?"

"It is, and Lulu probably made it," Gloria agreed. "Franny wasn't much into sewing."

They stepped back to admire the quilt with its border of hand-quilted tulips and ivy in red and dark green fabrics. The center had a dark brown calico background and muted squares of red, green, and brown. It was a striking piece of fabric art.

"Nice heavy quilt too," Theresa said, lifting the corner. "Lulu used really nice quality fabric. I wonder if anyone will fight over this."

"Who knows?" Gloria grumbled. "I'm sure we'll find out soon enough."

Theresa's gaze dropped to the cedar chest at the foot of the bed.

"Should we take a look?"

Gloria shrugged. "Why not?"

CHAPTER 12

Marc paced, the phone to his ear. The agent had left him dangling on hold for the last ten minutes.

"Mr. Stevens. I have that information now," a gruff voice broke through the silence.

"Great. What's the latest then?"

"We have made progress on the background check. I just need to go over the extent of your relationship with your brother, Jeremy Aiken, once more."

"He's my half-brother, and I don't have a relationship with him, as I stated previously."

"But you did visit him in prison, and you attended his trial. Is that correct?"

"Yes. It is."

Marc closed his eyes, remembering the handful of times he'd ever seen Jeremy. The gaunt face and hate-filled eyes of the young man, ten years his junior, were burned into his memory.

"Jeremy was introduced to our family when I was about eighteen. He was seven or eight. His mother tried to coerce my mother to take him in. She had a new boyfriend who didn't like Jeremy. My father was out of the picture for them and us. I felt sorry for him. He was a just a little kid, but it would've been crazy for my mom to do that. His mother was a piece of work. She had a lot of nerve coming to our house."

"Was that the only time?"

"No. I attended his trial with my father. The old man hadn't bothered to be involved with Jeremy until then. He was sick and was trying to make amends with his children. I went because I was curious to see this monster who'd been a cute kid on our doorstep eleven years earlier. Then I visited him in prison to tell him that Dad had died. I felt it was the right thing to do, whether he cared or not. That last time was a little over two years ago. It was in March."

"All right. Thanks for the information. I hear congratulations are in order for you."

"I guess so. Thanks. The big day is coming up in a few days."

"Well, all the best. Try not worry about this. We're on top of it."

"Any idea of the timeframe?"

"It won't be much longer, but I can't give you an exact date, of course."

"Of course. Thanks."

Marc shoved the phone into the clip on his belt. If they'd been on top of it, he wouldn't be answering the same old questions again.

***

Gracie sat in the kitchen, sorting through the mail. Several cards addressed to her and Marc were interspersed with the junk mail. Most likely wedding wishes. She put them off to the side for later. She and Marc could open them together. He should be coming to work on the yard any time. The sound of a tractor growled down the road, and the accompanying smell of the load behind it overpowered the pleasant cinnamon-scented air freshener. Haley trotted to the kitchen door, whining.

"You probably want to go roll in that."

A deep familiar bark corrected her. A German shepherd, with a lolling pink tongue, appeared at the kitchen door. Max and Marc were here.

Marc barely escaped the colliding dogs, who jumped and woofed playfully, tags jingling. The pair ran for the French doors. Gracie hurried and let them out to play in the yard.

"Everything okay?" Gracie asked, standing on her tiptoes to kiss him.

He nodded and wrapped his arms around her, holding her close before releasing her.

"I talked to the agent who's working on the clearance today. I had to answer the exact same questions about Jeremy again. I don't think they believe me."

"Have they made any headway?"

"I think so, but he won't say how much longer. Let's hope it's soon, like this week. I need a job."

Gracie was loading the dishwasher and immediately stood upright.

"I know you do, but you've got to relax. I'd like to enjoy this wedding week since everything is under control. You'll be gone a lot once you take the job with DACO. I like having you around. Can't we both appreciate this lull in activity?"

Marc's tense jaw relaxed, and he gave her a tenuous smile.

"We can. Guilty on being too jumpy. Now, what do you want me to do about the lawn?"

***

The mower shot out grass mingled with yellow and brown leaves, scenting the air with a rich, earthy fragrance. Gracie grabbed the rake leaning on the screen of the patio and quickly formed manageable piles for transfer to the composter behind the fence. The dogs seemed reluctant to move from the back corner, where they were sniffing intently. Marc had to get off the mower and shoo them away. They trotted back to the patio, and after a minute of circling, the

Lab and shepherd finally flopped to the paver floor. Gracie stopped raking and took a moment to enjoy the domestic scene. It was so normal, so right. In a week, they'd both be living here, making a new life together.

Marc finished the lawn, and they loaded the clippings into the wagon. The lawn looked good. The cool weather would keep the grass from growing too quickly, although a frost was predicted for at least two nights before the wedding. Everything would be perfect for Saturday afternoon.

She pulled her hair back from her face, holding it behind her head. The short summer style she'd had for the Arizona vacation had grown out, and the unruly auburn curls were back. Digging into her jeans, she found a hairband in the pocket and wrapped her hair snugly in place.

The rumble of the mower stopped. Marc reentered the yard.

"All done. Good enough?"

"Perfect. We're ahead of schedule. I'm sure that's the last time it'll need to be mowed anyway. How about a cup of hot chocolate? Some cards came in the mail today too."

"Sounds good on both counts," Marc said, wiping his feet on the mat before he followed Gracie inside.

The dogs pushed through and relocated to Haley's bed in front of the fireplace.

"I think I need to order a bigger bed for them," Gracie said, laughing.

"Haley will still hog it," Marc said, shaking his head at the black Lab's stretched-out body, which left a mere speck of space for Max.

"Most likely. She does the same thing with me."

"Uh ... She's not going to be joining us, is she?"

"No way. She's permanently banished, unless you're away, of course. Haley won't take it well, but things change." Gracie grabbed two mugs from the cupboard by the sink.

"Those cards are on the island. Go ahead and open them, while I fix the hot chocolate."

Marc slit the envelopes with a small silver letter opener. "Here's one from the Strouds," he said.

"That's nice," Gracie answered, watching the Keurig stream hot chocolate into a cup.

Marc abruptly sniffed the air.

"Do you smell something funny?"

"The hot chocolate smells funny?"

"No. Something a little rotten."

"The honey wagon went by earlier. Or are you making disparaging remarks about my housekeeping?"

She sniffed and didn't notice anything strange. The sweet chocolatey aroma was the only identifiable scent.

"I would never entertain that thought. Must be my imagination or that manure spreader," Marc said.

CHAPTER 13

The chest was unlocked, and Theresa sorted through several ordinary satin-edged blankets. Pulling them out, she discovered two dark-colored quilts in the bottom along with an old photo album. No fabulous *broderie perse* quilt appeared.

"Here," she said, handing the album to Gloria.

Gloria opened the nubby-textured black scrapbook.

"This looks like a history of the missing quilt," she said, fingering the brittle pages.

Theresa leaned over for a better look.

The photos began in 1867, according to the faint penciled inscription on the back. The sepia portrait was of Emma Lou Stederman standing next to the exquisite quilt, which hung from a rail mounted on a wall. The woman looked a bit grim in her shirtwaist and striking hairstyle. A thick braid wound around Emma Lou's head and was caught up in netting with a sprig of what looked like baby's breath tucked behind her ear.

"Why was everyone so unhappy back then?" Theresa chuckled.

"I think it was those corsets they wore all the time. How could women breathe?" Gloria commented.

"Good point. I'd never have survived."

They sat on the bed and flipped through the rest of the album. The last photo was of Franny at the American Quilters Society show three years prior. Another woman of about the same size, who looked a few years older, stood on the opposite side of the quilt.

"I wonder if that's Lisa Kronk's grandmother," Theresa said, looking carefully at the woman's features. "I think there's some resemblance to her."

"Could be," Gloria answered, taking out a yellowed envelope stuck in the next page. She carefully extracted an equally yellowed letter from the fragile container. "This is interesting. Listen. Hopefully, I can make all of it out." Gloria squinted at the faded ink.

"The Stederman quilt was handstitched by Henrietta Messner Stederman and Ada Drummond, her cousin. It was completed on the 21st day of November, 1803. Ada was joined in holy wedlock to Henrietta's brother-in-law, Mason Stederman, in 1804. The materials for the quilt were procured by Mason and Charles Stederman while in France in 1802. As merchants of dry goods and sundries, they obtained the silks and the threads through their most excellent and prolific supplier, Messrs. Lafayette and Girard."

Gloria turned the paper over.

"The purchase of silk was to make two quilts and two gowns for Ada and Henrietta. Misfortune took one cask of cloth, which was dropped overboard when the ship docked at Block Island. In the spirit of charity and sisterly kindness, Henrietta and Ada agree to share the quilt as follows: in the odd numbered years of our Lord, Ada will retain use of the bedcovering, and in the even numbered years of our Lord, Henrietta will retain its use. It is our wish that the quilt be thus shared between our oldest sons or daughters and to theirs in perpetuity. It's signed by Henrietta and Ada in 1821."

Gloria and Theresa looked at each other. Theresa whistled a low note.

"What a crazy agreement," she muttered.

***

The bright and crisp fall morning, along with an early call from an Investigator Hotchkiss, inspired Lulu to replace the zipper in Theresa's dress before a second cup of coffee.

The loss of Franny was devastating, but the autopsy had revealed that a massive heart attack had taken her life, not the jumble of plastic containers. None of the consequent bruises or the broken wrist had been life-threatening. Her conscience was partly assuaged. There was no way to determine if Franny's heart gave out just as she pushed the boxes or if fear had brought it on. She would never know. That was the hard part. Franny was more than a neighbor or even a friend—a sister—but things had changed so much over the past year.

She blew her nose before testing the zipper, which ran smoothly. Good as new. She snipped the stray threads and shook the dress out. Rather than have Theresa invade her space again, she'd walk over and deliver it personally. She should start walking again anyway. Getting in shape for the next phase of her life was a priority over the next few weeks. She slid the dress back onto the hanger and pulled the thin plastic cover over the ensemble.

Just as she opened the front door, a white SUV drove slowly down the street, stopping in front of Franny's. A dark-haired woman took a long, hard look at the house. Locking the door, Lulu wondered if she should ask if the lady was lost. The vehicle looked familiar. Maybe it was the one that was parked in the driveway the day before. An urge to ask if the driver needed directions crossed her mind, but she decided to stay out of any sort of limelight. Under the radar— that's where she needed to be. Swinging the dress over her shoulder, her finger hooked around the hanger, Lulu walked toward the Clarks' house.

***

After dropping off the dress, Lulu felt a bit lighthearted, seeing Theresa's surprise when she'd answered the door. It had gone well. Theresa didn't mention the Mexican currency, which had accidently spilled from the cabinet. The *faux pas* had almost given her a heart attack herself. She had been painfully circumspect in avoiding local banks and had exchanged dollars for pesos at banks in Rochester. Her transactions would have provoked too many questions locally. Now, she'd been careless and changed the hiding place to her own detriment. Fortunately, with Gracie's wedding just days away, Theresa should be plenty busy. No time to stop in for another visit and maybe she'd forget ever seeing the money.

She met no one returning to her house—another plus. The SUV was nowhere in sight either. The curtains of Franny's upstairs bedroom seemed to sway, although no face was visible in the window. Popping in the front door, Lulu clicked the lock behind her. Was someone sneaking around in Franny's home? She wondered if she should call the police. Sometimes people read or heard about a death and stole things out of the dead person's residence. On the other hand, the curtains were probably her imagination running wild. She was so used to seeing Franny surveilling the outside activity. That must be it.

***

Gloria sat at her kitchen table, watching her husband go over the insurance claim form with the adjuster. The adjuster had been thorough. With a practiced routine, he searched the cedar chest and examined its lock, as well as checking the locks on Franny's doors. Nothing had been forced, which matched the information given on the police report. The album with the quilt's history was of interest, but the man decided not to take it with him.

Neither Albert nor Gloria could offer any additional help to the man about where it might be. Franny's elderly sister,

Martha, hadn't shed any light either. She'd given the "blasted thing" to Franny when they were young. Martha hated it. In her opinion, it was ugly as sin and a family burden. She didn't care how much it was worth. No one had observed the original agreement about sharing the quilt since the late 1800s. The quilt apparently had gone to the fleet of foot when the current owner died. Martha and Franny's mother, Sally, had been at the bedside of the last cousin, when she left for Glory. Sally had wasted no time securing the quilt into a suitcase she'd brought along for just such an opportunity.

Albert tried to answer the adjustor's questions about why Franny didn't have better security. There was no reason to have more security, especially in Deer Creek. Who locked their doors, especially if it was just a quick run to the post office or a chat with a neighbor? The adjustor had asked about the accusation against her friend. Both Albert and Gloria had been adamant there was no proof of Lulu's involvement and that the police hadn't found the quilt in the search of Lulu's garage after Franny's mishap. The adjustor, a rather stern-faced man with a receding hairline and dark nose hairs that begged to be trimmed, looked the form over before slipping it into a file folder.

"All right, Reverend. Once you receive those documents officially appointing you as executor of the estate, give me a call to sign the form. Because of the size of the claim, there will be another review. We have our own investigator who'll do some digging around."

"How long will this take then?"

"It could be several months," he said, closing up a battered black briefcase.

"Several months? I don't understand," Gloria spouted, instantly regretting her hasty words.

"We need to do our due diligence on this claim. That includes further investigation. That isn't a problem, is it?"

His beady eyes narrowed, and Gloria had the distinct impression they were now under the microscope, thanks to her. She looked at Albert, who seemed unruffled.

"No. Of course not. I had no idea Mrs. Walczak had nominated me as the executor of her estate. I don't have any experience with any of this. We've never even had an insurance claim. Right, dear?" He looked at Gloria with steady, calm eyes.

"No. Never. Everything about Mrs. Walczak has been a shock," Gloria managed.

"I'm here to help you. Don't worry about anything. All of this is standard procedure. We must verify that the claim is in order before payment. It *is* a significant claim."

Gloria nodded. It certainly was hefty. More than what Theresa said the quilt was worth, which the adjustor had assured them was normal. However, the amount only created questions for her. Had Franny over-insured the quilt, or had she been coy about the value with Theresa? It also seemed to be no coincidence that a relative was hunting down the heirloom. Was there more going on than a stolen quilt? She couldn't wait for the insurance man to leave. Maybe she should do a little research at Franny's.

CHAPTER 14

Tom, along with Kelly and Emma, stood waiting for Gracie and Marc after the worship service at Deer Creek Community Church. While most of the congregation milled toward the Fellowship Hall for coffee and pastries, the Clark contingent had other plans.

"Joining us at Midge's for lunch?" Kelly asked.

"Not today," Gracie answered, looking up at Marc.

"No. I was just informed there's a bit of a plumbing problem at the house," Marc said.

"Plumbing problem?" Tom questioned.

"My tub drain is running really slow," Gracie said.

"Oh. A little Drano should fix it."

"Well, I tried that last night with no luck. It's probably a hairball of gigantic proportions, so Marc's going to try and clean it out."

"Good luck, then. Everything okay on the wedding front?" Tom asked.

"Couldn't be better." Gracie grabbed Marc's arm. "Let's go. I really want that drain fixed."

Marc smiled with raised eyebrows, following Gracie out the side door. After a quick greeting to Reverend Minders, they fled to Marc's truck.

"Does this have anything to do with the funny smell I imagined yesterday?" Marc asked once he started the engine.

"It might. After you left, I smelled something a little off myself. It wasn't the refrigerator, and this morning, the water didn't empty out of the tub right. Hopefully, it's just a clogged drain."

Marc maneuvered the truck from parking lot.

"Well, I can take a look. I'm no plumber though."

"Maybe if you plunged it, along with using Drano. You've got a little more muscle than I do."

Marc grinned, giving her a sly look, and turned on his left signal, stopping at the intersection before pulling out onto Main Street.

"Sure. You only want me for my handyman skills. But we don't need a problem with the plumbing this week."

"No, we do not. Isabelle will be all over it if there's even a hint of trouble. She's lurking in the shadows to take over. I can feel it in my bones."

"Speaking of Isabelle. Has she ever said anything about Kevin and his intentions?"

Gracie rolled her eyes. "That again? I am shocked at your interest in Midge's gossip about my cousin's boyfriend. Other than being perfect and the total opposite of Tim, which apparently isn't true—no."

"Kevin isn't a murderer though."

"I'll give you that—at the moment. I want to feel bad for her that she's made another miscalculation in selecting a man, but it's Isabelle. Her ego is boundless—massive. She's bossed me around for my whole life. Kevin will eventually show himself to be the rat he truly is—if he does have another girlfriend."

Marc shot her a questioning look.

"Do I detect a grudge? You really hate her that much?"

"Sorry. I don't really hate her—much. She's difficult, bossy, narrow-minded—"

"Your cousin," Marc supplied.

She huffed. "My cousin. Yup. I'll stop venting now."

"Thanks."

***

The drain resisted Marc's vigorous efforts with the plunger. Soapy water remained in the tub.

"Do you have a snake somewhere?" Marc asked, kneeling over the tub.

"This needs more power. Eww ... smells pretty bad." He backed away, and a brown liquid burbled up in the tub.

"Oh my gosh, it smells like sewer," Gracie cried, leaning over him.

"It sure does. This may be a bigger problem than a clogged drain."

When the toilet gurgled and more smells emanated from the vanity sink, Gracie ran to find the number for Ace McGowan's Septic Service.

***

"You've probably got roots in your leach system," Ace said, looking at the back corner of the yard. "It's wet here."

Ace was a slip of a man and Midge's brother. Lean and all business, just like his sister, he surveyed the lawn with a practiced eye.

"And not smelling too good," Gracie complained.

"That's why the dogs were so interested in the back corner yesterday when I was mowing," Marc observed.

"Great. What do you have to do?"

Gracie saw dollar signs drifting high into the cerulean sky.

"We're gonna have to dig it up. When did you have the tank pumped last?"

Gracie shook her head. "Never. Didn't think about it. I've been concentrating on upgrading the kennel and remodeling the house."

"How long you been here?"

"About three years, I think."

"Well, every three years is the rule of thumb, but I say your leach system is the problem. Lotsa trees back here—roots everywhere."

"Okay. When can you fix it? We're supposed to be married out here on Saturday."

"This coming Saturday?"

"Yes. Is that a problem?"

Gracie looked frantically at Ace's face, trying to determine if he was about to give her good news or bad.

"Well," he drawled, scratching the small gray beard on his square chin. "I'll pump the septic tank today. That'll help. I can start digging up the leach in the morning and ..."

"And what? What day can you have this fixed?"

"Now, hold on, Gracie. I'm trying to figure it out. Depends on what I find. If Marc here can start doing a little diggin' today to uncover the tank, we'll have a good start. I might need to bring in a backhoe. If tiles are broken or somethin' more serious is under there, it could take a week. You're not my only customer, you know. I'm pretty booked up right now."

"This is really important, Ace. My wedding, you know."

"Don't get in a lather. I know. I'll bring the pumper over here and start this afternoon. We'll go from there."

The chug of the pumper truck gave her some relief. No laundry and no dishwasher until the problem was fixed, Ace warned. Marc dutifully began digging with Ace looking on, while Gracie searched for the septic plans that were stored in the kennel office.

***

Ace looked over the drawings, a frown wrinkling his face. He pointed to the large birch and then back to the drawings.

"See that tree? It shouldn't have been planted back there. It's right on top of the leach. And so is the fence for that matter."

Gracie's stomach flip-flopped.

"What does that mean exactly?"

"That tree needs to come down, and ... well ..." He scratched the beard again. "I guess the fence's okay, but we might have to take a section out if the leach system is messed up."

"Are you kidding?"

The outdoor wedding under the blazing fall colors was fast becoming a dim possibility.

"No sirree! That tree's gotta come down too, or you'll have the same problem again."

"It could wait until after the wedding, right?"

"Sure. If you want. I can get you through the week."

Ace pulled a ribbed wide blue hose from the top of the septic tank and hauled it through the gate to load it alongside the tanker truck.

"Be back in the morning," he said, tipping his dirty Buffalo Sabres cap.

***

The chili and warm cornbread hit the spot after a more strenuous Sunday afternoon than planned. Jim joined Gracie and Marc in front of the TV, catching the last football game, with Denver and New England playing.

The two men discussed the merits of the two quarterbacks, which was way beyond her interest level. She took the dogs out to the backyard for one last run. Earlier, she'd dragged some old folding chairs to cordon off the tank area, which had been nicely excavated by Marc. At least, Ace shouldn't have to do a whole lot to check things out.

The air was nippy, her breath visible in the darkness. She shoved her hands into the warmth of the jacket's pockets, making sure Haley and Max stayed well away from the smelly area.

Everything had seemed perfectly under control for the wedding only days ago. She'd felt pretty proud of herself for handling the logistics, keeping everything simple. It certainly wasn't trouble-free as of today. Could they really be married here on Saturday? What would her yard look like? Did they need to move the ceremony somewhere else? Gracie wanted this wedding to be different from hers and Michael's. She'd had the big church wedding. This was supposed to be intimate. The fall colors were the backdrop, rather than stained glass. The dogs would be their attendants, carrying the rings attached with ribbons to their collars. It was a straightforward and even elegant plan. A headache had blossomed behind her eyes, making her feel sick. She really needed some sleep and for others to stay out of her plans.

The dogs ran happily back to the patio, tails waving. They seemed to be settling into life together. Would it be as easy for her and Marc?

She bent and hugged both dogs, who whined anxiously to go back inside.

CHAPTER 15

Midge's Restaurant was a cacophony of clanking dishes, sizzling bacon, and conversation. Jim sat sipping his second cup of coffee, reading the *Pennysaver*. It was amazing what people sold in the weekly publication. Someone was offering a 1984 Reliant that didn't run for a mere three thousand dollars. The price seemed a little optimistic. The seller must have thought the car was a valuable classic. Someone else had buckets of hinges, nails, and what have you for sale at best offer. That actually might be worth looking into, Jim thought. You never know when you might require "what have you."

"Hey, dreamboat, you need any more coffee, another stack of pancakes?"

Midge, the owner of the only restaurant in Deer Creek, sidled up to him with coffeepot in hand. She beamed, batting her eyelashes in jest.

"No. I've reached my limit on all accounts, adorable."

"Too bad. I have so much to give," she continued with a wicked smile.

"I *give* you a lot of my hard-earned money," Jim laughed.

Midge waved a hand nonchalantly. "Rightly so. You can't cook a lick. Everything all right with Gracie and Marc? Wedding still happening?"

Jim nodded. "All set. A little issue with the septic though. Ace has to dig up some of the backyard today."

"I know. He told me about that last night. That'll stress her out. Ace'll take care it though. He knows his stuff."

"I'm not worried. But, you're right, she *is* stressed about it. Hopefully he'll have it all back together by this afternoon."

"Did I hear you say that Gracie has a plumbing problem?" Isabelle Browne-Baker stood at the cash register next to Jim's place at the counter.

His heart dropped like a rock. Gracie would kill him for letting that slip.

"Yeah. A little backup issue. But, like I said, Ace is working on it today."

"Her yard will be in ruins if they're digging it up. It was already a mess anyway. She can't have the wedding there. I'd better run over to the house and give her some help. I knew something like this would happen. She doesn't have event experience." She pulled out a twenty-dollar bill from her wallet.

"Uh, I wouldn't plan on that," Jim started. "She's really busy."

"Of course, she's busy. We're all busy. Which is why she needs my input. Her decision-making skills are dismal. The wedding's only six days away, and it won't come off with any flair at all, unless I do something about it."

Isabelle, in her black leather car coat, perfect hair, and airbrush-quality makeup, was a formidable adversary. One which gave Jim chills. Let the women hash it out. He'd tried to stop Isabelle ... Well, sort of.

Midge managed not to interject any comments before ringing up Isabelle's check. As soon as she breezed out the door, the diminutive restaurant owner leaned over the counter with a smug look.

"What I would give to see that meeting."

"What I'd give to have kept my mouth shut," Jim groaned.

Midge straightened herself to her full five feet. She dismissed his comment with a shrug. "Isabelle would've found out anyway. Can't you hear her rant the day of the wedding if there was a little dirt pile in the yard?"

Yes, he could. Unfortunately, he could.

"Any sweet rolls left?"

The least he could do was bring some sort of peace offering. Midge snatched a box from the shelf next to the large flattop and quickly filled it with gooey cinnamon rolls.

***

Ace and two of his men carefully removed the section of vinyl fencing as Gracie watched from the patio. The fence was so new and sparkling white. They'd better not stain or break it. She held her breath while the three men gingerly laid the sections near the edge of the field that abutted her yard. They pulled the posts from the ground and laid them next to the panels.

Ace drove the backhoe into the yard, the tires sinking slightly into the soft earth. Ruts. There would be ruts in her yard. Gracie nervously tugged at her sagging ponytail. The broken and clogged tiles were a real mess in the leach system. Ace was trying to clean everything out and replace the tile by Wednesday. The backhoe bit into the lawn, ripping turf, leaves, and dirt away. She looked at her watch. It was almost lunchtime, and she needed to be working at the kennel. Marc was on his way to the airport to meet his mother, sister, and brother-in-law. She'd sent two loads of laundry with him in the hopes he'd wash them at his house before returning. Now her soon-to-be mother-in-law and sister-in-law would see her home in a state of dishevelment. What would their take be on the predicament? Her phone rang, vibrating the back pocket of her jeans.

***

Theresa pulled up to the front of the Minders' two-story colonial. She admired the corn shock tied around a wrought iron gaslight near the sidewalk. Gloria had placed several pumpkins and a pot of red mums in the center for extra oomph. It was a nice touch.

Gloria opened the door almost immediately, a look of relief on her face.

"Are you okay?" Theresa asked.

Gloria looked uncharacteristically harried.

"Not really," Gloria answered, quickly shutting the door. "Art Walczak just left."

"Why was he here?"

"He came to claim rights to Franny's estate. He has some sort of promissory note, which says he's owed thirty thousand dollars. Can you believe it? Of course, Albert's already out and about. I had the distinct pleasure of talking with him."

"You're kidding!"

"I wish. Come in. The coffee's on in the kitchen."

Theresa trooped into the kitchen, sitting down in the breakfast nook. The old-fashioned kitchen, with a restored cast-iron range that had been converted from wood to gas, was a one-of-a-kind treasure. The kitchen also boasted a bay window, which overlooked their backyard. The cozy table for two was tucked into the angled spot.

Theresa unbuttoned her jacket and admired the dining set, which was a spectacular tiger maple, one of Gloria's best finds at a yard sale a few years back. She ran her hand over the beautiful wood grain, still a little envious.

Gloria set a large brown mug in front of her, along with the sugar bowl, before sitting across from Theresa.

"Is this promissory note legitimate? Why would Franny go into debt to an ex-husband?"

"Good questions. I told Art he'd have to give it to the attorney, which went over like a lead balloon. I think he expected Albert to write him a check."

"Hmm. Maybe the note's a fake then."

Gloria shrugged. "It had Franny's signature. I wish Albert hadn't agreed to be the executor. He should have let the attorney do it. He's the substitute."

Theresa stirred two teaspoons of sugar into her coffee.

"I'm sure he's feels duty bound to Franny."

"Always. He can't help himself." Gloria managed a wry smile. "Along with Art, the quilt dispute, and insurance claim, he will more than earn every penny of the executor's fee. And who knows if there are any assets?"

"What about the house?"

"Mortgaged to the hilt. The bank will take everything, unless Art wants to buy it. Her car was paid for, thankfully."

"I had no idea. I thought the house was paid off long ago."

"It was. She took out a big home equity loan right before their divorce for some reason. Such a mess."

Theresa set the mug down quickly, sloshing coffee on the placemat.

"I wonder if Art is still gambling. Maybe he's run up some debts."

"Albert will talk to Kevin at the bank. I'm sure he'll have the whole story."

"What about a funeral?"

"Well, this is strange, but Franny's last wishes were to be cremated and her ashes strewn over the gorge in Letchworth Park. No service. No calling hours. No fuss. We didn't need to pick out that outfit either." Gloria frowned.

"Really! So, what are you doing?"

"We're going to the park early tomorrow morning and toss Franny over the wall."

Theresa nearly choked, suppressing a laugh and feeling shocked all at once.

Gloria's face softened, instantly repentant. "I'm sorry. This thing has me so upset."

"Don't worry. Should Bob and I come? What about Lulu or Art?"

"You can come, if you want. We'll be at the Wolf Creek picnic area at nine. I let Art know. He should have the opportunity to be there. I think he'll show up. Of course, her sister isn't able to come, but once the urn is emptied, I'll give it to her, if she wants it."

"And Lulu?"

"I was going to stop in and see her after we did some inventorying in the house. There will have to be an auction for the household goods and car. East Koy Auctions is meeting us there this afternoon with Art. He wants to make sure his property is identified."

"It sounds like you have it under control. I'll see if Bob wants to go. I'll be there in any case."

"We'd both appreciate that." Gloria frowned. "Didn't Franny tell you the quilt was worth fifty thousand dollars?"

"Yes. Why?"

"It was insured for twice that."

Theresa's eyes widened. "Really?"

"Really." Gloria drummed her fingers nervously on her mug. "I guess it's standard practice, according to the adjustor. I wonder how they determined the value to begin with. Wouldn't Franny have had some sort of appraisal that would determine the insurance value?"

"That would be my guess."

Theresa rose and took her mug to the sink. "I'd better run. Gracie has a crisis at the house, and apparently, Isabelle tried to help. I may have to referee. I wish those two would figure out how to get along."

"I hope it's nothing serious. Probably wedding jitters."

"We'll see."

***

Theresa pulled away from the curb, abruptly remembering the foreign money she'd spotted in Lulu's sewing cabinet. She wanted to ask Gloria if she'd seen it. Oh, well. She'd ask in the morning.

What a peculiar turn of events! No funeral, lots of debt, and a stolen quilt. Franny must have been working on some scheme to fix her serious money troubles.

Then there was Lulu with her own version of quirky. Why did Lulu have foreign money in her sewing cabinet? Would she steal Franny's quilt? Nothing made a lot of sense. The two women had been best friends for years. They'd been through thick and thin. Assorted illnesses, Franny's continuing marital problems, and Lulu's bereavement in the last year. Neither woman had had children. They'd always been like sisters. Something didn't feel right. Theresa couldn't decipher what the real deal was and it was driving her crazy.

***

"Am I glad to see you!" Gracie called to her mother as Theresa opened the car door. She held her kitchen door open and felt the stinging chill of a north wind.

"What's the emergency? You said something about the septic, which must be the case, since Ace's truck is here." Theresa pointed at the pickup parked next to her sedan. The dogs surrounded her, pink tongues hanging out. She scratched behind their ears and walked toward the house, the dogs bounding back inside.

"Unfortunately, it's true. It gets worse."

Gracie's face felt hot, despite the wind, which blew wisps of red hair around her face.

"Tell me inside. It's freezing out here."

93

The dogs ran through the kitchen and pressed their noses against the windows of the French doors that led to the patio.

As soon as they were inside, Gracie cut loose. "My leach bed is clogged, and Ace's backhoe broke down about a half hour ago. The stupid thing is partially stuck in the backyard. I think I need another place to have the wedding. I don't know what I'm going to do. Marc's in Buffalo, picking up his family, and Isabelle was here earlier, trying to take over—again."

Theresa held up hands in a pleading gesture. "Whoa! Hold on a second. We've got a few too many irons in the fire for my brain."

Gracie sighed and sunk onto a stool at the breakfast bar.

"It's a real jam, Mom. All I wanted was a simple wedding in my backyard. What is going on? It's only six days away."

Theresa took off her coat, draping it over a kitchen chair. She joined Gracie at the granite counter.

"Tell me what's happening with the backyard, first of all," she said calmly.

Gracie offered the gory details of the dysfunctional septic system.

"To top it off, the ground under the backhoe started sinking on one side. Ace says it won't be too bad to get out, but the lawn is a wreck. As if that wasn't enough, a few minutes ago, something happened, and the backhoe quit. He's on the phone right now, trying to locate a part."

"All right. So, your backyard isn't going to be a good place for people to be wandering around in on Saturday."

"Right. It was supposed to be an easy fix. Dig up a little grass, repair the problem, and cover it up. What if he can't get the part?"

"What's Marc say?"

"I didn't even call him. He's focused on picking up his family. He hasn't seen his mom and sister for a couple of years, so he wanted to be there."

"Of course, he should be there. You should have gone with him."

"Not with Ace here."

"That's true," Theresa agreed. "Are we all getting together before the wedding? You haven't said anything."

"Well, we might have everyone over. I don't see how we could now, but we really haven't talked about it yet. There's been a lot going on."

"We could whip up something, I guess. It's a little short notice now."

Gracie sighed and rubbed her forehead. Her nerves were frayed, and she didn't want to lose it with her mother. "I know. Let's figure it out once Marc's back. That's the least of my worries. At the moment."

Theresa frowned, picking at her cuticles, which to Gracie signaled disapproval.

"You said something about Isabelle?" Theresa looked up at her daughter.

"Yes. That's the other problem. She somehow heard about my issue and flew in on her broom, offering to host the wedding at her house. There's no way that's happening."

"Why not? She has the perfect spot in her back garden. The gazebo, big yard, and her flowers are gorgeous. If it rains, she has that huge enclosed patio."

Theresa slid off the stool and joined the dogs at the French doors to survey the disaster.

"That's the problem," said Gracie. "It *is* perfect. She will throw this favor in my face until ... until the Bills make the playoffs again. Izzy rescued my wedding. Saved the day like Wonder Woman. It makes me sick." She joined the group at the doors, truly feeling ill when she saw Ace leaning against the backhoe, talking on his phone.

"Gracie! You should be grateful for options. Isabelle is only trying to help her cousin, who does have a big problem. The way I see it, even if Ace does finish the repairs in—let's say two days—your yard will still be a mud pit for the weekend. Not a great backdrop for your pictures."

Her mother was right. Pictures. Wedding photos. Wedding photos. She gasped. Oh no! She'd forgotten the photographer. She'd meant to call Jesaro Photography, who'd done Tom and Kelly's wedding. Somehow it had disappeared from her radar. How could she have missed that important detail? Selfies with her phone wouldn't cut it. She groaned, hitting a palm against her forehead.

CHAPTER 16

Marc was sandwiched between two mini-vans full of noisy teenagers, who were dragging out a never-ending stream of luggage from the back of each vehicle. He tapped his fingers against the steering wheel, enjoying Carrie Underwood's latest tune on the radio. It was taking forever for his sister and brother-in-law to appear from the underground rental car garage. His mother was stretching her legs, walking around the short-term parking area when Miranda and her husband, Larry Holcomb, drove into view. They could finally get underway. It had taken over an hour for his brother-in-law's rental vehicle transaction. That had been the most painful part of the reunion so far.

Unlike the Clarks, the Stevens family thrived on separation. It always took at least a couple of days for Marc to adjust to familial bonds. He never knew what to say to his sister especially. They'd been close as kids, but adulthood had taken them in very different directions.

Larry rolled down the window and gave Marc a weak smile.

"Sorry we were so long. The line was killer."

"No problem. Ready to head for Deer Creek?" Marc responded cheerfully.

"How far to the house? I need to lie down after all that turbulence. I thought we were going to crash," Miranda griped.

"About an hour," Marc began.

"An hour?"

"Oh, Miranda. Don't turn on the drama. It was a little bumpy. We're here in one piece. We have all our luggage too," Violet Stevens said sharply, opening the passenger door of Marc's truck.

"It was awful. My nerves are shattered," Miranda whined.

"Did you take a pill?" her husband asked. "Take the pill, and we'll be on our way. Right, Marc?"

Marc nodded with arched eyebrows. This was going to be a dilly of a visit. While Miranda squinted at a brown prescription bottle, Larry waved and followed Marc out to Route 33. Within an hour, they were on Wethersfield Road, not far from Marc's home. His mother had insisted they were going out to dinner as a family during their leisurely drive through the rolling hills and dairy farms that dotted the highway. Gracie still hadn't answered his text, which he'd sent right before they'd left the airport. Crossing the railroad tracks into Rock Glen, his phone buzzed in the dash holder and went to the Bluetooth connection.

"Hey, I got your text." Gracie sounded uncommonly businesslike.

"Good. We're in Rock Glen. We're dropping off luggage at the house first, and then we'll be over. Mom wants to take everyone out to eat tonight. I hope this doesn't mess up any plans."

"Well ... no. That's great. My mother will be pleased. She was concerned about meeting everyone."

"Hi, Gracie. I can't wait to meet you and your family," Violet interjected.

"Uh ... oh ... hi. Yes. I can't wait to meet you either."

"Probably a half hour and we'll be there."

"Good. One thing though. Ace wasn't able to finish the job today. His backhoe is sitting in the yard, broken down for the moment."

"Really?"

That wasn't a good sign. No wonder she hadn't called before.

"Yes. Really. He needs a part that won't be here until Wednesday. Which means limited water use until then. And it means we need a new location for sure."

"It's okay with me if the yard looks a little rough. We can—"

"I'll talk to you about it when you get here. I need to go. And don't forget the laundry."

"Right. The laundry."

It was sitting in the washer at his house. Had he turned the machine on before leaving for the airport? He'd have one very unhappy fiancée if he hadn't.

"I'll bring it."

"Good. See you in a bit."

The called ended, and Violet looked expectantly at her son.

"Is she all right? A little stressed maybe?"

"A lot stressed. Leach field problem and the guy fixing it has to repair his backhoe."

"Isn't the wedding in the yard?"

"It is or *was*, at this point. Sounds like we'll need to find a new place."

"That's awful. Is there a church or a town hall you could use?"

"We'll figure it out, Mom. Don't worry. We just want a casual wedding. It can't be that much of a problem to find another place, compared to surviving a week with Miranda."

"Marc, please. Miranda had some sort of breakdown this year and is medicated out the wazoo. Her real and imagined issues are getting to me and poor Larry. This is a lot to handle for all of us. Your sister is an emotional wreck, and I'm starting to feel a little shaky myself. Day after day, it's another problem. I had high hopes that your wedding would snap her out of whatever is really bothering her."

"That's a lot of pressure for Gracie and me. Should Miranda be here? If she's not stable—"

"She'll be fine. A nap and a few pills."

Marc turned up the paved driveway, which wound around a small apple orchard, and deposited them in front of a small, ranch-style house. A stand of pine trees flanked the rear of the property. Marc parked his pickup outside the attached garage, with Miranda and Larry right behind him.

"Here we are," he announced.

"It's been quite a while since I was here. The house looks nice."

Marc smiled. "Thanks. I'm hoping it'll sell quickly in the spring."

"It's too bad you and Gracie can't live here." Violet stood taking in the serene property. "Such a pretty house and yard."

Marc looked at his mother quizzically. "You understand about the kennel business, right?"

"Yes, but it's too bad you have to give up your home."

"I don't have a problem selling. It's okay. Besides, you'll love Gracie's house. She's worked hard on remodeling, and even adding on, in the last couple of years."

Violet didn't look convinced. She drew her jacket closer, her slight frame shivering in the chilly breeze. Marc chewed the inside of his cheek, hoping that his mother and Gracie would hit it off. His mother was on the defensive for some reason. The look in her stormy brown eyes was a warning for those who knew her.

Miranda and Larry joined them, Miranda stretching and yawning. She had aged since he'd seen her last. Maybe it was because she was wearing glasses now. Apparently, the meds had kicked in. There was hope she'd settle down. He carried his mother's suitcases and set them on the small porch.

"Mom, you've got my bedroom on the right. Miranda, you and Larry have the last room on the left down the hall. You can rest if you want. I need to run Gracie's laundry to her, but I'll be back," Marc said, unlocking the door.

Miranda gave her brother a puzzled look. She rubbed the back of her neck, yawning again.

"You do her laundry?"

***

"Let's wrap it up," Jim called to Gracie, who was just locking the office.

"I am. I am. I want to check on a couple of the dogs before I leave though."

They'd decided to close early with the light boarding traffic. Besides, the logistics of having the Stevens and Clark families meet, along with the lack of a photographer, had put Gracie almost over the edge.

"Is there a problem with somebody?" Jim asked, winding a hose onto the metal holder fastened to the wall.

"I hope not. Peace-of-mind check in Corridor C."

"Let me turn the lights back on," Jim said, striding down the darkened hallway.

Once the lights went on in the kennel corridors, dogs vocalized enthusiastic greetings, while Gracie and Jim made sure each boarder was snug. Gracie stopped at the run with Rhett and Scarlett, a couple of rat terriers who'd been skittish during the day. It was their first time in the kennel. She opened the door for them, and they dashed out to freedom. The lively black and white dogs yipped and spun in circles in their excitement. They ran and licked her face when she squatted down to pet them. They spied Jim farther down the corridor and ran full tilt, launching themselves into the air.

"Catch them," Gracie called. "They expect to be caught."

Jim managed to snag the small wiggly dogs just in time, balancing them precariously on his crossed forearms.

"Wow, guys! That was a bit of a surprise."

Gracie laughed. "Those are the Bascoms' dogs. Mike taught them the leaping trick, which isn't popular with his wife. Good work. They're pretty fast and a little unpredictable."

The dogs jumped to the floor as Jim bent down.

"I guess. Circus time is over," he said with a chuckle.

"They seemed pretty scared when they were dropped off today," Gracie said. "It seems they've recovered nicely. Come on, little ol' Scarlett and Rhett. Time for you two to settle down and go to sleep. Tomorrow's another day, and I have to find a photographer on very short notice. Everyone seems to be booked. Imagine that," she said, snapping her fingers.

She and Jim walked side-by-side to the reception area, flipping off light switches as they went

"A photographer? Somebody cancel on you?"

"I wish. I totally spaced it. Have no idea why. My mother is supposed to be making some calls too. As long as she doesn't call Isabelle, we'll be fine."

Jim laughed. "I'll bet you a dollar she's called her. And speaking of Isabelle, the word on the street is that her boyfriend has somebody on the side."

"Marc said the same thing. Where is this information coming from?"

"I heard it at the hardware today when I returned that defective heater. Darlene Evans told me some woman has been visiting Isabelle's house at odd times."

"How would she know that?"

"Neighbors always know what's happening in the neighborhood. Isabelle lives next door to the official neighborhood watchdog—"

"Benny Crowder," Gracie finished for him.

"Exactly. You know how seriously he takes that vital job."

"Ha! Well then, it may be true. I do feel sorry for Izzy if it's really happening." She twirled a strand of hair, contemplating how to open the topic of Kevin with her mother, but more importantly, she had to change out of her kennel clothes and pass muster with Marc's family. It was surprising her mother hadn't at least left a voicemail about the photographer search. Pulling the phone from her jeans pocket, she swiped the screen. Nothing happened. Great! Her battery must have died.

***

Gloria followed Albert, who trailed after Mike Shultz of East Koy Auctions. He shambled along, hulking and older than Gloria thought he'd be. Mike reminded her of an elderly bear. Art Walczak had already left, his nose out of joint over Franny's disinheritance. He had only debt handed to him; the mortgage was on the verge of foreclosure. The sale of the house might take care of the obligation, but Gloria wasn't confident of that. Art didn't seem to be in a position to pay off the mortgage and regain the house.

"We can put you on the calendar for the second week of November," Mike said.

"That would be good," Albert said, stopping in the gloomy living room.

"How much do you think the auction will bring?" Gloria asked, standing next to her husband.

"Hard to say. Maybe five thousand on a good day, probably less." Mike's paw-like hand scratched his longish dark gray hair. He pulled a ball cap from the pocket of his plaid flannel coat and stuffed it over his untidy locks.

She exchanged a look with her husband.

"That's all, huh?" Albert asked.

"Yeah. There are a few decent antiques, but nothing special here."

"What about the quilts in the bedroom? We found about six in all." Gloria had hoped for a better answer.

"Who knows? They're all right, but it depends on the crowd. I'll have Edna call you with a date and time. My crew will organize everything here, and it'll all be removed the day of the auction. You won't have to worry about anything."

"Thanks, Mike. I'll be expecting Edna's call," Albert said, shaking the man's hand.

The Minders stood looking around at the worn, but comfortable furniture.

"Still glad you said you'd be the executor?"

"Now, Gloria, it was Franny's last wish."

"I know, but you're so busy. Why not back out and let the attorney handle everything?"

The pastor took off his wire-framed glasses and rubbed a white handkerchief over the lenses before setting them back on his face.

"Let's go see Lulu," he said.

CHAPTER 17

The somber group bowed their heads during Albert Minders' prayer, committing Frances Walczak to the tender mercies of God. The sound of Wolf Creek burbled in the background, and a few birds added a couple of measures of warbled notes, befitting the occasion. Theresa, Bob, the Minders, Art, and Lulu lifted their heads at the "amen."

"And now, we complete Franny's wish of remaining in the park she loved so much," Albert continued, carrying the copper urn. Silvery butterflies adorned the top, and thin silver bands circled near the neck of the jar. He set the urn down on the stone wall. He tried to unscrew the lid and grunted when it didn't move.

"Is it on a little too tight, preacher?" Art asked, examining the lid.

"I don't know. It seems to be stuck."

"Here, let me try." Art lifted the gracefully shaped container and wrenched on the top without success.

Lulu, Gloria, and Theresa looked at one another and then at Bob.

He sighed and strolled over to take a look.

"How many men does it take ..." Lulu began with sheepish look.

"I know," Theresa giggled. "Poor Franny."

"You hold the urn, Art, and I'll give it a twist," Bob said. Artie stood by the wall with the lid pointed outward, and Bob grasped the lid with both hands. "Hold it tight."

"Got it," the dumpy man said, hugging the urn.

Bob attempted to rotate the top, groaning. "It's no good. Must be cross-threaded."

Theresa came forward and examined the container. "Are you sure?"

She stifled a laugh. A thin layer of wax was evident on the top metal band.

"Here," she instructed, reaching for the urn. Scraping the additional layer of security with her thumbnail, she handed it back to Art.

"Oh. That will help," Art said. "Well, here goes."

After brushing off the remaining bits of wax, he quickly unscrewed the top of the urn. "Should I go ahead?" he asked, looking back at the group.

"Yes," Albert Minders said, looking relieved. He patted at his silver hair, which had ruffled in the early morning breeze.

"Good luck, Franny," Art said with a little sob, the powdery cremains drifting in the air above the Genesee River.

The rest joined him, Lulu placing a hand on his shoulder. He tapped the jar on the wall before screwing the top back on and handing it to Gloria.

"Now, preacher," he said, turning a determined face to Albert, "we need to talk about that money that's owed me."

***

Theresa's phone chimed with a text notification on the way to her car. Poor Albert and Gloria were still "chatting" with Art, who seemed to think his dubious promissory note had priority over the bank and anyone else.

The text was excellent news that refocused her thoughts on the wedding. Isabelle had, indeed, come through with a photographer in the nick of time.

Isabelle had worked her magic to snag Adriana's Photography. A personal favor, Isabelle had noted. Of course. Family comes first. Isabelle knew her priorities. How could Gracie have been so scatter-brained? At least one wedding crisis was solved.

Now, if her daughter and niece could only be civil to one another for a few days, the wedding location issue would be resolved too. Isabelle could be difficult, but the poor girl had been through a lot. Except for her two college-age children, her entire family was gone. Two of the three murdered, which most days was too much to think about. At least, Tim, Isabelle's late husband, couldn't do any more damage. If Kevin would just make her an honest woman, then all would be put right.

Once home, Theresa was irritated that Gracie still hadn't answered her two text messages. Maybe she'd turned her phone off. Marc's family was probably taking up her time, but why didn't she have a moment to call her mother? Maybe Gracie had found another photographer. That would be a mess. Maybe she should drive to the kennel. She checked the soup in the crockpot, which was bubbling nicely.

The WCJW weather report blared from the kitchen radio, forecasting Indian summer weather tomorrow through Sunday. She was hoping that the weatherman was right for once.

That was another thing. Gracie's determination to hold an outdoor wedding in October. They didn't live in Tahiti. There could be snow, or at the very least, freezing temperatures.

"Bob, I'm taking some soup to Lulu," she called to her husband, who was seated at the dining room table, staring at his laptop screen.

"All right," he answered distractedly. "I'm paying the bills and then picking up my suit from the cleaners."

"Good," Theresa replied, thankful for one less errand before the wedding.

Hefting the crockpot from the kitchen counter, she made a mental list of things that had to be done by the end of the day. The most important one was talking to Gracie to find out if there were any other wedding details that hadn't been handled.

But, first, a visit with Lulu was in order. Gloria Minders had agreed to meet her there with a pie. After the memorial, Lulu had left quickly without a word. Her lack of emotion had them worried, and Gloria's ears had perked up when Theresa mentioned the foreign money. Maybe Lulu was planning a trip abroad. After last week's bizarre events, maybe Lulu was ready to talk about what was really going on.

Gloria was waiting curbside when Theresa pulled up. She held a Tupperware pie carrier in her arms. Her cream-colored wool scarf rippled in the steady breeze, flapping against the sleeve of her black tweed coat.

"Ready?" Gloria asked, tucking the scarf snugly inside the coat.

"I think so. Did you call her?"

"I did, and she sounded really quite happy to have us visit. I'm surprised, after her aloofness at the park."

Theresa pulled a face. "I am too. Let's go then."

The steamy warmth of Lulu's kitchen was welcome. Fresh brewed coffee was waiting. Lulu looked downright cheerful, and the kitchen was now decluttered. Everything was spick and span, as it had been before Ed's death. Quite the change from only days before.

"You're looking so much better," Gloria chirped, setting the pie container on the table.

"Better? I'm fine," Lulu said, lifting the plastic lid. "Is it apple?"

"Apple and pear," Gloria said, shedding her coat and hanging it on the back of the chair.

"Sounds good. Thank you, Gloria. I will really enjoy it. How about some coffee?"

Theresa plugged in the crockpot next to the coffeemaker.

"I'll get it," she said. "You sit down, Lulu. I'm sure this morning was very difficult. These mugs all right?" she asked, pointing to the row hanging from hooks under the cabinet.

"Those are fine," Lulu said, sitting across from Gloria. "The soup smells wonderful, Theresa."

"It's beef and barley." Theresa grabbed three mugs and filled them before placing them on the table.

"Thank you both for thinking of me."

Theresa pulled out a chair and found a pile of papers, which she scooped up and lay on the tabletop.

"Oh, sorry! I didn't have time to take care of this stuff," Lulu complained, snatching the papers and placing them in her lap.

"No problem," Gloria said with a smile. She took a sip from the black cup.

Lulu struggled with the mishmash of papers that threatened to slide onto the floor. "I'm glad you invited me to Franny's service."

"Of course. It wouldn't be right not to have you there." Gloria said.

"Art was a surprise though. He and Franny were really on the outs. He'd been hanging around again, and there were a couple of pretty loud arguments on the front porch before ... Well, you know."

"That's too bad," Gloria said.

Lulu rose, clutching the papers to her body. "I'll just put these stupid ..."

The papers fluttered away from her, and Gloria bent to collect them. Lulu's face reddened.

"I heard him say some awful things to Franny the day—" she began, tearing up. She stooped to collect the stray papers and magazines from Gloria.

"It's okay. Let me help," Gloria said graciously.

She deposited the stack onto the counter and reseated herself.

"Which day?" Theresa asked.

"The day of the accident in the garage," Lulu supplied with a catch in her voice.

"Did he ever say anything about the quilt?" Theresa found herself tensed for the answer.

"No, I don't think so. Art always wanted more money. He was constantly after Franny for it. I do think he was in my garage the night ... well, when Franny had the ..." Her voice broke, tears welling in her eyes. She shook her head mournfully.

"Are you sure?" Theresa gasped. "Did you see him in there? You should've—"

"I didn't see him, and I couldn't swear it was his voice, but I'm almost certain there were others in the garage with Franny. But I didn't tell the police. I was so upset. I might be wrong."

Gloria's and Theresa's eyes were wide. Gloria put a hand over her mouth.

Theresa forged ahead. "Would Art or another family member take the quilt? Did he know where she kept it?"

Lulu stirred powdered creamer into her coffee. She tapped the spoon against the mug's rim before laying it down.

"I don't know. There were family squabbles about it once in a while. Artie probably knew where it was, like I did. I'm not sure who else would have that kind of information. Franny was pretty careful what she shared about the quilt. What about those women who were over there a few days ago?"

Theresa nodded. "One of them is a relative of Franny's, but not a close one. She was insistent on seeing the quilt—something about her grandmother being the rightful owner. But now that Franny's gone ..."

"It's become Albert's problem," Gloria finished. "Lisa Stederman Kronk called right away about the quilt. He had to give her the news about the insurance claim."

Lulu shook her head sadly. "It's a beautiful work of art. Priceless in many respects. It must have taken forever for those two women to sew it all by hand. I wonder if that article will still be printed about the quilt's history. Franny was pretty excited about the historical organization's interview. The photographer took lots of pictures too. A very attractive young woman who really knew her stuff."

"That's a good point. It sounds like there have been quite a few people in the house to see the quilt in the last several months."

"Yes. Franny told me back in September that there was a lot of interest in the quilt again," Lulu added.

"That may be why the family dispute has reared its ugly head," Gloria sighed.

Lulu began looking around, as if anxious for them to leave. Theresa glanced at her watch. She did have plenty to do herself. As if on cue, Gloria concurred.

"Let's go, Theresa," she said, rising from the chair. "We both have lots of errands to run."

"That's for sure," Theresa agreed, catching Gloria's signal. "My next stop is to talk to the bride."

"Give Gracie my congratulations. I'm so happy for her," Lulu said, scraping the chair back from the table.

"I sure will. Take care of yourself, and if there's anything you need, just call."

"I will, Theresa. Thank you both for coming."

***

Gloria walked Theresa to her car, smiling and waving to Lulu, who stood at the storm door, watching her guests depart.

"I believe Lulu really does have a trip in mind," she said in a hushed voice.

"Really? You think so?" Theresa replied, surprised.

She unlocked her car and slid into the seat, her mind racing. Lulu never went anywhere outside the state. A trip to Rochester was a big deal. Ed had traveled because of his job and took his annual fishing trip to the Adirondacks, but Lulu was perfectly happy in Deer Creek.

"Yes. A trip to sunny climes," Gloria continued. "Those papers had a couple of travel brochures mixed in."

"For where?"

Gloria arched an eyebrow at her friend. "Mexico and Costa Rica."

***

"Mom! Am I glad to see you," Gracie gushed, opening the storm door.

"Didn't you get my texts?"

"Sorry. Marc and I were busy with his family last night, and then this morning I realized my phone was dead. I can't believe that you found a photographer. I came up empty with the ones I called."

"You can thank Isabelle for the photographer. It's a good thing she has connections. You're one lucky bride. Now, let's go over my checklist and make sure we don't have any other ugly surprises."

Gracie screwed up her face, her fears realized. Isabelle now had a foothold on her wedding. She resigned herself to the checklist scrutiny. Theresa plunked herself on a stool at the granite-topped breakfast bar, pulling a notebook from her handbag. Gracie settled in next to her, determined to be pleasant. She was relatively confident that there would be no other bombshells to derail the wedding.

"All right. I think it's all covered now," Theresa said, ticking off the last item, "thank you notes," on her list. She slid off the stool and walked to the French doors.

"I told you—" Gracie started, trailing behind her.

"Except for the venue. Your yard is out of the question. Be realistic."

Ace's backhoe sat silent and still, awaiting a miraculous mechanical organ that would bring it to life again.

"I know. I know. I suppose Isabelle's offer still stands."

"I would make a call to her, if you still want that outdoor wedding."

***

Isabelle's eyes gleamed, her fingers tracing the white railing of the classical garden fixture. "I think the gazebo is the perfect place for you and Marc. There's plenty of room for Reverend Minders to even have a little podium. I did have an entire string quartet here."

"I remember," Gracie replied acerbically. "It was quite the event—that food fight and all."

Isabelle avoided Gracie's eyes and sniffed. "Anyway, mi casa is su casa."

Gracie ate a generous bite of crow and nodded. Marc wandered around the yard, rubbing his cold hands together, uneasily waiting for the negotiations to be finalized.

"I really appreciate this, Isabelle. Your yard is lovely."

It was the truth. Velvety grass, masses of red-and-gold mums, purple asters, the gazebo, and flagstone walkways and patio screamed first class—*Better Homes and Gardens* all the way.

"And as long as it doesn't rain, it'll be perfect."

"It won't rain," Isabelle verified with a confidence that made Gracie wonder if her trying cousin had power over the weather. "There's a high pressure area over Western New York from tomorrow through Sunday morning."

"I see."

Marc reappeared, a questioning look on his face. "Everything settled?"

"Of course. There was never any question that this is where your wedding should be from the start. Gracie's lawn isn't close to being ready for any formal event. It never was." Isabelle pursed her lips and offered a pained smile. "You did talk with Adriana?"

"Yes. And thank you for that help too," Gracie gulped.

She had absolutely no pride left. It was all in a deep hole in her backyard.

"Adriana is the best. She's been photographing the house for a spread in the *Historic Homes* magazine. I'm being featured in the January issue. Kevin knew her in college. They went to Syracuse, you know. She was selected to work with some of the finest photography artists there."

"Interesting that Kevin knew her then. Wasn't he in finance?"

"Kevin has so many interests. He's crazy about fine art. He has some wonderful connections in the art world." Isabelle looked practically beatific speaking about Kevin. "Anyway, Adriana is top-notch. You should see some of her work. It's gallery quality."

Marc's face blanched. "What's she charging us?" he whispered to Gracie.

Gracie shook her head slightly. "Not now. It's okay though."

"Adriana is worth every penny she charges and more," Isabelle confirmed.

Gracie smiled and followed her cousin across the lawn to the house.

"Now, Gracie. We need to talk makeup and hair. What about the musicians? Have you booked any?"

Marc put a hand over his mouth, stifling a painful laugh, and peeled off in the direction of the driveway. Waving, he called out, "I'm going to pick up pizzas with Tom for tonight."

What a coward!

CHAPTER 18

Lulu carefully fingered the quilts stacked in her sewing room. The batting in each was sufficient. The stitching was even and perfect, the clamshell pattern simple, but so effective with its little pockets for her purposes. The subdued color schemes for each of them should keep the quilts from drawing attention. However, the last quilt would be special. She was already stitching the small pieces together to create the complex pattern. She smoothed out the paper with the instructions for laying out the design. It was the "Blushing Bride Stained Glass" pattern. Carefully refolding the quilts, she stacked them in a plastic tub and shut the lid.

She sat at the small computer desk to check her email. It was there! She opened the message and scanned the contents. Everything was still on track for November. Printing it off, she deleted the email before shutting down the laptop. Once she finished the last quilt, the entire plan would be in motion. She would finally be on her way out of Deer Creek. The adventure of a lifetime was on the horizon in a little over four weeks. The humdrum life in a small town would be over. Why she hadn't considered this before was shocking.

Lulu went to the kitchen and made herself a cup of coffee. Even though the loss of Franny was heartbreaking, she must focus on her own future. It was providential that the police had closed the investigation surrounding Franny's death. Providential indeed. The other people that must have been with Franny in the garage were still a mystery. Had Art been there? It seemed like his voice at one point. The other voice was totally unfamiliar. Should she say something to the police? It wasn't wise to pick a scab though. Poor Franny. Those plans had come to nothing now.

She wandered into the living room that was now clear of all boxes. There was plenty of space once again. She pulled the Reinvent and Recycle Company appointment card from the pocket of her sweater. The recycling company had agreed to return to finish cleaning out the garage next week. Once the building was emptied, it might ease her mind. Maybe.

Lulu gazed out the window, automatically checking Franny's property. It now had the look of a vacant house. Her heart sank, and then she remembered that the quilt was still hidden. Franny had refused to tell her where she'd stashed it, so there would be no way Lulu could be implicated. Where was it? Should she tell someone about that? She had already told so many half-truths and outright lies to her friends. They'd never forgive her. Her head hurt. Life had become way too complicated.

***

Tom and Kelly's home was lively with chatter and country music in the background. Several pizza boxes were open, strewn across the kitchen counters. Emma, Tom's teenage daughter, dumped chips into a large glass bowl and spooned dip into a matching small bowl, slipping it into a metal hanger on the side of the bowl. Kelly lined up bottled water and sodas on the table next to the chips.

"Looks like we're ready to eat," she said to Emma, whose dark hair flowed over her shoulders.

"Good. I'm starving. That pizza smell is driving me crazy."

"Me too. All right, everyone. Come and get it."

The Clark and Stevens families were no slackers when the dinner gong sounded. The group descended on the kitchen immediately, loading plates with pizza, chips, wings, and a smattering of raw vegetables from the huge tray Theresa had brought.

"When is Aunt Gracie getting here?" Emma asked her father, who was stuffing himself with a mouthful of pepperoni and cheese pizza.

Tom held up a finger, requesting more time. Emma laughed.

"Pretty soon," he managed after washing the pizza down with Mountain Dew.

"Which means she'll be really late," Emma said.

Tom nodded. "There are a lot of last-minute things when you're getting married," he said. "You know how it was with Kelly and me."

"Ugh. You guys were a mess," Emma groaned. "I thought Aunt Gracie would be different."

"I guess not," he said, catching Kelly's eye. His wife leaned against the range, giving him a wink.

He wasn't sure how Gracie would survive Isabelle's help. Three days—that seemed doable. Marc seemed relaxed though. Of course, he might be in denial. And Isabelle and Kevin were invited to this informal bash tonight. No wonder Gracie was late. He'd have done the same, if he could.

Marc's family was nice enough. His sister seemed a little high maintenance. He liked the brother-in-law, Larry, and Marc's mom. Both appeared to be easygoing and down-to-earth. Larry was in technology, testing anti-hacking software for banks. Violet still worked part time at a law firm. Her specialty was legal research. The doorbell rang, and Kelly opened the door for Isabelle.

***

Gracie left her seat at the picnic table at Inspiration Point and walked over the stone bridge to the lookout spot. There wasn't much to be seen now that it was dark, but she wasn't ready to leave Letchworth Park yet. Placing her hands on the wall, she leaned over, staring into the inky, deep gorge below her. The soothing sound of the Middle Falls was comforting and peaceful. An owl hooted nearby, and she heard wings flapping overhead. Instinctively, she ducked and saw the large bird veer off into the woods down the trail to the south. In spite of her near-death experience not far from where she stood, the location had always been where she went to think. From the time she'd been a teenager and able to drive, if something was bothering her, she headed for Inspiration Point for perspective. She loved the limestone and shale walls that towered over the Genesee River, which wound northward through the park.

The generosity of William Pryor Letchworth had given her this unique retreat. He'd gifted the spectacular stretch of river gorge and his Glen Iris home situated by thundering falls to the people of New York State in 1910. Three generations of her family had enjoyed the state park with innumerable picnics, hikes, and family reunions over the years. The history and the beauty of the place were woven into her. A part of her identity. It was easy to picture Mary Jemison, The White Woman of the Genesee, on a trail or an Iroquois brave hunting in the dense woods that followed the river to the Mt. Morris dam.

She zipped up her fleece jacket. Her breath was white in the air. The afternoon's long phone call with her cousin necessitated some time to clear her thoughts and regain a pleasant attitude before she clobbered anyone within arm's length. Her head was still buzzing with instructions and critiques from Isabelle. Makeup, hairstyle, no iPod music, more flowers, more everything. She'd politely refused further assistance, but saying "no" didn't always dissuade Isabelle from her perceived mission.

Her family and Marc's were waiting for her at Tom and Kelly's. She'd been here since the kennel closed, which was over two hours ago. The crisp air filled her lungs, and her brain felt energized after two draining days of chaos and a backyard full of problems. A couple of cars drove past on the main road, no doubt heading to the park's exit. She walked quickly to the red RAV4 and turned on the ignition.

***

The lights in Deer Creek were warm and homey, the streets predictably quiet. She drove down Oak Street, which would take her to Ivy Lane, where Tom and Kelly lived.

Before the intersection with Ivy, she noticed a man dressed in a dark hoodie and matching pants jogging on the sidewalk, slowing as he passed the Walczak house. For a moment, she thought he looked familiar. He was familiar. The athletic silhouette looked a lot like Kevin. He was supposed to be at Tom and Kelly's. She couldn't be sure who it was. The runner sped up again. A beagle appeared from the darkness, running ahead of the man, as her phone rang.

On the other end, an excited Ace jabbered his good news. The part for the backhoe would be delivered in the morning. If he coaxed the equipment into running by noon, he was pretty sure the work would be done before dark. Her yard might be a little muddy, but her bathroom situation would be fixed. Hallelujah!

CHAPTER 19

The phone interrupted Theresa just as she was pouring coffee at the breakfast table. Bob was, as usual, oblivious, his nose buried in the *Daily News*.

"Hello," she said, holding the carafe with one hand and cradling the handset to her ear with the other.

"Hi, Theresa!" Gloria said brightly. "How's the mother of the bride?"

"Still alive," she bantered. "I'm making phone calls to everyone today, letting them know about the wedding location change. What a week!"

"Good thing it's a small wedding." Gloria chuckled. "I know you're going crazy, but I really need a favor. I hate to ask."

"What do you need? I won't be on the phone all day."

"Well, there are a couple of quilts that have to be mailed to the orphanage in Mexico today—the birthday ones we finished last week. I don't think I'll have time. Albert has a doctor's appointment in Rochester, and I never know how long it'll be."

"Sure, as long as I can mail them from Deer Creek. I don't need to go to Warsaw or Geneseo, do I?"

"No, you can mail them from here."

Bob peered out above the newspaper with questioning eyes, pointing to himself. Theresa shook her head "no." Bob's head disappeared behind the paper again.

***

The line at the post office was slow. Theresa finally had to set the awkward box on the floor outside the lobby. There were at least eight people ahead of her, which was unheard of this time of year. Before Christmas was horrible, but not October. The clerk must be new, she decided, watching the unfamiliar young woman behind the counter. Where was Rudy the postmaster? He'd move the line along.

As if on cue, Rudy appeared. He had a string-bean physique, a prominent Adam's apple, and sported a goatee, which was a recent development. The next person in line made a beeline for him and dropped a large rectangular box on the counter. It was Lulu. She'd been hidden from view until now. She had forms, and the transaction took several minutes.

"Hi, Lulu," Theresa greeted her as the tall woman brushed past the line.

"Oh, Theresa. Hi. Sorry, can't chat."

Lulu kept her head down and hurried out to the street. Apparently, Lulu was on some sort of important mission. At least, she was out of the house.

Finally inside the lobby, Theresa hauled the package onto the counter so Rudy could weigh it.

"Got your customs form?" he asked, eying the scale.

"Yes. Right here," she replied, pulling it from her coat pocket.

Gloria had been organized enough to have it completed when she'd dropped off the package.

"Tierra and Cielo Orphanage," he said, reading the label. "Pretty popular place lately."

"Why is that?" Theresa asked.

The sewing circle sent quilts and other gifts a couple of times a year. Rudy looked down at her, sliding the box off the scale.

"You ladies are sending a bunch of stuff to them, that's why."

"A bunch? This is our first package since June."

"Oh. I thought ... Lulu just had another . . ."

"Lulu? She's sending something?"

Rudy cleared his throat. "Forget I said anything," he said, pressing the plastic sleeve with the customs list onto the box.

"Sure. A lot of packages?"

"That'll be $45.50. You need any extra insurance?"

"No. I don't think so. Does Lulu get extra insurance?"

"Mrs. Clark, that'll be $45.50. And no, she doesn't."

She handed her debit card to Rudy.

"I'll need a receipt."

Theresa couldn't decide how to proceed with this new information about Lulu. Despite Rudy's reluctance to comment on Lulu's mailing habits, it didn't take a genius to figure out she was mailing something to the orphanage. On the one hand, maybe Lulu had merely chosen to continue helping the orphanage on her own. But why stop working with the sewing circle? Ed's death had set her back, changed her personality. She was awfully secretive, and the hoarding was certainly peculiar. On a positive note, her house was returning to normal. Then there was Franny and the stolen quilt. If truth be told, she wasn't exactly sure the quilt was stolen. What did Howie Stroud think about the claim?

***

Gracie had the phone on speaker as she printed off an invoice for a dachshund named Dashiell, Dash for short. He was currently sitting on her lap, waiting for his owner to appear. Freshly bathed, he wore a green sweater with a rather dapper deerstalker cap. Dashiell wasn't exactly pleased about the cap, but tolerated it since there were several small liver treats on the desk.

"You should be at the house to have your hair and makeup done by one o'clock on Saturday," Isabelle directed.

"I don't need any help with my hair," Gracie insisted. "And makeup and I don't really get along."

"You can't do your own hair. Makeup isn't optional. Think of your photos. I've booked my stylist to be here. He can do both."

"The wedding isn't until four."

"That's cutting it fine. Kelly needs hers done too, but I'm just not sure there'll be enough time to do both of you."

"Please don't add extra work. Really, we want it to be low key."

"Gracie, take my advice and don't be stubborn about this. It's my treat." There was a hint, just a hint of softness in Isabelle's voice.

Gracie had the distinct feeling there was no way to win.

"Okay, Isabelle. Whatever you say," she sighed, hardly believing she was saying it. "Good-bye."

Gracie hit the speaker button and glared at the phone. She set Dashiell on the floor.

Cheryl popped her head into the doorway. She was dressed in jeans and a red long-sleeved T-shirt with the Milky Way Kennels logo.

"Dash's mom is here," she said.

"Perfect. He's all set."

Gracie picked up the trailing lead and handed the dog off to her slender, dark-haired assistant manager. She snatched the invoice from her desk. "And don't forget this too."

"Right. Are you okay? Wedding jitters?" Cheryl's worried brow and kind eyes made Gracie smile.

"I'll admit to the jitters. Too many last-minute additions, I guess."

"I thought you were having a simple wedding. Still in the backyard on Saturday, right?"

"No. It's not. Sorry, I forgot to tell you and Marian. It's at Isabelle's because of the excavation going on. Which reminds me, I'd better check on Ace. I hope he'll finish today."

She used the kennel's rear exit and jogged up the driveway to the house. The welcome sound of the backhoe chugging away greeted her ears. She opened the gate to find that Ace had cleared the roots and was checking the tiles. Approaching the bent-over man, she yelled, "Everything copasetic?"

Ace straightened himself and took his hat off. Sweat trickled down his cheeks, and he swiped a sleeve across his face.

"Lookin' good. So far. I told you I'd be done by dark."

"Great. Laundry and running the dishwasher are at the top of the list."

"Shouldn't be a problem."

She shivered as the wind picked up. It was supposed to be warm, according to the weather report. Where were the Indian summer temperatures? Leaving Ace to his digging, she decided to have an early lunch, as long as she was at the house, and ponder how Isabelle had so smoothly taken the reins of their wedding day.

CHAPTER 20

The day at Niagara Falls had started out mostly uneventful, for which Marc was grateful. Miranda seemed cooperative and even happy, which was a pleasant change from her moping and two meltdowns over nothing in particular. He wondered if there was another guy in the picture. She seemed to have her phone glued to her hand. However, everyone did, so it might be nothing.

Larry deftly played the part of the long-suffering husband, encouraging and prodding Miranda to cheer up. Marc felt like shaking her out whatever funk that was holding her prisoner. His mom kept her opinions to herself for the most part. Tension was evident in the short spurts of conversation. At least, this family day gave Gracie some time to work on her own family issues, of which Isabelle was chief. The wedding was two days away. He'd received a timeline email from Isabelle before leaving the house with detailed instructions for every moment of the wedding day.

The four of them were packed together with the press of the crowd in the Observation Tower, watching the mighty Niagara roar, the falls crashing with tons of power on the rocks below the falls.

"Ready for lunch yet?" Violet inquired, maneuvering away from the front to give room to newcomers anxious for their spot.

"I am," Marc said.

"Where are we eating?" Miranda asked, stepping away, holding Larry's hand.

"Let's drive over to Goat Island to the Top of the Falls Restaurant. That way you'll have the full tourist treatment," Marc said.

"Sounds good to me," Larry agreed.

Marc checked his phone as he slid behind the wheel of Gracie's RAV4, which he'd borrowed for this excursion. Two missed calls. Both were from DACO. Maybe this was it.

"Sorry, but I've got to return a call. It's from DACO."

"Of course, Marc. We're in no hurry," Violet said, settling into the front passenger seat. "I hope it's good news."

Marc nodded, redialing the number and exiting the SUV.

"Marc Stevens, returning your call," Marc said to DACO's receptionist.

"Mr. Stevens. Let me connect you with Mr. MacElroy."

"Stevens. Good. I wasn't sure we'd be able to get in touch with you."

"I'm sorry I missed your call."

"No problem. We have a once-a-year training that starts next Wednesday, and I really want you to attend. It includes your dog and is pretty intense."

"Next week? Has my clearance come through?"

"No. We're confident that it will be finished this week, and from our perspective, you're good to go. Our corporate background check is clear, as of today. The government part adds another layer, which always takes longer."

"You know, I'm getting married on Saturday." Marc's thoughts were swirling into a dark vortex. He'd leave Gracie only days after their wedding. How would she handle immediate separation? How would he handle that?

"I realize the timing might not be the best for you personally. The date is the date though. You'll meet the other newcomers to the K-9 security force too."

"How long's the training?"

"It's three weeks in Maryland. We'll make your travel arrangements, and you can take the dog ... uh, Max, right on the jet with you. It's a company jet. Flight's at oh-six-thirty Wednesday out of Buffalo."

"Well, sure. I'll be there. Uh, what will I need?"

"I'll shoot you an email. We've set up a secure account for you. My assistant, Diane, will call you later with the info.

The call ended, and Marc stood looking at his phone. He closed his eyes; his appetite had vanished.

His mother gave him a worried look as he reentered the vehicle.

"Everything all right?"

"Yes and no," he answered, turning the key in the ignition.

***

They were seated quickly at the restaurant, and once they'd ordered, Marc filled in the curious group on the phone call.

"Bad timing," Larry commiserated. "How's Gracie going to feel about that?"

"I don't know how I feel about it," Marc stated, tapping his fingers on the tabletop.

"Three weeks? I'd be pretty upset," Miranda added. "Wouldn't you, Mom?"

"Probably, but you both knew the job would be demanding, right? Violet queried, her brows drawn together.

"I need to talk to Gracie about this."

"Of course. We can go back to Deer Creek as soon as we finish lunch. You don't need to entertain us the rest of the day," Violet said, putting a hand on her son's shoulder.

"It's countdown time," Larry joked. "I'm surprised your bride let you out of her sight. I know mine wouldn't." He patted Miranda's hand, who offered her husband an uncomfortable smile.

Marc's phone rang just as the food came to the table.

"Marc. It's Emily. I wanted to let you know that the sheriff is retiring on the first of November."

"Really. Then it's official," Marc said, looking at the pile of fries and a multi-level burger with a steak knife spearing it.

Things had just gotten way more interesting.

"Yes. I can't offer you a permanent position until at least spring, but I've talked with the sheriff and the board of supervisors about a special contract position for you. I'll need an answer right away. I'd like you to start on November second."

"I'm out with my family in Niagara Falls right now. I really need to talk to Gracie before I give a final answer. DACO called earlier and ..."

"Oh." After a pause, the investigator replied, "Sure, Marc. Close of business today then?"

"Absolutely."

He'd already signed up for DACO, but the sheriff's department was a known quantity in many ways. It wouldn't be for the money, but he'd be home much more often.

***

Gracie and Kelly spread their dresses out on Gracie's bed. The trial run was underway, and Gracie wriggled into the high-waisted tummy control shapewear, guaranteed to make you look two sizes smaller in minutes. Minutes could turn into hours though if you couldn't put the darn thing on. It was stuck in a roll around her hips.

Kelly burst out laughing when Gracie dropped onto the bed, yanking in earnest to get the Lycra straight jacket to budge.

"What is wrong with this thing?" She rolled on her side, working at the lump of material. She felt like a fish flopping on a creek bank.

"Are you sure you really need to wear it? The dress fits, right?"

Kelly stepped into the navy long-sleeved lace dress.

"Yes, but it would be nice to look a few pounds lighter for the pictures," she grunted, finally pulling the garment into place. "There," she announced triumphantly, standing to look at herself in the full-length mirror.

"Can you breathe?"

Gracie took a shallow breath and then a deeper one.

"I can. Not bad. All right, now for the dress," she said, unzipping the champagne-colored dress. The metallic brocade added elegance to the knee-length V-necked sheath.

Kelly zipped up the dress, and Gracie turned to every angle in front of the mirror with a critical eye. The bedroom door swung open, and Haley ambled in, pink tongue hanging out, tail waving.

"Girl, you need to stay out of here," Gracie said, bending to shoo the dog out the door. "You're way too dangerous around these dresses."

Haley looked disappointed, but acquiesced to the banishment. They heard her lie down against the door, tail thumping on the wall. Kelly and Gracie chuckled.

"We have to practice with those dogs after this, you know," Kelly said. "I brought the ribbons for them."

"That's next on my list," Gracie said, slipping on the long matching jacket.

The cuffs and collar were trimmed with seed pearls and Swarovski crystal stitched in three rows of scallops. The neckline of the dress had the same beading.

"Gracie, you're really gorgeous. The dress is you all the way," Kelly said.

"I think it works," Gracie agreed, smiling at her reflection. Her freckles, now faded from the summer sun, were hardly visible.

"The color really sets your eyes and hair off well," Kelly added. "Good choice."

Gracie nodded. Her auburn hair and brown eyes were complemented by the champagne. "I hope so, since you did help me pick it out."

"Mutual good taste. It's always good to have it confirmed," Kelly countered, smiling. "Speaking of good taste, Isabelle sent everyone an email with a timeline for Saturday."

Gracie rolled her eyes. "Sorry. She's officially taken over, although I put my foot down about the dogs. She's afraid they'll soil her yard or bite someone. I told her that was non-negotiable."

"She asked about makeup and hair, and I let her know that I was covered."

"Me too. By her stylist. I think she has some possible altruistic motives this time. At least, I hope they are."

"I'm surprised to hear you say that," Kelly said, turning her back to Gracie. "Unzip, please."

"I really like this dress too. I brought you a pashmina to match my dress if it's chilly. Rats! I left it in the living room."

"Don't go out there with your dress," Kelly warned.

"No one's here," Gracie said, looking at Kelly over her shoulder.

Haley rose to greet her as her stiletto heel caught in a crack in the wooden threshold. Grabbing at the doorframe, Gracie managed to stay upright, her face bent down to an ecstatic Haley, who slurped her cheek.

"Oh boy," Gracie breathed, retreating into the bedroom.

Kelly's eyes were wide, her mouth puckered in an "o." "Let's put it back in the bag before something happens."

"Right."

The sound of a vehicle in the driveway sent Haley and Max to the door.

***

"Two job offers on the same day?" Gracie asked, slipping a coffee pod into the coffeemaker.

"Yeah." Marc sat at the kitchen bar, folding and refolding a paper napkin. "It's decision time. There are cons with both jobs. I really don't want to leave you less than a week after we're married. It's next week—really fast. The sheriff's department is a known quantity, but if things don't work out for Emily, I could lose my job. And then there's the money part."

Gracie took a seat on the stool next to him. She didn't want to sway his decision. It needed to be his, with her complete support. Each job was dangerous. DACO as a company was a mystery. The Defense Advantage Company contracted with the U. S. Department of Defense. She had little knowledge of what they really did, other than provide surveillance and security systems for military installations. The fact that the company's executives required personal security with dogs trained to detect explosives was disconcerting, at the very least. That meant lots of visits to Afghanistan and Iraq. Neither organization fit the parameters of her comfort zone. She'd experienced enough danger just as an interested bystander helping the sheriff's department ... well ... helping in *her* mind. Investigator Hotchkiss was of a different opinion.

"And, what are you going to do?" She reached for his nervous hands, now shredding the napkin.

Their fingers intertwined.

"What do you want me to do?" he asked softly.

"Oh no, you don't," she firmly countered, shaking her head. "This is all you. I'm not a fan of being separated, first thing, but I'll deal with it. It's not months. It's three weeks. And you love working as a deputy, and it's the chance to move up to being an investigator. The ball's in your court."

She hoped her expression remained neutral, not revealing her preference for him to stay local.

"I wasn't holding out much hope for the security clearance, but it should be okayed by tomorrow," Marc said, pulling his hands away. "I wish the calls hadn't come on the same day. I could've told one or the other, I'd already gone to work." He sighed, starting to pace the kitchen.

"I guess you need to decide if you really want a career change. You had a lot to say about that when I was in Arizona with you." She swiveled around on the stool, watching him finally turn and look at her.

Marc smiled. "I sure did. That's when breeding Belgian Malinois looked like my best career move."

"Which it wasn't." She had momentarily considered offering him kennel space for that business. He'd be around all the time that way. The idea evaporated as quickly as it had come. It didn't suit him.

"No, it wasn't the right move. I do want a change. That's what's a little scary. The opportunity with DACO is once in a lifetime though. Max is ready for action after the private training we had over the summer. I am too. The bonus is DACO has continuous K-9 training for us. The salary can't be matched by anyone either."

Gracie nodded. He and Max had worked hard to complete another level of protection training and had passed with flying colors only a few weeks ago.

"I will support your decision—whichever one is lucky enough to employ you," she offered bravely. There could be no regrets or complaints she reminded herself, as the words came from her lips.

Marc's intense blue eyes met hers, and he rubbed his jaw, the dimple in his chin seemed even more pronounced than usual.

"DACO. I want to take this chance and see where it leads."

She smiled, slipping from the stool to be caught up in his arms.

"Then DACO is it," she said, kissing him. A sick feeling was swirling in the pit of her stomach, and she forced herself to sound enthusiastic.

CHAPTER 21

Isabelle glared at Haley and Max, who sat panting under her spectacular Japanese maple. Gold ribbons hung from white satin collars.

"On Saturday, the rings will be tied to the ribbons," Gracie explained.

"This won't work," Isabelle griped, pushing back a lock of blond hair in the warm autumn breeze.

Her gaze swept to the gazebo, which was already festooned with branches of maple and oak leaves tied with champagne-colored burlap ties. White folding chairs were stacked on the platform.

"Sure it will. We've been practicing at home, and they'll be fine. They just have to learn the route. Jim will have both of them on leashes," Gracie said, hands on hips.

Isabelle's arms were crossed, and a frown marred her face. "It won't. You have no idea what they'll do. They could do ... do something embarrassing on a guest or chase a cat in the middle of the ceremony. This will be disastrous."

"Regardless, the dogs are in the ceremony."

"All right, but if something goes wrong, I don't want any blame."

"I wouldn't think of it, Izzy," Gracie crooned sweetly.

She gave a furtive eye-roll and called the dogs to her. They trotted eagerly from the shade by the RAV4. "Come on, guys. We have to practice," she said, grabbing Haley's collar.

Jim and Marc strolled toward the women with weak attempts at straight faces.

"Are you two ready?" Isabelle demanded.

"Sure," Marc said, regaining his composure.

"You'll already be in the gazebo, Marc, with Reverend Minders." Isabelle pointed to the structure. "Then Kelly will progress down the aisle, followed by Jim and the dogs. The music for them is *The Water is Wide*. Then Gracie comes in when the guitarist begins playing Debussy's *Clair de Lune*. I did get the music selections right, didn't I?"

"Yes. They're both right," Gracie agreed, the knot in her stomach tightening. The melodies of both songs always brought tears to her eyes; they were so romantic. They'd been choices for her first wedding, but the church organist had insisted on more traditional music. She looked at Marc and Jim, who were now much more serious. Max whined, jumping on Marc.

"All right," he laughed. "It's time for a test run." He clipped on a short lead to a chain collar underneath the decorative satin one.

Gracie did the same with Haley. Jim put Max on his left, with Haley on the right.

"Come on, you two," Jim said.

The dogs pricked up their ears, sniffing at his pockets.

"Bacon treats, right?" Gracie asked, standing on the steps of the gazebo.

"Absolutely. Nothing but the best," Jim answered. With a canine on each side, he strolled toward Gracie.

"You'll need to join Marc on the platform, Jim," Isabelle directed. "And keep those animals under control."

"No problem," Jim confirmed, ascending the two steps to the gazebo's deck. The dogs sat on command, enjoying their reward. Their eyes glued on both Marc and Gracie.

"This is it," Marc said, gazing at Gracie, who was now a bit flushed.

"Well, Saturday actually," she corrected.

"Might be easier to see if Reverend Minders could slip over here this afternoon," he teased.

"I'm tempted to agree, but the train has left the station."

Jim sighed in mock distress. "I guess we'd shouldn't even think about jumping the rails now. Isabelle would ..."

Isabelle walked closer to the group, with her hands on her hips, taking in the arrangement. Her white shirt, accented with a teal scarf, and black pants fit her perfectly. In fact, Gracie thought her cousin looked a little trimmer of late. How did she do it?

"I still don't think the addition of the dogs will work, but that's on you," Izzy reiterated. "I won't be held responsible for their actions."

"We understand. No problem," Gracie responded, taking Haley's leash from Jim, looking up to see a long-legged and voluptuous redhead stride across the lawn, a camera in hand.

"Hi, everyone," the woman greeted them with a low, husky voice.

"Adriana. Good, you were able to make it," Isabelle said, turning to her.

"Of course. I need to talk with the bride and groom," she said with a broad smile at Gracie and Marc.

After introductions, Gracie mostly agreed to Adriana's suggestions and felt her stomach tighten again. For such a small wedding, it was suddenly crammed with lots to do. Wedding nerves were coming on strong. Marc managed to escape with Jim and the dogs, ostensibly leaving the details to the bride. Cowards, both of them.

"I'll leave you with Adriana," Isabelle called to Gracie, walking toward the driveway. "I have an appointment with Lulu Cook, and I'm already late."

***

Isabelle parked her Lexus SUV in Lulu's driveway, astonished at the pile of storage containers and cardboard boxes next to the garage. She had no idea the woman had so much junk.

Lulu appeared from the kitchen door, lugging a dark garbage bag down the steps.

"Oh, hi, Isabelle."

"Hello. Quite a lot of ... things you've got here."

"I know. I know. It will all be gone by the end of next week."

"I hope so. I had no idea of the amount of ... stuff you had. I didn't see this before."

Isabelle's face darkened, her eyes narrowed with laser accuracy at the older woman.

Lulu settled the garbage bag next to the boxes. Brushing her hands off on her jeans, she sighed. "I'm cleaning out everything as we agreed, Isabelle. It will be totally empty before the closing date next month."

"I hope so. I'd hate to have to penalize you on the purchase price."

The icy statement snapped Lulu to attention. "There will be no need of that, I assure you. I want to make sure you're ready to close the deal without any hold-ups. My plans are to leave right after the closing."

"There are no issues on my side. There will be an inspection the day before, as we agreed." Isabelle replied, inching her way to the garage.

"I'm working on the garage as well," Lulu said, following Isabelle, who seemed to be examining the building's paint job.

"Fine. I was sorry to hear about Franny," Isabelle said, placing her hand on the doorknob of the side entrance. "It was her heart, from what I understand."

Lulu pursed her lips, eyes round. "Yes. It was her heart. She had angina."

"I see. What about these accusations she made about a stolen quilt?"

Lulu backed away, avoiding eye contact with Isabelle.

"A misunderstanding is what it was. I don't know why Franny said those things."

"Awful for you. Her dying in the garage and all."

"It was terrible. My best friend ..." A sob caught in Lulu's voice. "I'm sorry. I have to get back to cleaning," she said quickly.

"I wouldn't want to hold you up," Isabelle said, moving away from the door. "I have another appointment that's out of town. Oh, by the way, do you know what's happening with Franny's house?"

***

Lulu sat down heavily onto a kitchen chair after Isabelle left. What was the woman up to? She was certainly interested in purchasing Franny's house too. It might be a good thing for Reverend Minders to have an instant qualified buyer though. She rubbed her forehead and stood. No sense in wasting time. If she could clear another bedroom today, she'd be one step closer to freedom. She tried to push the vision of Franny lying on the floor of the garage out of her mind without much success. The voices she'd heard arguing with Franny that night kept coming back, nagging at her. One had sounded like Art, but the other wasn't as easy. The voice had been unfamiliar. Maybe a young man. Had Art and a minion threatened Franny? Had they frightened her, or even worse, assaulted her that night? Who could she tell? Her part in this deception made her guilty of ... Well, she was guilty on so many levels. In way too deep. She preferred to put that out of her mind too.

CHAPTER 22

Gracie sat in front of Isabelle's mirror watching Ryan, Isabelle's personal stylist, work his magic on taming her incorrigible curls. The straightening wand, gel, and spray were liberally applied to her tresses, which, for the first time ever, were behaving themselves. How long would it last though? Until the four o'clock wedding? She had doubts, when Ryan, with his own curly-hair issues, bent to tuck the last hairpin that swept her shoulder-length hair into a French twist, with tendrils oh-so-romantically framing her face.

"Perfect, if I do say so myself," the short, russet-haired man said. He smoothed an immaculately groomed goatee, eyeing her from every direction. "Now for makeup."

"I really don't want to be spackled," Gracie warned him.

He arched dark eyebrows and then laughed.

"I promise you, absolutely no spackle. However, your freckles need a bit of evening out. I think you'll be pleased with the result."

A knock at the door turned their attention from the mirror.

"Gracie. It's me," Kelly said, entering the room. "Oh, you look fabulous," she cooed.

"I told you. It's perfect," Ryan said, returning his attention to Gracie.

"Thank you. I agree. I'm hoping it will last until after the pictures are taken."

Kelly carried a dress bag over her shoulder, with a pair of pumps in her other hand. Her short, brown hair framed a tanned angular face.

"Guaranteed to last until the wedding night begins," Ryan said officiously. "I make no such promises after that."

The women exchanged looks and giggled.

Another knock on the door brought Isabelle, with a tray of mimosas in fragile crystal flutes, plus fruit and tiny tea sandwiches.

"Ryan, you've done it again," she said appreciatively, eyeing Gracie's hair. "I don't think you've ever looked better—once your makeup is finished."

Gracie bit back a sharp reply. No sense in starting any conflict today. So far, everything had gone according to plan. Her quiet breakfast with Haley had set the tone for a leisurely pace on her wedding day. The yard was back together and the birch tree that had caused the septic disaster removed. Jim had taken Haley to join the men while they prepared for the zero hour. Now her hair was perfect. She grabbed her phone and took a selfie for posterity. Just in case.

"You aren't posting that on Facebook, are you?" Isabelle fussed.

"Of course not. Just keeping a record of a bona fide hair success," Gracie said, grinning at Kelly.

"Good. Now, everyone eat a little something. No fainting at the wedding. You'll ruin your dresses with grass stains if you do."

"Thank you so much," Kelly jumped in, taking the tray from Isabelle and setting it on the vanity. "This looks delicious. You've thought of everything today."

Isabelle gave her a condescending smile. "You're quite welcome. Weddings require a skilled hand. Now, I need to get ready myself. It's already 2:30, Ryan. You really don't have a lot of time to finish up."

"All under control, Ms. Baker. Ms. Andersen will be perfection itself very soon."

Isabelle glanced at her watch and looked out the bedroom window. "Where are those men? They are supposed to be here."

"I'm sure they're on the way," Gracie soothed. "We have plenty of time. Really."

Isabelle sucked in a breath and went to the door. "I'd better call—"

"Oh, don't bother. I'll call Tom and see where they are," Kelly offered. "I'm sure they'll be here any minute. They have the dogs, so it may take them extra time."

Isabelle glared at Gracie. "Those dogs are going to be a problem."

"Uh ..."

Before Gracie could formulate a reply, Isabelle had vacated the room, closing the door with a smart little slam for emphasis.

"Ah ... if only my yard could have been ready for today," Gracie sighed.

She selected a cucumber sandwich, cut in the shape of a heart, and sipped the mimosa.

Ryan helped himself to a drink and eased down on the bed.

Kelly already had her phone to her ear, nodding. "Okay then. Isabelle may go nuclear if you aren't here in the next two minutes."

"Where are they?" Gracie asked, taking another sandwich.

"They're almost ready to leave Marc's house. Looks like Max and Haley were playing and knocked over a lamp. Marc's sister tried cleaning up the broken lightbulb and cut herself. Apparently, she's not real stable. Is that true?"

Gracie closed her eyes. "No. She's not. Is she all right?"

"She is now. They'll be here in a few minutes." Kelly snagged a cluster of red grapes and an orange-juice-and-champagne cocktail.

"Not too much bubbly, ladies," Ryan warned, returning to the vanity. "No tipsy brides or matrons of honor today. Now, let's finish your makeup before the photographer appears."

***

Jim opened the club cab up for the dogs to jump in the back. Max eagerly pushed Haley out of the way and sat, panting, while Haley entered the truck with a bit more dignity.

"All right, we're off, lady and gentleman," Jim practically sang as he slid behind the wheel.

He began whistling "I'm Getting Married in the Morning." Haley immediately began to howl, and Max was quick to join in. Marc and Tom were close behind, hanging coat bags in their vehicles. Both began laughing as Jim's truck rolled down the driveway, with howling dogs hanging their heads out of the open windows.

The three pickups rolled into Isabelle's driveway, where they were met by Kevin, who directed them to the patio. Jim kept the dogs in the truck bed under a large maple. The temperatures were unseasonably warm, but a cool breeze kept the air comfortable.

"The boss says you all need to stay here and not go upstairs for any reason. Bad luck, you know." Kevin smirked, following them into the screened area.

Marc nodded. "No surprise. Don't worry, we'll be fine out here."

"You guys lucked out on the weather. What a great day," Kevin commented, reaching for a bottle of Scotch that stood on the counter of a small wet bar. "Drink, anyone?" he asked, pouring a shot for himself.

"No. Not for me," Marc said. "I need to keep my wits about me today."

"I'd take a Coke or ginger ale," Jim said. "I'm in charge of the dogs, so I definitely need to be on top of things."

The men had settled into the Adirondack-style furniture with their beverage of choice when Adriana Keller appeared in the doorway, a camera slung around her neck. All eyes were fastened on her as she stepped down to the patio level, taking candid shots, moving cat-like, until she took a seat at the wet bar on a leather-covered stool.

"Gentlemen, you all look astonishing," she purred, resting the camera on her knee. "Let's take some group shots near the gazebo while the ladies are putting on the finishing touches."

The dogs joined the all-male gang, and Adriana created a montage of groupings, before making her way upstairs. Kevin stayed on the patio, sipping another drink, and Tom ambled around the yard, while Marc and Jim secured the dogs in the back of the truck. Isabelle appeared with a tray of hors d'oeuvres, just as the trio rejoined Kevin. The men eagerly helped themselves.

"I knew you'd be famished. Like I told the girls, no fainting during the ceremony. You need a little something to eat." She moved to Kevin and massaged his shoulders. He smiled, looking relaxed, and allowed her to continue.

Marc laid a slice of cheddar on a multi-grain cracker, while he took in the wedding site. Isabelle hadn't disappointed. The white chairs were arranged in an intimate curve around the gazebo, which was now fully decorated with fall flowers of purple and gold, with creamy roses entwined in the arrangements.

"Hello, everyone," Reverend Minders called out, striding down the walk to the patio entrance.

"Pastor, good to see you," Marc said, opening the sliding door for the gray-haired man.

"Have a little something to eat," Isabelle offered, stooping to pick up the food tray.

"Oh no. I never eat before a wedding. A glass of water would be good though."

While Isabelle fulfilled his request, he ran down the checklist with Marc. After placing the water glass on a nearby table, Isabelle disappeared into the house.

"Ring?" the Reverend asked.

"I've got it," Tom said, drawing a simple gold band from the breast pocket of his suit.

"Good. Now, we'll need you and Kelly to witness the license and the certificate right after the ceremony." He looked at his watch and out to the gazebo.

"We'll be there," Tom assured him.

"Brave men, you two," Kevin joked, rising from his chair. "You won't catch me in that honey trap."

The pastor jerked his head toward the man in surprise, as did the rest.

"You're missing out," Tom responded with conviction. "Marriage with the right person is the good life."

"I think mine is just fine without the marital obligations." Kevin's face was flushed, and Marc wondered how many shots the man had consumed.

Jim opened the door to the yard. "I'm going to let the dogs have a little exercise before they have to be on their best behavior. Okay, Marc?"

"Sure. I'll come and get Max though. He's probably still amped up after that photo session."

Tom and the pastor went off to the gazebo, while Marc and Jim left to take care of Max and Haley.

"He's blasted," Jim said, lowering the tailgate of the pickup to allow the dogs to jump out.

"I think you're right," Marc agreed. "I'd also say those rumors about his having another love interest are right. Did you see the way he looked at Adriana?"

Jim nodded. "No question in my mind."

The sound of vehicles coming down the street caught their attention, as family members turned into the wide, circular drive. The guitarist arrived in the midst of the procession into the Baker residence. Running late, he practically ran to the gazebo.

Isabelle swept out of the front door, directing everyone to the backyard. Kevin straggled behind her, looking a bit rumpled. The sounds of classical guitar set the mood, while the trickle of family and friends found their places, with Isabelle's precise and Kevin's somewhat unsteady direction.

The pastor rounded up Marc and Tom and herded them to the tastefully decorated shelter for last-minute instructions. Jim, meanwhile, adjusted the white satin collars on Haley and Max, beside themselves with excitement that something was, at last, afoot.

Kelly stuck her head out of the front door.

"Hey, Jim, here's Marc's ring. Are you ready for it?"

"Sure. Just tied Gracie's on Max."

She hurried across the black-topped driveway and handed him a plain gold band. "Don't lose these whatever you do," she warned.

"I've heard that speech more than I want to over the last week," Jim complained. "I think I can handle it from here."

Kelly grinned, her head bobbing in agreement. "I know. Let's be really happy that in an hour we're just in this thing for fun."

"Amen, sista, amen," Jim said, putting an imitation Southern drawl into action and wiping imaginary sweat from his brow.

She laughed and disappeared inside. Adriana strolled through the front door, the shutter on her camera clicking softly.

"Those dogs are the absolute best," she said, walking across the grass toward Jim.

She wore a black pullover sweater and black pants that fit her lithe form like a second skin, showing off some lovely assets. Her dark red hair (no doubt from a bottle) was shoulder length, cut in jagged layers. Jim straightened up, grasping the two leashes firmly.

"They are characters," Jim answered. "Let's cross our fingers that we can pull off the ring bearer job without any incidents. Isabelle is pretty fidgety about it."

Adriana's brown eyes crinkled with humor. "Her panties are always in a twist about something." She put a hand over her mouth. "Was that out loud?"

Jim chuckled. "I guess you have our hostess pegged."

"Nailed to the wall. This photo shoot at the house has been a challenge. When she was around, I hardly got any work done. Kevin was kind enough to let me come over when she was out showing houses."

Jim's eyebrows raised slightly. "Really? You're doing a magazine article or something on this house, right?"

"Yeah. It's finished now. The house has quite a history and should make for an interesting feature."

Before Jim could respond, the guitar volume rose, catching their attention.

"That's the signal," Adriana said. "Show time."

She slipped back into the house as Jim wrangled the dogs into position.

Haley sniffed the ground, while Max, with ears pricked forward, stood watching the cluster of people find seats.

"Heel, dogs," Jim commanded, taking a step forward. Haley kept sniffing, and he gave the black Lab's leash a quick yank. "Come on now."

***

The procession had begun. Marc and the pastor were already standing in the gazebo, while Larry led his mother-in-law, Violet, on one arm with his wife, Miranda, on the other.

Adriana was positioned at the patio door, her camera shutter whirring with each entrance. Tom, dressed in a well-tailored black suit, white shirt and gray tie, smiled down at his mother as she took his arm. He gave her a wink.

"Nice outfit, Ma."

"Thanks, son," said Theresa. "Don't let me trip whatever you do."

He saluted her with a bit of flair, and she giggled nervously.

Tom started down the grass path between the chair sections as soon as Larry sat down between the two women. He glanced over to see his wife, Kelly, standing on the patio, looking downright beautiful. Her dark blue dress accented her fair coloring and sparkling brown eyes.

"Tom, I sit here," his mother hissed, pulling on his arm.

"Sorry, Mom. A little distracted," he whispered as he bent to kiss her cheek.

He joined the men on the platform as the guitarist began playing the familiar folk song, *The Water is Wide.* Jim edged closer with the dogs, making them sit, as Kelly made her way down the grassy aisle. The anxious dogs followed behind on very short leads, Jim's face shining with perspiration. He dragged them into position, off to the right side of the gazebo steps, leaving plenty of room for the bride to make her way to the groom.

The music transitioned to *Clair de Lune,* and Bob led his daughter from the shelter of the shady patio into the afternoon sunlight. Adriana's camera captured each step as Gracie clung to her father's arm, smiling, her heart pounding.

This was really it. She was about to become a wife again. The dogs whined, wriggling in the down position, and Haley tried to greet her when she approached the wedding party. Jim tossed a couple of treats onto the grass to refocus the pair. She smiled. So far, so good with the dogs. She felt Isabelle's approving scrutiny as she took in the champagne brocade dress and jacket. Her one-rose-for-a-bouquet strategy had been replaced by one wine-colored rose and creamy jasmine, accented with ferns, which was simple, yet more sophisticated than her original intention. She must have clutched her father's arm tighter, because he patted her hand, smiling.

Marc greeted her with an appreciative look and a warm smile. She took his arm as the music ended. Taking a deep breath, she exhaled slowly, savoring the scene.

The dogs waved their tails with enthusiasm when she and Marc bent to untie the gold bands from the ribbons. She saw relief wash over Jim's face after the successful ring delivery. He was quick to make a hasty about-face to secure the dogs on the patio before rejoining the ceremony. A momentary flash of her first wedding came and went when Marc slipped the ring over her finger.

"Do you, Grace Marie Andersen, take Marc Jeffrey Stevens to be your lawfully wedded husband ..."

Her mind blurred as she responded, and she heard Marc promise to love, honor, and cherish her as long he lived. Tears threatened, and she blinked furiously, hoping the waterproof mascara was the real thing. The vows were spoken, and her longtime pastor pronounced her a wife for the second time. As she and Marc kissed, the tiny congregation erupted into a standing ovation. She heard Jim's piercing whistle over the applause.

***

A section of the lower dining floor of the Glen Iris Inn was walled off with accordion doors, providing the reception with some privacy. The sun filtered through the trees overlooking the Middle Falls, the multi-hued leaves catching the last of the day's amber rays.

"A toast, everyone," Tom announced, clinking a table knife against his water glass. He stood and raised a champagne flute. "To my little sister, Gracie, and her very lucky husband, Marc. Much love, joy, and domestic tranquility as you begin a new adventure."

"Hear, hear!" the crowd agreed, glasses clinking.

Gracie felt like her face was cracking from the amount of smiling she'd been doing. Wasn't it a fact that smiling took fewer muscles than frowning? It didn't feel like it at the moment. She might have a permanently upturned mouth after this. That would be weird.

Marc turned to her and whispered, "When's it over ... the dinner and everything?"

She giggled. "Easy, boy. Not yet. Not quite yet. We need to cut the cake."

"Right. There's no time like the present." He winked and kissed her hand.

"Come on, give her a good one," Larry, Marc's brother-in-law, urged, tapping his water glass. Others immediately chimed in. Gracie and Marc happily obliged.

The whole day had gone without a hitch. Isabelle had been tolerable and even kind to her today. The dinner had been excellent. Adriana continued to work the room, capturing candid memories of the evening. The kennel staff was all present and having a great time. Marian, the groomer, had managed to coax her husband Al into a suit. Cheryl Stone, her assistant kennel manager, had brought along her teenaged daughter. Her Aunt Marlene and Uncle Beau were in animated conversation with Cheryl and her daughter. It really had been a perfect day.

A stifled scream came from Marc's sister, who knocked over a candlestick as she rose from her seat. The wax splattered onto the white linen tablecloth.

Miranda looked around at the roomful of faces and rushed from the table, her napkin sliding to the floor.

"What's going on?" Gracie yelped, lurching to her feet. Marc did the same.

Larry followed after his wife, tossing his napkin on the table. Violet came to her son's side. The rest of the crowd gaped at the dramatic exit.

"I need to go after them and find out what happened," Marc's mother said quietly.

"I do too," Marc said. "She's been looking at her phone ever since we got here. Is she involved in something bad or being threatened?"

"I don't know, but it appears to have come to a head," Violet answered, closing her eyes and sighing. "Maybe that would explain her strange behavior and these unpredictable emotional outbursts. Miranda's refused to talk about why she went into counseling."

"Go find out," Gracie directed. "We'll cut the cake when you come back."

Marc followed his mother from the room, and the party switched their gaze to Gracie.

"Keep eating, everyone. Nothing more to see," she said with a weak chuckle.

"I don't know if I believe you," Jim said, sliding into Marc's chair.

"I'm lying, of course. Marc will find out what his sister's problem is. It's been brewing for a while."

"She's a bit jumpy, that's for sure."

Jim rejoined Tom and Kelly, leaning over the table to inform the Clark family, as well as Gracie's mother's brothers and their wives. She hadn't seen her uncles in several years, but they'd been excited to make the trip from Ohio. Both were dairy farmers and didn't often have the opportunity to leave their responsibilities.

Isabelle left Kevin, who looked like he was dozing. How much liquor had the man swilled? He'd been wobbly at the wedding. Now he was almost, if not already, passed out. Isabelle better be prepared to dump him in the backseat. Some boyfriend. She actually felt sorry for her high-maintenance cousin. This was something the late Tim Baker would have done. Izzy might want to reconsider her co-habitation arrangement after Kevin's performance today.

Gracie was about to check on the Stevens family disappearance when Marc strode through the door, his face dark with anger. She met him in a corner of the room, afraid of what he'd say. Maybe Miranda had had a psychotic break or something. They'd need to call an ambulance, and that would be a mess.

"Is Miranda all right?" Gracie asked, grabbing her husband's arm.

"No. She's not."

"Do we need to call an ambulance or take her to the hospital?"

Marc closed his eyes, his jaw tense.

"No. I need to talk to you outside though."

The side exit from the room led them onto the Glen Iris' lawn. The roar of the falls seemed amplified in the twilight. Mist from the water rose from the river gorge, keeping the observation area by the fieldstone wall wet.

"Okay, what's the deal, Marc?"

"I should have known everything was going too well," he said, loosening his silver necktie. "Miranda's been threatened by some associate of Jeremy's for the last several months. Apparently, Jeremy tried to start a correspondence with her. When she didn't reply to his first two letters, he sent another that blamed her—all of us actually—for his miserable existence. She did respond to that one, telling him to stop writing. That's when someone named Adam started stalking her and sending threatening texts … all sorts of things."

"Hasn't she told the police?" Gracie asked.

"No. My sister is a private person. She's never been one to let others be involved in her life."

"But what about Larry? Does he know about it?"

"A surprise to him too. She's internalized the whole thing, hoping it would go away if she ignored it."

"This is why she's on meds?"

Marc nodded. He took a few steps closer to the old-fashioned wrought iron light near the walkway. Gracie followed, feeling a touch shaky and chilly. The night air was quickly cooling off after a warm day.

"What happened tonight?"

Marc stopped and turned to her. "This guy has threatened her again. He said he'd burn down the house with her and Larry in it."

Gracie gasped, feeling sick.

"Oh my gosh! No wonder she reacted that way."

"I know. I've contacted the FBI. They'll call anybody else necessary to investigate."

Gracie took a step back, looking into the darkness falling over the gorge. Shadows were beginning to stretch out over the lawn from the lights along the sidewalks.

"Will she be safe?"

Marc wrapped his new wife in his arms. "She will and so will the rest of us. This guy will be caught. He's left a big trail to his door."

Gracie snuggled into the warmth of Marc's shoulder, hoping his words were true.

CHAPTER 23

Gracie squeezed her mother's hand as she accepted Theresa's kiss on the cheek.

"Well, Mrs. Stevens, it's time for everyone to leave you two on your own."

Gracie gave her mother a wry smile. "It's about time, Mom. I thought you'd never go. Everyone else has."

The reception's celebratory atmosphere had deflated somewhat after Miranda's emotional departure. Everything had smoothed out though when they'd cut the cake, except when she'd tried to plate a piece for them to share. The slice of white cake had flipped off the knife, landing on her shoe. Marc had gallantly removed it with a dramatic swipe of a napkin. Her second try was successful, and Adriana snapped the traditional shot of the cake feeding for posterity.

"It was a beautiful wedding, Gracie," Theresa said.

"I think it was," she agreed. "And, before you say anything else, Isabelle was fine. I'm glad we moved it to her house. My backyard really wasn't ready for primetime."

"I may faint," Theresa said, fanning her face dramatically with her hand.

"Come on, enough chit-chat," Bob urged his wife.

"Yes, dear," Theresa agreed, grabbing her purse from the table.

Gracie turned to find Marc on the phone. "What's going on?" she asked.

He held up a finger before ending the call. "I had a call back from the FBI. They're locating this Adam character right now. Miranda's nightmare should be over."

"Good. I hope we can focus on other pressing matters."

"I'm focused," he answered, putting his arm around her waist, leading her upstairs to their room.

***

Isabelle poured a second cup of coffee for herself, forlornly watching a bleary-eyed Kevin read *The New York Times* at the kitchen table. He was doing his best to ignore what must have been a raging hangover.

"I need to talk to you about the Walczak house," she said, taking a sip from the blue-striped china cup.

Kevin looked up, the bags under his eyes and wan complexion verifying his overindulgence of the night before.

"Not much to say. It's pre-foreclosure, at the moment."

"I want to buy it then."

"Why do you want another old house? You've already got the Cook house on that street and two on Railroad."

"It's a good rental, that's why. I intend to have eight properties by next year."

Kevin messily folded the newspaper and placed it in front of his untouched bowl of granola. He sighed. "I think there's already someone interested in the property. It's in probate now and there are a lot of penalties to be paid off. I don't think it's a good deal for you."

"I'll be the judge of that. I find it hard to believe that Frances Walczak would have let things go in arrears. Or is her ex-husband involved with the house?"

"Mrs. Walczak took out a home equity loan to buy out his share when they divorced. The debt is hers. At least, that's what I've been told."

Isabelle dropped a spoonful of sugar into her coffee, stirring it thoughtfully, and sipped again.

"Oak Street is a good neighborhood. It won't be hard to rent either house."

Kevin pushed the ladder-back chair away from the table, looking at Isabelle, who leaned against the black granite counter.

"There's a bit of an issue on Oak Street and with the Walczak house. There's that stolen quilt and the owner's death across the street from the house that you almost own. Aren't you a little concerned about that?"

Isabelle sniffed. "I don't see what that has to do with buying the house. Someone stole the quilt ... allegedly. It has nothing to do with selling it."

"The Cook woman is accused of stealing it, you know. She may be hiding stolen goods."

"I don't believe it for a minute. It's absurd. Someone else stole it, or maybe she washed it and ruined the thing. Besides, Lulu is leaving on a cross-country trip with some tour group. She'll be out of the house in a few weeks. That is, if she cleans out the rest of the junk she's accumulated. It's unbelievable."

"Is she really cleaning out the house?"

Kevin rose and put the bowl in the dishwasher. He grabbed a mug from the cupboard and slipped a K-cup into the coffeemaker.

"She is, but the garage is a disaster. Of course, her friend met with ... well, an accident in there. Lulu might be avoiding it until the end."

"Yeah. That's right. That was a shame. I'm surprised that Mrs. Cook wasn't investigated for foul play."

"Are you kidding? You don't know these people, Kevin. They aren't capable of something like that." Her eyes hardened as she looked at him. "You don't know *me*, as a matter of fact. And maybe I don't know you." She glanced around the kitchen, before turning her gaze back to Kevin. "What are we doing here anyway?"

He folded his arms across his chest. "Oh no, you don't. Your cousin's wedding's put ideas in your head." His face spread in a wolfish grin. "We agreed that marriage wasn't on the table, remember? This is a mutually beneficial business arrangement with special advantages—for both of us."

He smiled charmingly at her, which had no effect on Isabelle's dour mood, and took his seat at the table.

"That's not the way I see it," Isabelle said in a biting tone, placing her cup in the sink. "You do live here at my pleasure."

"Of course, it's pleasure," Kevin agreed with a smirk. He quickly rejoined her at the sink and started nuzzling her neck.

Isabelle backed away, pressing her hand against his chest. "Not now, Kevin."

"Your loss." He shrugged and walked to the side window in the large kitchen.

The sky was overcast, leaves blowing in swirls across the lawn.

"Good thing the wedding was yesterday," he said.

"Timing is everything," Isabelle replied, pulling her fluffy powder-blue robe closed. "It's chilly in here. Did you turn up the heat?"

***

Suzie had just plugged in the big coffeemaker in the Fellowship Hall at Deer Creek Community Church. Margaret was arranging brownies and cookies onto plastic serving trays. Gloria appeared in the kitchen and greeted her friends.

"Enough cookies?" she asked Margaret.

"More than enough," Margaret replied. She straightened up, helping herself to a brownie.

"How did the wedding go yesterday?" Suzie inquired, pulling a pile of white paper napkins from the cupboard.

Gloria nodded, smiling. "It was beautiful. Gracie was lovely, of course. Isabelle did a wonderful job of turning her backyard into an autumn country-wedding venue. The chef at the Glen Iris outdid himself with an absolutely delicious meal. She and Marc looked so happy, and they make such a handsome couple."

"He seems much different than Michael," Margaret commented. "They were so close. Always together."

"I know. I hope they'll be happy," Suzie added.

"I'm sure they will. Gracie has changed quite a bit since Michael's death. She's much more independent now," Gloria confirmed, helping Suzie with the napkins, while Margaret set out the plastic spoons.

Margaret placed spoons in a small wicker basket lined with a napkin. "I always thought she and Jim would get together. To tell you the truth, I'm a little surprised they didn't."

Gloria frowned. "Surprising or not, Gracie and Marc really are a solid couple. You know Jim Taylor can't commit. He's always been that way."

"I guess the most handsome men like to play the field forever. He should think seriously about settling down soon. He's no spring chicken anymore," Suzie said.

"None of us are," Gloria agreed. "Now that the wedding is over, I'm glad Albert can focus his energies on settling Franny's estate. He's been bone-tired with so many things going on. I do worry about his heart."

"I would too," Suzie agreed. "He needs to slow down."

"Have you found the quilt in the house?" Margaret asked, her hand resting on the old Formica counter near the big double sink.

"No. I have no idea where it could be. Theresa and I took a good look through all her linens."

Suzie stacked the paper hot cups on a corner table. "Do you think Lulu really has it?"

Gloria sighed and rubbed the back of her neck. "I don't want to believe that, since Franny met with such a horrible accident in Lulu's garage."

"I know ... it was ..." Margaret began.

"Good morning, Lulu," Suzie loudly greeted the long-absent congregant who stood in the doorway.

CHAPTER 24

Gracie woke, snugly wrapped in her husband's arms. Marc still slept, and she hesitated to break the embrace. The room was dark even though the clock on the bedside table said 8:30. He murmured and rolled over, releasing her, which was probably a good thing. The call of nature wouldn't wait much longer. When she returned, Marc was peering out the window at the gloomy day.

"Breakfast in bed?" he asked, reaching for her.

"I think that's an excellent idea. I don't want to have to get dressed for breakfast."

"Dressing for breakfast is overrated," he said, chuckling.

She had to agree, following him back to bed, while they waited for their order to arrive.

***

The dogs were ecstatic when they arrived home. Max barked joyously, and Haley butt-tucked around the dirt piles in the yard. Jim had taken them with him for the night and had deposited them in the backyard when he came to oversee the morning routine at the kennel.

"Holy cow, dogs! You'd think we'd been away for a week," Gracie exclaimed, finally corralling a wriggling Haley. "Let's wipe off all four paws before you go inside."

She threw a small towel to Marc, who caught it and began working on Max. Haley was uncooperative and dashed

160

off once more, before deciding it was in her best interest to have her feet cleaned.

"Finally. You are a crazy dog today," she said, exasperated. She tossed the towel on a chair.

Haley merely wagged her tail, pushing ahead of Max through the French doors into the living room. The house smelled homey and warm, the aroma of a roasting chicken wafting throughout.

"Your mother's been here already," Marc said, sniffing appreciatively.

"I have no doubt. But I'm grateful for that today. Cooking is not high on my list of priorities."

"Nor mine," Marc said. "We need to say good-bye to my family in about an hour. Will dinner wait that long?"

Gracie opened the oven door and checked the meat thermometer. "Not a problem. Are they coming over, or are we going to your house?"

"They'll stop here before they head to the airport."

"Good. At least, we can relax today then. I have a feeling we'll be busy getting you ready to leave."

"Don't even talk about next week. We're in the moment." Marc's smile was a bit weak, and she wondered if he was having second thoughts about DACO.

"I'm all about the moment," she agreed.

The dogs began growling and barking a few minutes later as a car rolled into the driveway.

"They're here already," Gracie called out.

She watched her new in-laws make their way up the sidewalk to the kitchen door. Marc quieted Max and opened the door for his family to enter.

"It smells wonderful," Violet exclaimed as soon as she walked in. "You're pretty amazing if you've already put a meal in the oven."

Gracie laughed. "I can claim no credit. It's my mother. We couldn't possibly miss a meal, especially on Sunday," she said, hugging her mother-in-law.

Marc took Larry and Miranda into the living room, while Violet found a seat at the counter.

"You and Marc are good together. I'm so happy for you both."

"Thank you. It's been an interesting journey to this point and will probably continue that way. His job will keep him away from home quite a bit."

"You'll adjust. It won't be easy, especially with his training that starts in a couple of days. What bad timing for a honeymoon."

"I know. But I want Marc to pursue his career, as I have mine. It will be tough, but I'm hoping the time goes by quickly for this training."

"It will," Violet assured her.

"What about this stalker of Miranda's? Did they catch him?"

"I think so. I'm sure that's what Marc is talking about with them. If only Miranda had said something. My children are the poorest communicators on the face of the earth— besides their father. Miranda has always kept things bottled up until they explode, and it hasn't improved with age."

Gracie nodded, remembering her tense conversations with Marc in Arizona. He'd held back quite a few things as well, not the least of which was the fact he'd lost his job with the sheriff's department.

"Now that it's in the open, and they've arrested the guy, maybe she'll get back to normal."

"I do hope so," said Violet. "Larry's been through a lot this year, trying to figure out if it was something he'd done or what. I hope Miranda hasn't damaged her marriage."

Gracie nodded solemnly, noticing that Marc seemed to have finished the private conversation in the other room.

"Time to run," Larry announced. "It's been a pleasure finally meeting you, Gracie. We wish you and Marc all the best."

He gave Gracie a peck on the cheek before shaking Marc's hand. Miranda hugged Marc, tears sparkling in her eyes.

"Thank you, Marc. I can't tell you ..." Her voice caught, and Marc grasped her shoulders.

"It's going to be all right now, Miranda. Don't pull another stunt like this again."

She shook her head sorrowfully. "You can count on that. I thought he'd just forget it and go away."

"You can't fix crazy or stupid," Marc replied firmly. "And this appears to be both."

Miranda brushed a tear from her cheek, a tentative smile curving her mouth as she hugged Marc again. She offered Gracie a rather stiff embrace, while Violet said good-bye to her son.

"Come and visit," Violet said as Larry opened the door.

"We will, Mom," Marc assured her. "Not sure when it'll be, but we'll plan on it."

"Don't say things just to make me happy," Violet teased.

"Of course not," Marc bantered back.

"We really will," Gracie added. "Have a safe flight home."

The car rolled out onto the road, and Gracie sighed.

"The invasion of the new in-laws is over," Marc said, laughing.

"You're perpetually stuck with yours," Gracie quipped, opening the oven door to check on the roasting chicken, potatoes, and carrots.

The fragrance was making her hungry, even after her hearty breakfast of eggs Benedict.

"One of the benefits of travel," he kidded.

"Really?" Gracie threw an oven mitt at him. "That's the real reason you wanted the DACO job?"

Marc grabbed her around the waist and kissed her. "I'm going to miss you like crazy," he whispered.

"You'd better."

A knock at the door brought the dogs tearing back into the kitchen, barking, tails wagging.

"Jim!" Marc exclaimed, throwing the door open.

"Sorry to barge in, but I wanted to let Gracie know that Marian had a fall today and broke her hip."

"What!?" Gracie almost dropped the plates she was taking from the cupboard. "What happened?"

"She was in the Geneseo Wal-Mart parking lot, just walking to the car, and must have tripped or something. Anyway, she fell. It was a good thing Al was right behind her. She's in Strong, having surgery right now."

Gracie set the plates on the kitchen counter. "Oh, poor Marian! That's terrible!"

"Right and poor you. Grooming appointments for the next week are already booked up."

Gracie pulled a pair of brown-checked napkins from a drawer and gathered flatware from another. "That puts a different spin on my schedule. We may have to cancel a few. I don't think I can handle all of them, especially with Marc leaving."

"I'll let you make the calls." Jim leaned against the door, hands folded across his chest.

Gracie sighed, placing a fork on top of the napkin. "I didn't need this problem. I really wanted to take Monday off."

"Don't stress about it," Marc said. "I'll be around. Can Cheryl or Trudy help you?"

"Some," she said, going back to the oven. "Poor Marian. This will keep her out of commission for some time."

"Probably," Jim agreed, opening the door. "Well, I'll let you lovebirds go back to whatever ... ahem ... you were doing."

"That's right," Gracie teased good-naturedly, snapping a dishtowel in Jim's direction. "We were having an excellent time until you showed up."

"Excuse *me!*" he said with a mocking bow.

Marc's cell phone sounded, and Jim slipped out the door.

CHAPTER 25

Theresa dumped the coffee grounds into the trash can in the church kitchen. Gloria wiped down the counters as Theresa finished cleaning the large coffee urn. The coffee time after the morning worship service had been lightly attended. Even Suzie and Margaret had made tracks, mentioning an afternoon trip to Naples for grapes. Theresa hoped to finish quickly, because a nap in her recliner was an absolute necessity. She'd been on the go since before the sun was up. She wasn't even sure why she'd rushed to come to church. Bob had declined to accompany her, opting for the newspaper and an extra cup of coffee. He'd disclosed his exhaustion as the father of the bride and couldn't understand why she was "on a quest to ride on the wings of the dawn." He was still throwing out poetic phrases, which was very strange.

"There. All done," Gloria said, rinsing out the dishcloth.

"Me too. Let's go," Theresa added, wiping her hands on a paper towel. "I'm beat."

"Theresa?"

The women looked up to see Lulu standing near some stray chairs next to the stacked folding chairs in the corner of the empty Fellowship Hall.

"Lulu. Is something wrong?" Theresa made a quick assessment of Lulu's demeanor. The woman was pale and looked frightened.

"Well ... uh." Lulu licked her lips and walked toward them. "I need to talk to someone. I'm not sure, but ..." She stopped and then took another couple of steps, grabbed the back of the gray metal chair, and crumpled to the floor.

Theresa waved the damp towel at Lulu's ashen face.

"Breathe, Lulu. It's okay," she instructed.

Gloria came running with a glass of water.

"Drink this." She handed the drink to Lulu, who took a quick gulp.

"I'm all right. I don't know what came over me. I really need to talk to someone." Lulu blinked rapidly, exhaling heavily and then sucking in a deep breath.

Theresa helped Lulu into the chair and pulled two more into a tight circle.

"Tell us what this is all about," Gloria said, wadding up the small towel on her lap. She put a hand on Lulu's shoulder, and she shrunk away.

"Really. I'm all right. But someone broke into my garage while I was at church. The place is a mess. They tossed quilts everywhere, dumped fabric ..." She closed her eyes. "It's awful. I'm sure it must be about Franny's quilt. I should've never . . ." The lanky woman sighed deeply, rising from the chair.

"Did you actually take Franny's quilt?" Gloria asked.

Lulu looked her in the eye. "No. I did not. I don't even know where the quilt is."

"But maybe it was meant to look like you took it," Theresa offered gently.

"Maybe." Lulu looked at her friends, as if trying to decide whether to elaborate. Finally, she said, "Yes. Franny and I hatched a plan to keep Art from selling her last asset. She needed money to get away from him for good. He was constantly hounding her for money she didn't have. He claimed to have a buyer who'd give them top dollar."

"Give them top dollar?" Theresa asked, puzzled.

"Right. That was the problem. Art expected a cut of the sale of the quilt as a finder's fee of some sort. Of course, Franny wasn't going to sell. It's a family heirloom. But she was having trouble making payments on the house ... and ..."

"Which means collecting the insurance money, while hanging on to the quilt, became a possibility," Gloria said.

Lulu shifted uneasily, looking at the floor. "Right. And I said I'd help her. She could blame me, and no one would find it, because I didn't have it. She wanted to sell the house and leave Deer Creek. Go where Art couldn't find her. He's not a nice guy, and Franny put up with an awful lot over the years. This was the last straw. She needed to get away from him."

"But they were divorced. Art didn't have any right to something that belonged to Franny," Theresa said, rising and returning to the kitchen where she hung up the towel on a knob.

"That wouldn't stop Art and hasn't. The more I think about it, I'm sure he was in my garage the night Franny was there, trying to find the quilt. It was supposed be a little skit for the neighbors. I'd yell at her for being in the garage, and she'd yell back and then go home. It all fell apart."

"Like Franny's act with us in your yard?"

Lulu nodded. When Theresa returned, Gloria had produced two more chairs, so they all could sit down.

Lulu cleared her throat. "There was another voice I heard that night. Art must have had someone else with him. I wish I could be sure though. But I am quite sure he was the one who broke into the garage today."

Gloria stood, chewing her bottom lip. "Which makes it difficult to report, with this backstory you've told us."

Lulu nodded, with a sheepish expression. "I had to tell someone. It's eating me up. I'm afraid he may try to break into my house next. What if he's violent?" She walked into the kitchen, dumping the rest of the water from the glass and placing it on the counter.

"Why is Art so strapped for money?"

"A good question, Theresa. He's perpetually broke and guilted Franny into helping him even after the divorce. He had a gambling problem at one time, maybe he's always had it, but Franny hated talking about him. It always brought on one of her spells. I just wanted to help her." Lulu pinched the bridge of her long nose, a pained expression on her face.

Gloria sighed. "This is a bit of a mess. The stolen quilt isn't stolen, but you don't know where it is. We need to stop the insurance claim right away, which means we'd better go talk to the executor, who's waiting for his Sunday dinner."

***

Albert Minders' look of astonishment was only outdone by his uncharacteristic outburst: "Are you kidding me?!"

Lulu shrank back from her usually mild-mannered pastor, looking like a trapped animal.

"I'm sorry, Lulu," he said immediately, adjusting his glasses. "Really. Let's sit down and talk about this."

Gloria busied herself in the kitchen, warming up a pot of leftover beef stew. She sliced into a dark loaf of pumpernickel bread, straining to hear the conversation in the living room. Poor Theresa must be grinding her teeth over missing this tête–à–tête. She'd demand a full report.

Albert regained his composure, and his voice was even and low.

"Let me understand this. The quilt really wasn't stolen. Franny and you wanted it to appear that way."

"Oh yes. I'm so sorry. I'm afraid it may have killed her. Her heart was bad, and the stress of Art pressuring her and making the insurance claim, the silly act to search the garage to make it look real—it was too much for her." Lulu sniffed and then blew her nose, sounding like a sick goose.

Gloria edged toward the doorway, listening intently and trying to decide if she should invite Lulu to stay for dinner. Deciding against it, she went back to the stove to give the stew a thorough stir and lowered the heat.

Albert scratched his head, ruffling his hair. He leaned back on the couch, his hands in a prayer pose, but fingers tapping against one another. Gloria impetuously joined her husband, perching on the arm of the couch.

"Well, you can let the insurance company know you're cancelling the claim. No harm, no foul, in my opinion."

The pastor shot his wife a sideways glance. "I'm responsible for all the assets of the estate. I can cancel the claim, but what about the quilt? Franny's relatives are very interested in obtaining possession of it, and it may be rightly theirs, after seeing the old agreement you found at the house. Then there's the promissory note that Art insists is legitimate. There's no way there are enough assets to pay off all the debt."

"I'm so sorry, Pastor. It's all my fault for going along with it." Lulu fidgeted, straightening a couple of magazines piled on the coffee table. She stopped and looked at the Minders. "There's an agreement about the quilt?"

"Oh yes," Gloria said. "Theresa and I found it when we were picking out an outfit for Franny. Ownership or use of the quilt was given to each side of the family, depending on whether it was an odd or even year."

Lulu looked puzzled. "She never told me about that. I wonder why."

Albert harrumphed, raising his eyebrows. "She was very attached to it," he stated.

"She was. But I'm not sure what to do about the garage break-in. Do I report it? I don't want the police at my house again. I can barely stand to go into the garage."

"You shouldn't ignore it," Albert said firmly. "You don't know for certain it was Art. Your safety is a priority."

"Maybe. I don't know. I'm having a service clean it out anyway. It's time to move on with my life." Lulu stared into the distance and then stood. "I'd better go." Her tone was brusque. Lulu was back to normal.

"If you need anything, please call," Gloria urged, seeing her to the door.

"I will. But ... oh, never mind," she finished quickly, hurrying to her car parked on the street.

CHAPTER 26

"My top secret clearance is official," Marc bragged, a broad smile on his face. He laid the cell phone on the kitchen bar. "Everything is a go for Wednesday, according to Mr. MacElroy himself."

Gracie pulled the roasting pan from the oven, setting it on top of the range. "That's good. Everything seems to confirm it was the right decision."

Max trotted into the kitchen with Haley right behind, her nails clicking on the tile.

"You two are scroungers. No chicken for you," she scolded the dogs, who sniffed and jockeyed for position around the stove.

Haley sat at Gracie's feet and put her front paws in the air, begging oh-so-very-pathetically.

"How can you tell her 'no' after such a touching performance?"

"No problem. She's getting a little too heavy. Marian is always giving her treats, which now won't be for a while. I will be stinking busy while you're away. That's probably good, because I'm going to be desolate without you."

"Double for me," Marc said, kissing the back of her neck.

She turned and put her arms around his neck. "We definitely need a real honeymoon when your training is over."

"Why is that? This one seems to be going just fine, plus we have a fabulous chicken dinner. When do we eat?"

She pushed him away, with a chuckle. "As soon as you finish setting the table, Mr. Stevens."

Halfway through their meal, Gracie's cell sounded. It was her mother.

"Not even one day of time alone," Gracie complained, contemplating not answering the call.

"She's probably making sure the dinner was okay."

"Maybe," she replied, swiping the phone's screen.

The chicken dinner wasn't on Theresa's mind, and it wasn't long after the dishes were placed in the dishwasher that the couple drove to Oak Street to pay a visit to Lulu Cook.

Theresa and Lulu stood on the side lawn, while Marc examined the broken padlock on the side entrance to the garage. Gracie followed Marc in and whistled. It looked like an explosion of cloth strewn around the old garage. The concrete floor was cracked and broken in a few places that weren't covered by quilts and sewing supplies. A single overhead lightbulb didn't help illuminate the area well. The majority of containers were open, and some were overturned, the contents strewn about.

"Ho-ly cow. Mom wasn't exaggerating. I can't believe the amount of stuff in here."

"It's a lot. Someone snipped the padlock and had themselves a heck of a time looking for something. I'm not sure if you could tell if anything had been stolen." Marc pushed to the back of the garage, batting at cobwebs.

"We should've have brought a flashlight," Gracie said, examining a couple of blue and yellow quilts. There was no doubt about it, Lulu was an excellent seamstress. "Do you think she should report it?"

Marc came back, brushing off his jeans and jacket. "Yes. But if nothing was taken, it won't be a priority. It could've been kids doing a little pre-Halloween mischief. I don't see anything to indicate who was in here."

"End of story then."

Marc shrugged. "Probably. But your Mom's friend is acting a bit peculiar. There might be more to this than meets the eye."

"She's a hoarder. That's plenty peculiar."

"Agreed. There's something else going on here, or we wouldn't have gotten a call."

Gracie stopped, righting a couple of Totes. "Absolutely correct, my handsome detective. Let me see if I can make them spill the beans."

Neither Theresa nor Lulu were forthcoming on many more details. Lulu restated her fear that someone was searching for Franny's quilt, which she adamantly maintained was *not* in her possession. Marc joined them on the lawn. The breeze was now icy, and thick clouds blew in from the west.

"It feels like snow," Theresa grumbled, thrusting her hands into the pockets of her navy wool jacket.

"I guess," Gracie agreed. "I'm really glad this held off until today."

Marc handed the broken padlock to Lulu. "Mrs. Cook, I'd report the break-in, but if you're sure nothing was taken, it will probably just be filed."

"Thank you for checking it out, Marc. I hated to bother you on your honeymoon, but Theresa was sure it would be fine."

Gracie glared at her mother, who seemed to be concerned with her shoes, which she scuffed on the grass.

"No problem," Marc assured her. "After my mother-in-law's gift of a delicious dinner, it's only fair. You might want to have motion lights installed out here and replace the lock."

"I will. Right away. Thank you."

Walking to the red RAV4, Gracie glanced back at the women, who were still talking while entering the house.

"I don't think she's going to call the police, do you?"

Marc huffed. "No. For some reason, she needed someone official to check out the garage, or more accurately, your mother wanted me to. I'm telling you, there's more to it than that."

Gracie turned the ignition on as Marc fastened his seatbelt. "I'll call her a little later and get to the bottom of it."

Marc frowned.

"Don't worry, that's all." She backed out of the driveway onto the street.

"I hope so. I'd hate to have to worry about you becoming tangled up in some bizarre sewing circle cloak-and-dagger thing. I'm kind of wondering about the company your mother keeps."

Gracie laughed. "Interesting women—all of them," she said, turning onto Main Street. "Let's go home and—"

Marc's cell phone interrupted with a loud buzzing.

"It's *my* mother now."

The conversation was brief, but Marc's expression turned from amused to solemn.

"Are you sure? How could they have not picked him up? All right. I'll call the agent."

Gracie slowed the vehicle to turn onto Simmons Road. "What's going on?"

"The FBI missed picking up this Adam Delaney, who's been threatening Miranda. They found out at the airport. An FBI agent actually met them at the luggage carousel."

"Oh no. I thought it was a sure thing."

"So did I. Apparently, it wasn't as simple as we were told. I'm calling the agent I talked to before they left."

He scanned his recent call list and selected the agent's number. The agent confirmed that Adam Delaney was still out there, but had left his phone at the location where they'd expected to arrest him. Marc rubbed his hand through his hair in agitation.

"It was too easy. I should've known," he said tersely. "They'd better protect Miranda and Larry and my mother."

"Are they?" Gracie turned the vehicle into the driveway, leaving it outside the garage.

"So they say. There are teams surveilling their homes. Miranda is probably having another meltdown, and I wouldn't blame her."

"Let's hope they track him down today," Gracie said, opening the door. "There's nothing more you can do, so let's try to enjoy what's left of the afternoon. The Bills are playing a late game today."

A few more phone calls throughout the football game broke up the monotony of three and out for the Bills. The FBI had regained its footing on locating Adam Delaney and expected to have him in custody before midnight. She was happy to see her husband's more relaxed demeanor.

He brought in a plate of nachos, setting them on the blocky square coffee table. "Need anything else, while I'm roaming around here?"

Gracie stretched out her legs on the leather sofa, feeling the fatigue of the last week catching up with her.

"No. I don't know if I can keep my eyes open much longer. I'm feeling dog-tired tonight."

Marc bent and kissed her forehead. "The salsa on the nachos will perk you up."

"Ha! I doubt it." She leaned forward and snatched a generously cheese-and-salsa loaded tortilla chip. "Mmm. Very good."

Her reaction brought the dogs to the coffee table. Max put a paw on the table and looked longingly at the plate. Marc grabbed a couple for himself and shooed the moochers back to the dog bed in front of the fireplace.

"Weren't you going to call your mother about the quilt lady?"

Gracie swung her legs off the sofa and onto the floor. "That's right. Totally forgot after the FBI manhunt thing." She yawned. "I don't want to do that now. My mind isn't working all that well, and my mother can be pretty cagey. There's always tomorrow."

CHAPTER 27

Lulu tossed the plastic bag into the kitchen's trash can and held the shiny new padlock. The walk to Evans Hardware this morning had been invigorating. The fall air was crisp, and she was one day closer to warm weather forever—if she could hold everything together for a few more weeks. She buttoned up her jacket and trundled out to the garage. Snapping the padlock on the hasp, she turned and found Art Walczak standing next to her.

"Art! You about scared me to death! What are you doing here?"

Art rubbed an unshaven jaw, his bushy eyebrows drawn together.

"I'm wondering when you're turning over that quilt."

"I don't have it. I never had it. In fact ..." She hesitated. Did she really want to be the one to tell him that the quilt hadn't been stolen?

"Franny would've never accused you unless she was sure." He dropped his hand to his side, making a fist.

Lulu edged away, calculating how far it was to the kitchen door. "Someone broke into my garage yesterday. They cut the padlock off, as a matter of fact."

Art's eyes flickered, and he thrust his hands into pockets of his dirty baseball jacket. "Are you accusing me?"

"Should I?" Lulu began walking purposefully to the house.

Art tagged along. "No. I wasn't in your garage. You can't prove it either."

"Didn't say I could. But you were in the garage the night Franny died, weren't you?" She stopped and looked coldly at the disheveled man.

He sucked in a breath and exhaled it into a white cloud. "You can't prove that either."

"Maybe not. I heard your voice and someone else's too. Franny wasn't in there alone. You and this other person could very well have—"

"You're the one who knocked those tubs over on poor Franny. No one else did that. That's the reason she had a heart attack. It's all on you. Handing over the quilt is smart. Otherwise, something could happen to you."

Lulu gasped. Clutching the top of her coat, she drew it around her throat. "You're threatening me? In my own yard? Get out, Art, and stay off my property."

Her voice was steely. The man's chutzpah knew no bounds. She'd had enough of his bullying.

"No problem. Give me the quilt, and everything will be fine. If you don't, I might let some people know you're still hiding it, hoping to sell it after Franny's estate is settled. The cops might be interested in searching your house, if that happens."

Lulu felt the color drain from her face, her courage gone. "Leave me alone. I don't have the stupid thing."

How she wished Franny had given the quilt to a museum or historical society years ago!

"Okay then. Whatever you say. This isn't over though." Art stalked away and walked down Oak toward Main Street.

***

A brush in one hand, her cell phone pressed to her ear with her shoulder, and a Yorkie dancing on the grooming table gave Gracie the appearance of an awkward juggler.

"Mom, the whole thing was strange yesterday with Lulu. What's really going on over there?"

"Someone broke into Lulu's garage. I thought if Marc stopped by and assessed the situation, she'd feel better."

"What about the stolen quilt? Has it been found?" Gracie laid the brush down and gathered a little fawn-colored topknot on the wriggling dog. She clipped a red bow on the impatient Dinah, whose pink tongue flashed in and out of her tiny mouth, trying to lick her hand. Once Gracie patted the dog's side, Dinah finally sat, enjoying the attention.

"Well ... there's a development about the quilt."

Here it was. The crux of the matter. She knew the defeated tone in her mother's voice.

***

Marc seemed unsurprised when Gracie filled him in at lunchtime.

"I knew something was going on. Insurance fraud is a serious matter."

"Pastor Minders won't be in trouble, will he? After all, he had no idea."

"No. I wouldn't think so," Marc said. He poured himself another glass of water from the pitcher at the kitchen bar.

"But Lulu could be," Gracie mused.

"Hopefully the insurance company wouldn't go after her. She didn't hide the quilt—so she says, and she didn't support the claim in any way."

Gracie placed her glass and plate in the dishwasher after rinsing it under the faucet. "Any news from your Mom?"

"No, but the FBI agent called. They do have the guy in custody. With any luck, they can keep him off the streets."

"Good. I've got to get back to work. The afternoon grooming schedule is full, and the rest of the week is just as bad. Plus, I need to order some flowers for poor Marian."

"I'll finish spreading the dirt and fixing the lawn today. It's one thing I can do for you before I leave."

Marc handed his dishes to Gracie and grabbed a hooded sweatshirt from the back of the dining room chair.

He disappeared through the French doors with the dogs, and Gracie wiped down the counter. Her cell phone buzzed in the back pocket of her jeans.

"Mom, what's up?"

"I hate to bother Marc again, so I thought I'd call you. Lulu had a scary run in with Art Walczak today. I was wondering if Marc might have a talk with him."

"You do know Marc isn't a deputy anymore?"

"I know. But Lulu's really upset. She doesn't want to call the police, so I thought—"

Gracie's patience had yet to appear on the horizon for the day. "Mom! Marc is busy. He leaves Wednesday morning. Tell her to call the police."

The silence on the other end stretched into an awkward one before Theresa replied. "You're right. Sorry. I'll talk to Lulu again."

"I'm sorry too. It's really hectic here. Tell her to call the sheriff's office if Art really threatened her."

"Sure. I will. I didn't mean to cause a problem."

The call ended. Gracie stood, staring at the screen. What in the world was Art threatening Lulu about? Was it over the missing quilt? She stuffed the phone back in her pocket and jogged down the driveway to the kennel.

***

Isabelle followed Albert and Gloria Minders into the chilly house. The pastor flipped a light switch, illuminating the gloomy living room.

"I'll take it from here." Isabelle's businesslike tone raised the pastor's eyebrows, but he kept a smile on his face.

"Certainly. We'll wait for you."

Gloria twisted her mouth into a disgusted expression, as she plopped into an armchair. Crocheted doilies were draped over each arm and on the headrest. The sound of a vehicle turned their attention to the front windows.

"That looks like Kevin's car," Gloria said, holding the curtain back.

The pastor called up the stairway, "Were you expecting Kevin?"

Quick footsteps came to the top of the stairs. "Kevin's here?"

"I believe so."

"I'll be right down."

Albert answered the knock at the front door, and Kevin stepped into the living room.

"I thought I'd catch up with Isabelle to look the house over," he explained, adjusting his blue-and-gray striped tie. "I'm not sure the house is right for her."

"Kevin! Are you following me around today?" Isabelle was not pleased to see her boyfriend. Her narrowed eyes and a disapproving frown were his greeting.

"I thought I'd take a look myself. It is in pre-foreclosure. Just looking out for the bank's interests."

The Minders looked at each other and back to the sparring couple. Gloria could feel the smoldering acrimony.

"Can I show you around?" Albert asked. "The furnace or …"

"Is there an attic in the house?" Kevin asked. "I'd like to check the insulation."

Isabelle shot him a suspicious look. "I saw an access panel in the hallway ceiling upstairs," she replied. "I'd like to see the basement, Reverend."

Gloria wondered about following Kevin upstairs and then decided to assist her husband. Empty canning jars sat in neat rows on two sets of metal shelves off to one side of the small basement. A crawl space yawned into blackness past the block walls that came halfway up to the floor overhead. Gloria stepped gingerly over a mousetrap, which fortunately was empty. She poked at a couple of cardboard boxes that seemed a bit damp. There were old pots and pans in one; the other held a few dishes. Nothing interesting. There were certainly no hiding places for an antique quilt. The dampness would mildew it into oblivion.

"That's all the mechanicals," Albert said, dusting off his hands. "The hot water tank looks fairly new. Did you want to have a look at the attic?"

"No. I'll put in an offer today and have my home inspector do that. I'll check out the kitchen and downstairs bathroom before I go though." Isabelle brushed off the tweed blazer and bone-colored blouse.

"Of course," Albert said, motioning for Gloria to join them in ascending the cellar steps.

Arriving back in the kitchen, Gloria expected Kevin to be finished with his attic inspection. No sound from above indicated he was upstairs though. She decided to check out his location, while Isabelle made notes on her iPad. His unexpected appearance had made her a bit skeptical as to his real reasons for stopping by. No one was on the second floor. The pull rope on the attic access door dangled a bit lower than before. No wonder. The mechanism hadn't gone completely back into place. Where had he disappeared to? Quickly making her way downstairs, she glanced out the window at the driveway and saw that Kevin's car was no longer there.

"Kevin left," she announced, joining her husband and Isabelle in the kitchen.

"Good," Isabelle answered with annoyance. "He doesn't think this house is a good deal for me for some reason."

"I think the house is sound and would be a good income property," Albert said, cleaning his glasses on his blue-and-beige, diamond-patterned sweater vest. "It may need a bit of work though."

"They all need work, Reverend. I'll have to rehab the house across the street and this one too. Outdated kitchens and bathrooms don't attract the best renters."

"The house across the street?" Gloria asked.

"The Cook house. I'm closing on it in a few weeks."

Gloria felt her mouth gape, and she instantly composed herself before commenting dispassionately, "I had no idea."

CHAPTER 28

The early morning farewell had been tough. Gracie's eyes were still red and unfortunately puffy. She patted a cold washcloth underneath them, hoping that the evidence of her brief crying jag would be erased before walking down to the kennel. Despite her heroic efforts, emotions had gotten the best of her when Marc and Max had driven away. Even Haley was droopy; the Lab's normal enthusiasm level had dipped significantly. Haley was curled up on the bed in front of the fireplace, rather than begging to go out and run. Marc had left for the airport before dawn with Max hyped up, ready for action. She wondered how the dog would react to flying and the training situation.

The sunrise stretched over the horizon. Tendrils of light illumined the red and gold leaves of the maples in the backyard. The doomed birch tree was now gone, a stack of wood ready to be seasoned for next year. It was shaping up to be a beautiful fall day.

Finishing her coffee, Gracie pulled on a sweatshirt and whistled for Haley.

"Come on girl. Time for work."

Haley thumped her tail on the floor, rattling the tags on her collar before making a dash for the door. The pair jogged down the driveway to the kennel, with Haley flushing out a cottontail near the storage barn. The dog seemed satisfied she'd made it run and continued to the kennel entrance. Unlocking the door to the reception area, Gracie swiftly keyed in the code to disarm the security system. A chorus of yips and woofing began, and Haley was off to greet the boarders.

The routine of making coffee and firing up the computer took a couple of minutes. She then printed off the schedule of grooming appointments. She'd be on the run all day shampooing and clipping as fast as she could. Yesterday's news that Marian would be out of commission for six weeks had her wondering if hiring a temporary groomer would be the best thing.

"Hey, Chief," Jim called, tromping through the reception area to the office.

"Morning, Jim." She turned her back to focus on the monitor and print out the arrival and departure schedule.

"Everything all right?"

"Yeah. Just a little preoccupied."

"And a touch upset by the groom's departure," Jim guessed.

She looked up after clicking on the print icon. "A touch," she agreed, her eyes suddenly welling with tears. "But it's a busy day, which is probably a very good thing since I won't be able to talk to him until the weekend."

"Really? What's up with that?"

"Orders. It's very military-like. No communication until they have some free time on Saturday."

"It'll go by fast," Jim said optimistically. He laid the morning paper on the desk and went for the coffee pot.

"Right. That's what I'm telling myself."

They sat in silence as Jim opened the newspaper and drank coffee. Haley came trotting in, rounding the corner from the grooming room next door. She sniffed in expectation.

"No Marian and no extra treats. I told you that it was now diet time for you, my chubby one," Gracie admonished the disappointed dog.

"You're so mean to that dog," Jim teased. Haley immediately went to Jim and sat, placing a paw on his knee.

"Right. It's for her own good. Anything interesting in the news?"

Jim rattled the pages. "Nothing much. Last movie of the year at the drive-in is coming up. Antique car rally at the Charcoal Corral. Oh, and there's a fabric art show coming up in November. It's in Batavia. Interested?"

Gracie shook her head. "Not really. What kind of art?"

"Fabric, it says. Embroidery, crewel and counted cross stitch, applique work, quilts, and much more."

"Sounds like something for my mother. Sewing of any kind was never my cup of tea."

"Ah ... well, I guess it's work, work, work for you." He folded the paper and handed the section to her. "Also, heigh-ho, heigh-ho, it's off to work, work, work for me. Kibble delivery is coming today, and Cheryl needs some help setting up the agility course stuff for tonight's class."

"All right then. You're helping with play times too, right? There's no way I can do them with Trudy."

"Absolutely. Somebody's got to handle the Irish wolfhound. I think he's a little big for Trudy."

"She's fine with him, but I'm sure MacGyver will be pleased to play with you." She flipped to the back page of the newspaper, an ad catching her eye.

"Did you see this ad for rentals in Deer Creek?"

Jim shook his head. "What rentals?"

"Houses in Deer Creek. Looks like my cousin is out to be a slumlord now. She's now DC Property Management."

Jim laughed. "I highly doubt Izzy would have anything to do with slums."

"Well, probably not slums, but she may take over Deer Creek. It could become her fiefdom."

"That I might buy, but no rest for the wicked. I need to—"

The bell on the front jangled. Trudy called out a cheery greeting, with Cheryl adding her "good morning."

"The troops are here," Jim said, slapping his leg for Haley to follow. "Let's rock and roll."

Two cocker spaniels sat in the drying area, while Gracie had a firm grip on a squirming beagle, who was boisterously unhappy about a pedicure.

"All right, Oliver. One more paw and you're free to go." She grimaced, adjusting her position to isolate his hind paw. The beagle whined, finally giving up on baying like he'd found a rabbit, and pulled his foot from her grasp. "Not so fast, buddy." She speedily filed down the long claw-like nails to their proper length with the new nail grinder, which obviated any blood-letting caused by clipping into the quick of an uncooperative canine.

She'd just deposited him in a separate area from the cockers, when her mother appeared in the doorway.

"Hi, Mom. What's up?" She took off her heavy apron and hung it on the wall hook.

"I'm just checking to see if Marc and Max got off all right this morning."

"They did. And I'm fine. Yes, it was difficult. But I'm fine."

Theresa made wry face. "Okay, smarty pants. I'm your mother. Inquiring mind and all that. For your information, you're not the only reason I stopped by."

Gracie groaned. It had to be the drama on Oak Street again.

"Is Art Walczak still threatening Lulu or something?"

Her mother hesitated, and Gracie feared another visit to Lulu's was in her future.

"Gloria heard that Isabelle purchased Lulu's house. She's also put in an offer to buy Franny's."

"I saw her property management ad in the paper this morning. Apparently, Izzy's on the move with real estate."

"She's an astute business woman. But the strange thing is that Lulu hasn't mentioned the sale to anyone."

Gracie walked past her mother, heading for the office. Theresa followed, pulling off her jacket and laying it on Jim's ratty green plaid recliner.

"No crime there," Gracie said, pouring herself a cup of coffee. "Want some?"

Theresa shook her head, picking at some pilled fibers from the sleeve of her blue shaker-knit sweater. "The hoarding and now finding out that she's sold the house don't add up to me."

"You're over-thinking it, Mom. She's probably ready to downsize and realized the house was too much to deal with. It seems like a good thing to me. She has to get rid of her stuff that way."

Theresa moved her coat and sat on the recliner. "That's what your father says." She frowned and continued. "I've known Lulu for a long time. She's never traveled and has always loved her house. I think something happened that triggered her hoarding mania."

"Her husband died, and she's been a little obsessed with her sewing, but now she's cleaning up her act. What are you worried about?"

Theresa stood, slipping the jacket on. "She didn't tell anyone she planned on moving away. That's unheard of. Well, I'd better run. I'm glad you're okay. Friday night fish fry, right?"

"Sure. What about Tom and Kelly?"

"They'll be there. Emma has some special SAT workshop, so she's busy."

Theresa hurried through the doorway, with Gracie on her heels to return to continue the grooming schedule.

"I'll see you then. Stay out of trouble, Mom."

***

Lulu stood in the garage, contemplating which container to begin with. She shivered and zipped up her old sweatshirt jacket. The dampness chilled her to the bone.

What if Franny *had* put the quilt in one of these tubs? The Stederman quilt was nowhere to be found at Franny's. The stupid thing needed to be located. The pastor was stressing about it; it was a major asset of Franny's estate. Poor Franny! What a stupid, stupid plan! Why had she agreed to go along with it? If Art found it first, he'd sell it in a heartbeat, although how he'd have connections to do that, she could not imagine. It must be on the most wanted quilt list somewhere. Then there was Franny's cousin who had laid claim to it. Maybe it should stay lost. The old thing had certainly become a huge problem—maybe even a curse. No way did she want to be in possession of it. Her own plans would be wrecked beyond repair if that happened.

She grunted, pushing a stack away from the workbench, and located a light that Ed had used when he worked on his truck. Plugging in the square, black work-light, she set it on the floor to shine on the container maze, the bright lamp revealed the full extent of her hoarding. What had she been thinking? She couldn't let the recycling company take anything unless she'd looked through it all. It could take forever.

"Lulu? Are you here?" Theresa called, stepping through the side door.

Two hours later, Lulu and Theresa emerged from the garage, smudges of dirt on their hands and faces.

"Franny's quilt isn't in there," Theresa confirmed, finding a tissue in her coat pocket and rubbing it across her dirty palms.

"Thank goodness," Lulu breathed. "I needed to be sure. The recycling company comes tomorrow."

"What about all the quilts and the sewing supplies?"

Lulu sighed. "I don't know. It's so overwhelming. I just want to get rid of everything."

"I'm sure the Red Cross or the homeless shelters could use the quilts. Or you could send more of them to Mexico. The church could help—"

Lulu eyes blazed. "Send more to Mexico? What do you mean?" she demanded.

***

Gloria handed a hot cup of tea to her friend. Theresa sank into the chair at the kitchen table, wrapping her hands around the cup. The warmth of the homey kitchen, smelling of fresh baked cookies, felt good after working so long in the freezing garage with Lulu.

"It was dumb, but it slipped out. I was only making conversation the day I mailed the package to the orphanage. She was really mad."

"Oh, Theresa. That is unfortunate." Gloria joined her, taking a sip from her forget-me-not patterned bone china cup. "I can't understand why she would be so upset though."

"Lulu was helping the orphanage on her own and didn't want us know, for some reason. Probably poor Rudy will hear about it, thanks to my loose lips."

"Well, let's hope not. And you didn't find the quilt?" she asked, picking up a warm chocolate chip cookie from a tea plate with the same blue flower pattern.

"The quilt is definitely not in the garage. She only has about thirty or forty others though, and bolts of fabric out the wazoo. Good grief! How she can throw them out is beyond me."

"It's a shame, but what can we do? Don't worry. In a couple of days, she'll calm down."

A knock at the front door interrupted the women's conversation.

CHAPTER 29

Gloria groaned, peeking through the front curtains. It was Lisa Stederman Kronk on the front steps, a manila envelope in her hand. Lucky for Albert, he was in his office at the church, writing Sunday's sermon. Bad luck for her to have answered the knock.

She opened the door, forcing a friendly countenance. At least, she hoped her expression was welcoming.

"Mrs. Minders. It's so good to see you," Lisa said.

Her black hair was pulled back into a bun, small gold hoop earrings accenting her business-like appearance of trench coat and black pumps.

"Mrs. Kronk. What a surprise!"

"Sorry." The woman's dark eyes seemed to indicate good humor. "I do apologize for dropping in without calling first. I lost your number somehow. I wanted to drop off a family document to Reverend Minders regarding the heirloom coverlet. The family attorney made a copy for him, and since it's not stolen, the agreement verifies that the Stederman family, my family, is the rightful owner."

Gloria hesitated and then opened the door wider to allow Lisa to enter.

"My husband's not here, but come in and have a seat. Would you like some coffee or tea?"

"Oh no. I really can't stay."

Lisa stood just inside the doorway, holding out the envelope, which Gloria took.

"We located an agreement at the house right after Franny passed away. I believe you received a copy of it from the estate's attorney."

Lisa smoothed her hair, tucking stray wisps back in place. "I'm afraid that's not the actual agreement. The one you found is a fake."

Gloria's eyes widened. "What? A fake? It looked quite authentic to us and to our attorney."

Lisa smiled, a patronizing look on her face. Gloria felt her own face redden. She wasn't about to be flimflammed by the likes of Lisa Stederman Kronk.

"My mistake," Lisa said smoothly. "'Fake' is too strong a word. 'Outdated' is more accurate. Actually, from the Stederman family documents, which my grandmother has in her possession, there was a superseding agreement about the quilt."

Gloria took a deep breath, hoping to regain her composure. "I see. Well, I'll be sure to give it to my husband and have the attorney take a look at it."

"Certainly. I believe you'll find it all in order. I would also like to have an opportunity to look through the house myself."

"I'm not sure that's appropriate," Gloria replied.

"You can understand our concern that this precious family keepsake is found and handled correctly." Lisa's expression was a muddle of congeniality and distain.

Gloria pursed her lips, thinking that the woman's supercilious behavior bordered on desperation.

"I'll pass along your request to my husband."

Lisa managed a tight smile, picking at loose thread dangling from a buttonhole on her coat. "Thank you for your time."

The wind gusted through the door as the woman exited. A relieved Gloria watched her drive away, glad to return to the safety of her kitchen.

Slapping the envelope on the table, she snatched a cookie from the plate.

"Another agreement. Really?" Theresa frowned and tucked gray hair behind her ear, exposing tiny pearl studs.

"I guess so," Gloria answered, sliding the copy from the envelope. "Let's take a look at what it says."

The old-fashioned language mirrored the other document in style only. The bequeathing of the bedding went to the Stederman line, with no mention of the Drummond family sharing it. It had been signed by Ada Drummond Stederman and Henrietta Stederman, just as the one found at Franny's. The date however, was 1825 and not 1821. Had there been a falling out between the cousins?

Gloria leaned back in the chair, looking at the document.

"What do you think?" she asked Theresa, who stirred her coffee absently.

"Interesting. Maybe the girls had a big fight."

"They both signed it though."

"True. But what difference does it really make if we can't locate the dumb thing?"

Gloria laughed. "Also true. I think we need to scour the house from top to bottom one more time before the auction and see if we can't ferret out Franny's hiding place. I'm sure the attorney will never agree to Lisa searching the house, and for Franny's sake, I don't think she should be allowed to paw through her things."

Theresa's eyes narrowed conspiratorially. "I agree. Maybe she's the one who broke into Lulu's garage. She seems pretty bold."

Gloria nodded slowly. It made sense.

Theresa looked at her watch. "Since Marc is away, it would be good for Gracie to help us. It'll keep her occupied."

"Her help would be appreciated. We can't ask Suzie and Margaret, because they're off on a bus tour to Boston tomorrow." Gloria gathered up the cups and the empty plate.

"I'd forgotten about that. We definitely need Gracie's help then. I'll have her go up into the attic. I hate heights, and so do you."

Gloria set the dishes in the deep black sink. "We'll have to do it before the auctioneer's crew starts sorting things. Do you have your calendar with you?"

***

Saturday afternoon found Gracie sitting in her RAV4 in front of the Walczak house, waiting for her mother and Gloria to appear. Her long-awaited phone call from Marc had come early, waking her before the alarm. He was working hard, as was Max. They'd been successful in locating explosive materials in all of the vehicles and buildings they'd been training on. Not one false alert from the brawny German shepherd. The pride in Marc's voice had made her smile. He was really enjoying the hard work, but he did miss her most painfully. She was glad to cross off another day on the countdown for him to come home.

How she'd allowed herself to be sucked into the vortex of the Holy Meddlers Squad was still a bit mysterious. The whole situation was odd and intriguing, which might account for her acquiescence. No matter the flimsy reasoning that had pulled her in, she was now well and truly stuck.

Theresa's sedan pulled in behind her, and Gloria's car followed. The super sleuths had arrived! Gracie brought up the rear as Gloria inserted the key into the front door.

"Here we are," Gloria announced, pushing the door open.

The trio gasped in unison at what met their gaze.

"What happened here?!" Gloria gasped.

Armchairs were tipped over. Cushions tossed around. Gracie stood feeling bewildered by the mess. What *had* happened? Gloria dashed to the bedroom with Theresa in tow. Gracie trailed after them and saw the bed was stripped to the bare mattress, sheets and the bedspread in a heap at the foot of the old bed. Dresser drawers were overturned, the contents spread on the floor. A muffled call for help filtered up to them from below.

CHAPTER 30

Isabelle's freshly manicured fingers drummed a staccato beat on her dining room table. Her almost favorite vases, a pair of nineteenth century French blue porcelain, were nowhere to be found. Hand-painted with intricate gold leaf scrolling and exotic birds, they'd been the last anniversary present from her late husband, Tim. The man had been scum, but his taste in antiques had been unimpeachable.

She repeated her inspection of the large china cabinet that held her best Waterford crystal, Royal Albert china, and her pride and joy—an extremely expensive hand-blown glass cologne bottle by Frederick Carder. He'd cofounded Steuben Glass in Corning. It had been a real coup to have scarfed it up at a charity fundraising auction. At least, the deliciously rippled copper-colored opaque bottle with stopper was in its assigned place.

Was it possible, with the comings and goings of people for Gracie's wedding, that someone had slipped the pair of vases out of the house? It seemed hard to believe, but one never knew about people. She'd learned that the hard way with Tim, trapped in his web of abuse and control. Or had they been missing for a while? She couldn't remember the last time she'd really taken the time to enjoy the collection.

The front door opened, and she heard keys drop onto the table in the foyer.

"Kevin, is that you?"

"Yeah. You're home early," he answered, sticking his head through the arched opening.

She watched him loosen his tie and take off his suitcoat. "I had a buyer cancel on a house showing this afternoon. You're a little early yourself."

"I had an unexpectedly short meeting in Warsaw this afternoon, so I decided to come on home rather than go back to the bank." He took off his shoes, walking into the dining room in his socks. "See, I remembered," he said, pointing to his feet.

She nodded, with a scowl. Isabelle found that his assumption her house was his home unexpectedly annoying. Seeing Gracie and Marc so happy on Saturday had her reconsidering the decision to allow Kevin to enjoy the benefits of matrimony without any commitment. He had a pretty cushy arrangement for himself. The same could be said for her. He was clever and handsome. A perfect companion for the social functions that took up so much time. Kevin was much more pleasant than Tim, and their goals of hefty personal bank accounts made them extremely compatible. Compatibility was so crucial to a good relationship. The arrangement had been immensely satisfactory until the wedding. Now she wasn't as sure. She strode into the living room ahead of him.

"Glass of wine, beautiful?" he asked, hurrying to give her a kiss on the cheek.

"Not now," she answered in clipped tones.

"What's the matter?" Kevin sank into a navy-and-cream striped wingback chair, swinging his legs onto a matching ottoman.

"My French vases are missing."

She perched on the arm of the leather sectional, looking at Kevin, who instantly sat up, his feet on the floor.

"What vases?"

Isabelle scrutinized his reaction. He seemed nervous, guarded.

"My blue vases that are always in the china cabinet," she replied.

Kevin's nonchalant manner flowed back into place. "I guess I don't remember them. Are you sure they're missing?"

"Of course, I'm sure. You didn't see any of the wedding people in there did you?" She'd explore that possibility first.

"There were so many people around on Saturday, I don't know. You had a whole entourage—the florist, hairdresser, the caterer, plus the guitarist. Your family and Marc's family. I hope you can trust all of them."

She rose without responding and returned to the dining room and opened the left door of the immense mahogany cabinet. The triple doors displayed the bounty of years of collecting. Every piece of china, glass, and ceramic had been selected with care. Her absolute favorite was the Frederick Hurten Rhead vase. The glazing was exquisite, the brown trees draping the graceful deep blue form perfectly. She smiled and ran her fingers over the surface lovingly.

"Well, the pair is gone, and I want to know what happened to them. They are rather valuable." She needed to retain her unflappable demeanor and not let anger get the best of her.

Kevin joined her, peering through the glass at the other end. "Are you sure you didn't put them in some other place?"

"Don't be absurd," she replied irritably. "You know that my entire collection is in here."

Kevin backed away, avoiding her gaze. "I'm just confirming. No need to bite my head off. Should we call the police then?"

"Should we?" she retorted, closing the door of the cabinet, as the doorbell chimed.

***

The three women scrambled from the bedroom, Gloria leading the charge.

"Someone's in the cellar," she cried, running to the kitchen.

They tried the cellar door. It was locked.

"Where's a key?" Theresa squawked.

The indistinct sounds from below had coalesced into a clear call for help.

Gloria rummaged in the drawer next to the sink, searching for a key.

"I think this is it," she said finally, brandishing a rusty key.

Thrusting it into the keyhole, she twisted and turned it until finally the lock clicked. She flung open the door and turned on the light switch. Nothing but inky darkness.

"Who's down there?!" Theresa yelled.

Gloria and Gracie frantically searched more kitchen drawers for a flashlight.

"Let's just use our phones," Gracie said, slamming a drawer shut.

"Right." Gloria and Theresa said in concert.

"Who's down here?" Theresa asked again.

"It's me," a weak voice called out. "Art."

Reaching the bottom of the stairs, the trio found Art Walczak propped up against a rough timber post. Gracie held her phone up to shine as much light as possible on the injured man.

"Oh, Art! What happened? Are you all right?" Theresa gasped.

Art's unshaven face was streaked with dirt, bruising apparent on his jaw.

"I think my leg is broken," he gulped. "I thought I was going to die down here."

"We're here now," Gloria soothed. "I'll call the ambulance."

Gracie stood at the front door, waiting for the Deer Creek Rescue Squad to appear. The siren announced their arrival from Main Street. She was relieved to see Cora Darling exit the vehicle first. Her curly gray head and solid, rotund figure hurried up the sidewalk, black case in her left hand.

"Right through here," Gracie said, leading the woman to the stairway.

"Thanks. You'd better show the boys back here too," Cora directed as she started down the steep wooden stairs.

The boys were the Harwood brothers. Their choice of community service had always seemed a bit self-serving, but they were skilled at both comforting the grieving, and giving aid to the injured. They nodded and smiled politely at Gracie, looking like a pair of off-duty butlers, dressed in white shirts and black pants. She showed the two men, who hauled a gurney between them, to the kitchen.

Staying well out of the way, she wandered back to the jumbled living room and then to the trashed bedroom. Had Art been searching for the quilt? Why would he make such a mess? More importantly, why was he in the cellar? There was a whole lot of weirdness going on here.

"All right, Artie," Cora said, following the gurney through the living room. "Emery and Phil have you snug as bug. You'll be just fine."

"Okay, Cora," a subdued Art murmured.

Theresa and Gloria appeared and went out onto the lawn to watch the ambulance crew load up the man for the trip to Warsaw.

"What happened?" Gracie asked, joining her mother on the leaf-covered lawn.

"Art says Lulu pushed him down the stairs and locked him in," Theresa said grimly.

"What?" Gracie was floored. "Why would Lulu do that?"

"Good question," Gloria said, frowning. "I can't imagine Lulu resorting to violence. Why would she be in the house? Someone else did this, not Lulu."

"Agreed. But who, and why's Art accusing her?"

In Gracie's estimation, it took a lot of nerve to shove anyone down the stairs and then lock the door so they couldn't get out. It looked like attempted murder to her.

"Possibly that cousin of Franny's. She's as tough as nails and awfully persistent about recovering the quilt," Gloria mused. "I can see her mixing it up with Art."

Lulu's front door opened, and she hurried across the street, a brown cardigan drawn around her mannish shoulders.

"Was that Art?"

Theresa and Gloria nodded. "He fell down the cellar stairs and was trapped down there."

"In the cellar? What was he doing in the house?"

"You didn't see him in the house last night?" Gloria asked tentatively.

Gracie closely watched Lulu's reaction.

Lulu's deep set brown eyes widened in surprise. "No. I didn't see anyone. In the house did you say? I haven't been in the house."

"Art must be confused then," Theresa said.

"Confused about what? I wasn't in the house, and I saw no one. Did he say I was in Franny's house?"

"He says you pushed him down the cellar steps." Theresa ran a hand over her hair, brushing her bangs from her eyes.

"What? He must be delirious or something. I haven't been anywhere near that house."

Gloria put an arm around Lulu. "Let's go inside. I'm sure Art must be confused. He had quite a bump on the head."

"No thank you," Lulu spat out, pulling away. "I'm being set up for some reason." She marched back across the street and into her house, slamming the front door behind her.

They watched her hasty retreat, and then saw Lulu's neighbor, Butch Novak, coming toward them.

He waved and called out, "Everything all right over here?"

Gracie shook her head. "A little accident, but we think he'll be all right."

"Was it Art?" Butch asked, stroking his bushy, dark beard.

"Yes," Gloria confirmed. "Did you see anyone over here last night, by any chance?"

Butch scowled, rubbing his hairy cheek. "Well, I was out walking the dog last night, and I heard some voices around the house. It could've been Art. Someone was with him though. I didn't recognize the other voice."

"Man or woman?" Gracie jumped in.

"Either one. Couldn't say for sure. They were talking pretty quietly. What happened to him?"

"He had a really nasty fall and might have broken his leg," Gracie said.

Butch shook his head. "That's too bad. Hope he'll be okay. You know there's been a woman hanging around. I've seen her a couple of times this week around dusk. It's when I walk Rocky."

"You don't know her?" Gloria asked.

"Never seen her before, but she was kinda bundled up in a big sweatshirt. Hard to see her face. I thought maybe she was the realtor or something since the sign just went up. Well, I've gotta get back." Butch was off before the women could ask additional questions.

"That was enlightening," Theresa commented.

"Yes. Interesting," Gloria agreed, turning for the house.

"If you want my opinion," Gracie said, scaling the steps to the front door, "Art is still looking for the quilt."

"That's obvious," Theresa answered with a dark laugh. "I want to know who's helping him look."

"We'd better get a move on to search ourselves," Gloria reminded them. "Come on."

Reaching Franny's bedroom, they surveyed the mess. Gloria scooped up the discarded bed linens and pillows and dumped them on the bed.

Theresa scratched the side of her nose, looking around. The closet seemed like the best place to start.

The master bedroom closet was unusually spacious for an old house. A set of shelves held extra linens and out-of-season clothing. Theresa shoved the line of clothes aside on the opposite wall, the thin metal hangers grating on the old metal rod. A creamy white wall of bead board was exposed. Brass hooks were affixed about every foot, each holding old handbags.

"Find anything, Mom?" Gracie bent over a storage container filled with winter clothes.

"No," Theresa answered, watching Gloria sort through a pile of sheets. "It looks like Franny started to panel the closet and then quit for some reason. This wainscoting idea is quite pretty, and I love the storage for purses. I have no idea why she'd save these ratty old things though."

Gracie stood and looked at the unfinished home improvement. "Too bad it didn't go all the way around. It's a nice touch," she said, running a hand over the wood. "Oh, look. There's some sort of ventilation grill in here too." She pointed at a long strip of wire mesh above the paneling, near the ceiling, that was painted to match the wood.

It seemed so out-of-place in the outdated décor. Gracie looked at the grooved wood again. She grasped the two hooks in the center and pulled.

CHAPTER 31

Adriana walked through the door, shedding her coat. Kevin took it from her, their hands momentarily touching in the transfer.

"I was hoping to catch Isabelle." Adriana smoothed her hair into place and picked up a portfolio case, which rested against the wall.

"You're in luck." Kevin winked, pointing toward the dining room. "She's in there."

"Oh, it's you," Isabelle said, walking to meet her, a glass of white wine in her hand.

Adriana flashed an enthusiastic smile, patting the case. "I have the galleys here. I thought you'd want to see the finished product before it went to press next week."

Isabelle relaxed, turning back to the living room. "Excellent. I was hoping to see them."

"The house photos are perfect, if I do say so myself, and I think the article really does justice to how you've restored such a historic Deer Creek home. Readers are going to love it."

Kevin poured a glass of red wine for Adriana while Isabelle examined the photo layout. Adriana crossed her long legs, which looked even longer in skinny jeans and the white sweater tunic.

"These photos are very good," Isabelle concurred. "You captured the character of the house, especially the dining room."

"I really wanted to feature it since you recently restored that space."

Adriana uncrossed her legs, leaning forward to admire her work, which Isabelle had spread across the coffee table.

"Yes," Isabelle said slowly. "You were able to shoot from every perspective." She picked up the magazine galley and looked at the photos again. "Very nice. When did you finish these?"

"About three weeks ago. I've had such tight deadlines for work lately. I have one due tomorrow that I need to work on. Another historical magazine." Adriana rubbed the back of her neck.

"You always manage to pull it off," Kevin said, chuckling. "You've always been a good time manager."

Isabelle glanced up at him, sliding the pages back to Adriana.

"What's the subject of that photo shoot?" Isabelle asked before sipping at her wine.

"Antique textiles." Adriana slipped the proofs into the portfolio. "I've been all over the countryside visiting old ladies who have all sorts of treasures lying around their houses."

Isabelle leaned back against the sofa. "Really? So embroidery—samplers, that sort of thing?"

"Yeah. Quite a few. But I think the larger pieces of fabric art are much more interesting."

"Larger? Like what?"

"Tapestries, rugs, and quilts."

"Quilts are considered art?"

Adriana nodded. "Absolutely." She eyed the handsome arts-and-crafts oak clock, with its decorative inlaid tile woodland scene. "I have to dash. I've got a gallery opening in Rochester tonight, and I promised to send a few wedding photos to your cousin Gracie by Friday." She set her unfinished glass of cabernet on the coffee table.

"I'll see you out," Kevin said, rising from his chair.

Isabelle flipped on the TV, changing the channel to HGTV, kicking off her high heels. She stared at the screen, chewing on her bottom lip, fingernails pressed into the palms of her hands.

***

"Holy smokes!" Gracie exclaimed, backing away from the hidden compartment.

The small crack she'd seen between the panels had opened up to reveal a concealed space, about two feet deep and five feet long.

Theresa's eyes were round. Gloria sucked in a breath.

"What in the world?" Theresa said, surveying the rectangular opening.

A slim wooden rod hung on two sturdy hooks near the top of the opening, and another rod crossed the opening halfway down, which held what appeared to be a white sheet. A heap of white cotton fabric was underneath them. The area was cedar-lined and smelled pungently of the fragrant wood.

Gloria poked her head into the opening, and nudged the cloth on the floor with her toe. "Why would she store a couple of sheets in here?"

"This is more than linen storage," Theresa guessed. "Look at it. Cedar and ventilation. I want to see what's so special about this sheet hanging on the rod. Help me with this, Gracie."

The heft and thickness of the sheet indicated that something more was inside as they carefully pulled it off the rod and took it to the bed. Buttons ran down two adjoining sides of the sheet, which Gloria quickly undid. She peeled back the covering to reveal a length of printed fabric in faded reds and blues. Birds and flowers were splattered across it.

"I recognize those patterns," Theresa gasped. "They're the appliques on Franny's quilt."

"No kidding," Gracie said, wondering what exactly they'd found.

Gloria lifted another white sheet. "There's more in here."

A yellowy silk fabric lay underneath, fold marks still evident, although it had been hung on the rod. Still another layer held a once-white piece of finely-woven cotton, now with brown stains and yellowing throughout, and a short length of cloth printed with exotic blue and purple birds.

Gracie went back to the opening and looked around the corners for any other hidden treasures. A small black wooden box was on the floor, which she brought out to examine. Opening the lid, the box's contents were spools of thread—red, white, blue, and gray. She set it on the bed beside the fabric. Gloria and Theresa looked at each other and then at the items on the bare mattress.

"I think these are the original materials for the Stederman quilt," Theresa said, running nervous fingers through her bangs.

"I believe you're right," Gloria agreed, standing back and gazing at their discovery. "Now what do we do?"

Gracie chewed the inside of her cheek. "If Franny stored this old fabric in that hidden space, do you think the quilt was in there too? Something was taken out, if the sheet on the floor is any indication."

"That's right. We'd better make sure it didn't just fall off the rod," Theresa said, hurrying back to the closet.

She gingerly brought the rumpled sheet to the bed. The same buttoned opening was sewn on it, but it was open, and nothing was inside.

"My best guess is that it had the quilt inside," Gloria said. "I wonder if Lulu knew about this hiding place. Or did Art? Art! Theresa, somebody needs to go to the hospital and see if he's all right."

Theresa blanched. "You're right. How could we forget? I'll go pick up Bob, and we'll go over. You let Albert know what we've found. Gracie, put this stuff back in. Be careful with it."

A bewildered Gracie stood in the vacant bedroom, wondering how she'd been left in charge of cleaning up.

CHAPTER 32

After a two-hour wait in the ER of the Wyoming County Community Hospital, Art's lower left leg was casted, and he was issued a pair of crutches. The official diagnosis was a broken ankle and a bruised ribcage. Bob helped him maneuver to the car, which was parked near the ER entrance.

"Did they give you any pain meds?" Theresa asked, opening the front passenger door.

"Yes, but I hate taking anything, especially if it makes you woozy." Art attempted to turn and deposit himself on the front seat. "I don't want to fill this prescription."

Bob took one crutch trying to position Art correctly without the cast hitting anything. "Careful," Bob warned him.

"Ugh," Art groaned, squinting his eyes.

"You'd better fill the script," Theresa advised. "You'll be sorry tonight if you don't."

Art made a face. "I just want to go home."

"We'll drop it off at the drug store. And, if it's going to take a while, I'll have Bob pick it up later."

"Well, all right," Art conceded.

"Now are you sure that Lulu—" Theresa couldn't help ask.

"It was Lulu, but I'm not pressing any charges against her. You don't know what she's really like. Greedy." Art looked straight ahead, his mouth in a firm line.

Bob slid into the driver's seat and shot his wife a warning look. Theresa clenched her fists, determined to heed her husband's silent admonition.

***

Lulu bustled in her kitchen, scrounging up some canned soup and a sandwich for her dinner. Streetlights winked on while she spread mustard on the bread and piled on some deli turkey. The street scene from the window over the sink was bathed in a dusky half-light. Butch was out walking Rocky, his beagle. They were like clockwork. Maybe she'd get a dog when all of this was over. Flickering sodium lights struggled to energize. Movement across the street caught her eye, and she thought a silhouette slipped behind a lilac hedge in Franny's side yard. Was someone back to continue ransacking the house? She took a chef's knife from the wooden block and cut the sandwich in half. Wiping her hands on a damp kitchen towel, she fumbled for the cell phone at the bottom of her purse. There was no way she was going to be blamed for trespassing at Franny's yet again.

***

The deputy's SUV came to a quick stop in front of Franny's house, which brought Theresa both relief and anxiety. She and Gloria stood on the sidewalk, huddled in their coats. Both husbands were fortunately entrenched in an emergency church board meeting over a roof issue, which was probably just as well. A young African-American woman in uniform exited the vehicle.

"I'm Deputy Shaw," she said, introducing herself. "There's a break-in here?"

"Maybe," Theresa answered. "We think there was one last night and—"

"And the neighbor across the street called us and said she thought she saw someone in the yard a few minutes ago," Gloria interrupted, pointing to Lulu's house.

"One last night and another tonight?" The deputy looked puzzled. "You didn't report—"

"It's a really long story," Theresa broke in. "Could you check on the house?"

"Of course. Does anyone have a key?"

Gloria handed the deputy a small keyring with a single key. "It's for the front door."

"You ladies wait here," she instructed.

Another sheriff's department SUV rolled up.

"Looks like we've called in the cavalry tonight," Gloria pointed out.

"Well, Lulu saw someone in the yard. She said Butch Novak has seen a woman around the property."

"And a couple of other things," Gloria hissed.

"Not a word about them," Theresa warned her.

The other deputy jogged to the front door, a flashlight in his hand. Minutes later, the pair returned, talking softly.

"Did you find anyone?" Gloria asked anxiously as they approached. She shivered, her hands in the pockets of her jacket.

"No, ma'am. The house is empty. No one is in there," the female deputy answered.

"What's this about a break-in last night?" the short deputy with a moustache asked.

"Well ..." Gloria began.

"Bart, I've got this," said Deputy Shaw. "Thanks for your help. Why don't you ladies come to my vehicle, and we'll talk about it?"

The strong-featured female deputy smiled, motioning for Theresa and Gloria to follow. The other deputy's vehicle soon pulled away, the red taillights of his SUV disappearing around the curve of Oak Street to Main.

Gloria and Theresa explained what had brought them to Franny's house, minus the details of the hidden closet and the discovery of the injured Art. They concentrated on the mysterious woman in the neighborhood and the trashed house.

"Is anything missing, Mrs. Minders?" The deputy stood with her notepad at the ready.

"Not that I can tell. It could've have been teenagers, just making trouble."

"Right. It could've been teenagers," Theresa quickly agreed. "You know stuff like this happens."

Theresa's doubts about the wisdom of calling in the police were growing. There were too many awkward facts to share with law enforcement.

"I think if we just change the locks on the house and check on it daily, it'll be fine," Gloria added.

"That's a good idea, Mrs. Minders. I don't think there's anything else—"

"Thank you for coming so quickly," Theresa said with a bright smile.

The deputy's expression made her nervous. Theresa waited for the other shoe to drop. Instead, Deputy Shaw retrieved a card from her vehicle.

"Here's my card, if you decide to elaborate on tonight's report."

Gloria tucked the business card into her purse. "Oh, sure. If we remember anything else that might help. Thank you."

Gloria and Theresa walked back to Gloria's sedan. Gloria turned on the ignition and cranked the heater, as the deputy sped away.

"That was uncomfortable," Theresa groaned.

"No kidding. I don't know what we should have done. Lulu wants to remain anonymous, and Art claims Lulu pushed him down the cellar steps. Now we've withheld information from the police. That deputy knows we didn't tell her everything."

"If Bob and Albert find out, we're in serious hot water." Theresa unbuttoned her coat.

Gloria lowered the speed of the blasting fan. "I'd agree with that."

"You'd better show Albert the closet compartment we found today. It sheds a whole new light on the Stederman quilt."

CHAPTER 33

Lulu contemplated her options after watching Theresa and Gloria pull into Franny's driveway. They were back again, and she had a nagging feeling they'd be showing up on her doorstep soon. Returning to the sewing room, she pinned another block together of the Blushing Bride pattern, sewing the pieces carefully. It would be a shame to ruin it by ripping the seams open, but it was the final one, containing the last shipment of money. Her other patterns had given her natural pockets and folds to secret the bills. The clamshell design, with its flap openings, and the one made from the pockets of Ed's old shirts had been the easiest to cram with cash. She'd placed buttons on each pocket to secure the cargo. This one was much more complex, because she would be carrying it in her luggage.

The walls of the house seemed to be closing in on her. She couldn't wait for the recycling guys to show up. Everything needed to go except basic furniture, which Isabelle had agreed to purchase with the house.

She sewed two more blocks onto the growing rectangle. At least, this one didn't need to be very big. She drew out a passport from a small drawer in the sewing cabinet, opening it to her photo. It was even a decent picture. She might never be able to use it if things kept going wrong.

Stuffing it back in the drawer, her laptop dinged with an email notification. Her heart jumped. It needed to be good news.

***

"Did you find anything in there?" Gloria asked, searching through an old bureau.

"No. There's nothing in this closet and no secret doors that I can find." Theresa shut the door of the small closet, hands on hips. "We looked everywhere. The attic is the only place left."

"Gracie's not coming, is she?"

"No. Marian broke her hip, and the poor girl is running six ways to Sunday trying to keep up."

"Probably a good thing she's busy, with Marc being gone."

"I think so."

Theresa gazed up at the access door in the ceiling of the hallway. The cord dangled just out of reach. Heights were not her thing, but Gloria would never go up there.

"Bring that step stool, will you?" Theresa asked.

Gloria positioned the beat-up white metal stool under the pull cord. Theresa stepped up and gave the rope a yank, and the ladder began descending. Unfolding it to the floor, Theresa took a deep breath and made the climb into the dark opening above. Her flashlight illuminated the rafters and insulation. Boards crisscrossed the beams leading to two storage areas, fortified with a solid wood platform.

"Someone was up here too," she called down.

"Is it a mess?"

"It sure is. Books and old clothes."

Theresa walked gingerly along the sagging boards to check out the items.

"Anything else?" Gloria's head popped through the opening.

"I don't think so. Old tax returns and junk, by the looks of it."

She turned around after examining the papers and tossed them into cardboard boxes. Nothing interesting.

"Well, Kevin was up in the attic the day we showed the house to Isabelle. Do you think he might have done this?" Gloria slowly crept down the ladder and waited for Theresa.

"I don't know much about Kevin, but he's a VP at the bank. I would hope he's trustworthy. Why would he want the quilt?"

"I have no idea. It makes me think that Isabelle's choice in men might not be all that good. Tim certainly wasn't," Gloria said, her brow puckered.

"I'll give you that," Theresa agreed, brushing dust from her shirt and jeans once she reached the safety of the floor. "Maybe we should ask him."

"I'm not sure about that."

"There's always Isabelle."

***

Art held the phone away from his ear, wishing he hadn't answered. He'd just managed to fix some lunch and was exhausted from the effort. He rested in a worn brown upholstered chair, his leg propped up on a folding chair. His crutches were clutched in his other hand.

"I want the Stederman quilt now. The buyer is way past patient on this. If I lose the sale, you're in even worse trouble."

"I know, and I've looked everywhere. You know that. And now, thanks to you, I can't search the house again."

There was silence at the other end. He heard a sharp intake of breath. "That was a mistake. You shouldn't have crossed me though."

"For telling you I couldn't find it? You didn't need to knock me down the stairs and then leave me! I could've died down there, you know."

"Forget the house. That Cook woman has it. I'm sure of it. She claims she doesn't know where it is, but she was your ex-wife's best friend. Of course, she knows."

Art shook his head wearily. "What can I do? I told her to hand it over. She keeps denying it, and I've looked in her garage."

"But never her house."

"No," Art said, closing his eyes. "It's a worse mess than the garage."

"I'll check out the house. You call her over to your place to discuss matters. That will give me time to take care of what you should've done long before this." The voice was low and dangerous.

"She won't come. Why should she?"

"She'll come if you tell her that you're pursuing charges against her. Assault is a serious crime."

"Yeah. It is. And painful too."

***

Theresa pulled up in front of Midge's Restaurant, scanning the parked cars along the street for Isabelle's white SUV. Her niece wasn't here yet, but she might as well find a table before the lunch crowd came *en masse*. Luckily, a corner table near the large front window was empty. She plopped her handbag onto one chair while she sat on the other.

"Need a menu?" The waitress was young with a pixie cut of chestnut hair. Her round face was friendly, and she held an order pad.

"No. But I'm waiting for someone. You're new, aren't you?"

"I just started here, but I've been waiting tables a long time."

Theresa wondered about the quantity of a "long time," since she couldn't be over twenty-one.

Isabelle swept in, handing Theresa's purse to her and sitting down. She looked dismissively at the server. "Give us a couple of minutes, but you can bring two waters with lemon."

"Actually, you can bring me a cup of hot tea and that new grilled cheese sandwich," Theresa corrected.

"Oh, pardon me. I'm so used to ... oh, never mind." Isabelle looked out the window across to the bank.

"You seem a little distracted. Is everything all right?"

Isabelle's gaze swung back to her aunt. "I'm sorry, Aunt Theresa. Just a lot of things on my plate at the moment ..." She hesitated and leaned toward her. "And I have a bit of a personal dilemma."

Theresa looked at her in surprise. "Oh dear! Can I help?"

The dammed-up apprehensions of Isabelle Browne-Baker flowed like the raging Genesee River in spring. Kevin took her for granted, and he didn't want to marry her. She thought he might be involved with Adriana, Gracie's wedding photographer. If that wasn't enough, Kevin might have stolen a pair of very expensive vases from the house. Isabelle's eyes welled up, but to her credit, she managed to avoid shedding a tear. The entire conversation took Theresa off guard. The unfortunate girl needed a shoulder to cry on or complain on, and that's what family is for.

After patting Isabelle's trembling hand, Theresa finished the last bit of Midge's newest grilled creation, a sourdough three-cheese sandwich.

"I'm so sorry, Isabelle. You and Kevin really need to have a heart-to-heart about all of this. If he is up to no good, you have to get him out of the house and pronto." Theresa's extended opinion was he should have never been living in her house to begin with, but young people—so careless about relationships. Well, Isabelle wasn't all that young, merely desperate.

"I know. But there are the social implications—so embarrassing. However, Greg and Anna have always disliked him, so they would be glad to see him go. They don't even want to come home for Thanksgiving if he's there." She sighed and looked at her untouched salad.

"You do need to think about your children. They've been through so much. How did you expect them to react when he moved into their house?" Theresa couldn't hold everything back. Someone had to tell Isabelle the truth.

Isabelle rubbed her forehead, closing her eyes. "I know. Even with the horrible, horrible things Tim did, I shouldn't have ..."

"If you want my opinion, you need to confront Kevin about the vases. Do you have proof he took them?"

"I think I have some. But I was hoping that Gracie's wedding photos would confirm my theory."

"I'm sure Gracie would be glad to have you look at the pictures. Adriana is a wonderful photographer. We can go right from here, if you like."

CHAPTER 34

Lulu could see that Art wasn't in very good shape. His skin color was a bit gray, and he gritted his teeth when he talked to her. His voice had been more menacing on the phone. At the moment, he sounded tired and a little panicked.

"I mean it, Lulu. I'll go ahead with those charges against you, unless you hand over that filthy blanket of Franny's."

At least, he couldn't harm her physically now. She paced around the apartment's small living room and glanced out at the street, glad she'd parked around the corner.

"I don't have it. Franny was trying to keep you from taking her last asset and asked me to help her. You've always been trouble when it comes to money. That hasn't changed, and you treated her like dirt. She didn't tell me where she'd put it. You have no right to it anyway."

Art's eyes were bloodshot and watery. The medication was probably fogging up his brain some, which was to her advantage—maybe.

"It's your word against mine. I was in the cellar, and I get to say who put me there. I say it was you. If you were home by yourself, then who's going to help with an alibi?"

He had a point. She had been home, sewing like a crazy woman.

Art grunted and adjusted his position, attempting to straighten himself. "You and Franny had some plan to spend the insurance money."

"Franny deserved every bit from that heirloom. Between your gambling and making her life miserable, she should've gotten something for her trouble."

Art smiled wickedly. "Like getting knocked over in your garage and dying? Is that what she deserved? Now stop playing games. If you don't hand over the goods to me by tonight, I'm calling the police."

Lulu threw up her hands. "I don't have it. I can't give you what I don't have. I guess you'll have to call the police." If he did, she was probably in a world of hurt. Maybe she should look for it herself.

"I guess that's what will happen, if I don't have it by six o'clock tonight—here in my hands."

She exhaled slowly. Think. Think. Stall him.

"What if I look for it myself? Give me some time though. There are people in and out of the house all the time now. It's for sale. Isabelle—"

"That's right. Mrs. Richey Rich Baker. She's buying your house, and I hear she wants mine too."

"It's not your house. And so what?"

"So, where are you headed, Lulu? Seems unlike you to move—or go anywhere, for that matter. Ed always said your apron strings were attached to that house. You wouldn't even go fishing with him. Maybe if you had that last time—"

Lulu rushed him, bending over to grab his shirt. "Leave Ed out of this!" she snarled. "And don't poke your nose in my business!" She released him, her chest heaving.

"Six tonight," he croaked. "Twice you've assaulted me. You're out of control."

***

Gracie seemed to dawdle as she opened the electronic folder labeled "wedding." Theresa wished Gracie would hurry. Isabelle was pressed for time and so was she. Computers were bad enough to endure, but Gracie seemed hesitant at her request. She edged closer to her daughter, peering over her shoulder.

"Here they are. Just click on the ones you want to see," she instructed, pointing at the photo icons.

"Of course," Isabelle replied, taking over Gracie's desk chair.

"I have a wash and style with a sheltie, so have a blast."

"That's quite all right, Gracie. Isabelle and I will just be a few minutes."

Theresa pulled up a molded plastic chair and joined Isabelle at the computer screen.

"Here's one in the dining room," Isabelle said, clicking to enlarge the photo.

The wedding flowers were strewn artfully down the dining room table. The china cabinet loomed in the background.

"I can't see anything clearly in there," Theresa said, squinting at the picture.

"Just a second. Let me enlarge it again."

"What side are they on?" Theresa pulled out her reading glasses from her purse.

"On the right ... and they're not there," she exclaimed, pressing an index finger onto the screen.

"And they were in the photo for the magazine?"

"Yes. In the place I've had them for years. I don't switch around items. Why tamper with perfection?"

"Indeed," Theresa answered, struggling to maintain a straight face.

"What do you think?" Gracie walked into the office.

"Oh, we've just ... um ..." Theresa floundered.

"What are you looking at? The flowers?"

"We saw something interesting in this one," Theresa said hurriedly.

"Right." Isabelle quickly clicked on another photo. "Oh, very nice, Gracie," she cooed over the shot of Gracie walking with her father. "Adriana is a true artist."

***

Just as they had breezed in, her mother and Isabelle were gone, apparently to check out something at the Baker residence. Gracie stared at the computer screen, wondering what was so fascinating about the flower photo. She looked at it again, enlarging it. Was there a bug on the arrangements or a wilted flower? Not seeing anything of interest, she closed the folder.

"Hey, Sammie's mom is here to pick him up," Trudy called through the office doorway.

"Sure. He's almost ready."

Gracie met Tina Harwood in the grooming room. Tina was a bubbly, brown-haired, bundle of energy, which matched the sheltie, but not her stoic husband, Emery, who ran the funeral home. Tina's hair was swept up into a ponytail, and she was dressed in jeans and a Letchworth School sweatshirt. She was a soccer mom, probably headed to a game.

"He's still damp," Gracie said. "Can you wait for about ten minutes?"

"Sure. I know I'm early." She bent to stroke the excited dog, who started barking in the drying area.

"Sammie, be quiet. Maybe we should leave him alone, or he'll keep at it."

"I've got some coffee and instant hot chocolate in the office," Gracie offered.

"No thanks. I'll hang out in there, if it's okay."

"Sure. How are things at the funeral home? Quiet, I hope." Gracie flashed a wry smile.

"Oh, it's always quiet," Tina said with practiced solemnity. "Congratulations on your wedding. How is everything going?"

Gracie quickly filled her in on Marc's new job and absence.

"I'm sorry about that. Tough break."

"Yup. Of course, not as tough as Franny Walczak."

"Oh, yes. Poor Mrs. Walczak. Isn't she a friend of your mother's?"

"Yeah. I was helping my mother and Gloria at the house."

"I felt so sorry for Lulu Cook. Losing her husband last year and then her best friend. Such a weird thing though."

Gracie's eyebrows squeezed together. "What do you mean? The quilt?"

"Huh? No." Tina settled into the plastic chair. "It's just kind of spooky about Ed Cook."

"Spooky?"

Tina nodded. "Right before Ed went on that fishing trip, he stopped by to see Emery. He gave him written instructions that he wanted to be cremated if something should happen to him."

Gracie shivered. "That *is* a little spooky, since he was incinerated in the accident."

"Just a dental bridge was left. Lucky they found it so they could identify him. I've wondered about that accident. Maybe it wasn't, if you know what I mean."

"Wasn't an accident? He didn't make a curve and went over into a ravine, didn't he?"

Gracie decided a cup of coffee might be in order. She snatched her mug from the shelf and filled it before returning to her desk.

"Yes, it looked like an accident, but Ed was kind of depressed. I wonder if he … well, you know, might have planned the accident."

"Really? I never knew him very well. Was he sick or something?" She blew on the steaming mug and took a sip.

"No. Nothing like that. Ed had told Emery at a Kiwanis meeting a few months before his death that there was a serious reorg planned at his company. They were going to phase out his job."

"Wow! He'd been at that insurance company in Henrietta a long time, hadn't he?"

"Around thirty years, I think. How can companies do that to people? I'm glad we're small potatoes here. No reorganizations for us."

Gracie laughed. "Not here either. We run lean and mean, although we're a bit too lean right now. Poor Marian will be out for quite a while." She glanced at the wall clock. "I'm sure Sammie's dry by now."

***

Lulu pulled into the driveway, contemplating how she'd gotten into such a mess. If she was arrested for assaulting Art ... She fought thinking about everything she'd lose. Oh, Franny, where is that stupid quilt? She slammed the car door and stalked to the house. She probably should call an attorney. That might make her look guilty though.

She'd begun to shove the key into the lock, when the door swung open of its own volition. The hair on the back of her neck prickled, and she had the urge to run.

Forcing herself to enter the house, she rushed to the sewing room. Fabric was strewn around. The doors on the wall of cupboards were open, as was the small sewing cabinet by her work desk. Swallowing hard, she peered inside the cabinet. Her stomach churned. The passport was gone and so was the Mexican cash. Frantically she sifted through the scattered material and sewing supplies on the floor. The navy-blue covered document wasn't there. She sat down on the floor and sobbed.

CHAPTER 35

Haley's tail thumped under the kitchen table, while Theresa dished up chicken and dumplings. Gracie stretched her legs out, stocking feet rubbing the Lab's belly.

"No dumplings, missy," Gracie stated to the dog, who nosed her toes insistently. Haley groaned and repositioned herself under the table.

"Thanks for calling. I didn't know Dad was out tonight."

"He's been going out quite a bit lately, with sketchy information on his whereabouts. If I were a suspicious person ..."

"Good grief, Mom."

"I know. He says he's working on a community enrichment program with some of the boys from the Legion. We'll see. They're playing pinochle is my guess."

Theresa sat down after ladling a generous amount of the chicken and gravy, laden with carrots, peas, and onions, onto her plate.

"Oh, well. At least he's around." Gracie dug into the rich gravy with chunks of breast meat.

"Yes, he is. What do you hear from Marc?"

The house phone rang, and Theresa pushed away from the table.

"Hello?"

Gracie watched her mother's expression change from humor to agitation. Theresa walked back from the kitchen counter to the table in the breakfast nook.

"Are you sure? Call the police, Lulu. Right away."

After another pause, her mother huffed impatiently. "All right. I'll come over." She placed the phone back in the charger.

"What's going on?"

"I'm not sure, but someone broke into Lulu's house, and she refuses to call the police."

"And she wants you to come over."

"Yes."

"What are you supposed to do? Chase off the burglar?"

Theresa sighed, looking at her plate. "Look for the quilt."

"Again with the quilt?" Gracie asked wearily, setting her fork down.

***

Haley sniffed around the remaining storage containers in Lulu's house, finally lying down on a throw rug in the kitchen. Gracie had dumped the contents of several tubs that were full of more patchwork covers than she'd ever seen. Theresa worked methodically through the sewing room with Lulu. Gracie blew through her mouth in relief. She'd checked everything that was in the living room. A stack of brightly colored blankets was ready to be returned to the bins. There was another stack of bins filled with newspapers and glass jars. No need to look through that mess. Why Lulu was saving recyclables was puzzling.

"I'm done in here," she called. "No extremely valuable bedspread in any of them."

"All right," Theresa answered. "We're almost finished in here."

The women gathered a few minutes later in the kitchen.

"We need to check at Franny's one more time."

Lulu's eyes lit up. "Has anyone checked the trunk of her car?"

"Not that I'm aware of," Theresa answered, shaking her head. "I can call Gloria and see if we can get the keys."

Now that it was totally dark, except for streetlights and the glow of lamps in windows, Gracie felt like a thief herself, skulking around. She kept expecting to hear sirens to haul Lulu away. Nothing had happened ... so far. It was hard to tell if that was good or bad. Art was a squirrelly sort of guy. Injured and on meds probably didn't help the situation. Who could've broken into Lulu's house? Certainly not Art. There was much more to this little dispute than met the eye.

Hopes were crushed when the trunk yielded a spare tire, a pair of gloves, and a half a bag of kitty litter. Gloria decided on one more search through the house, and then they were giving up.

"Do you know where Franny stored the quilt?" Gloria asked, pushing the door open and flipping on the kitchen light.

"In her cedar chest. I saw it in there a couple of years ago. It was right after some exhibition."

"Did you know about an alternate storage area?" Theresa broached carefully.

"Alternate area? No. Franny never talked about it being anywhere else other than the cedar chest in her bedroom."

"Come in here, and we'll show you what we found."

Theresa led the way into the bedroom, turning on lights as she went. Gracie straggled behind, still watching the street for the sheriff's department to arrive.

Traffic was minimal. A Mini Cooper drove by slowly, and then a man, walking his dog, strolled past on the sidewalk. Haley plastered her nose to the front window and uttered a weak "woof."

A little screech came from the bedroom. "I can't believe it!" Lulu cried.

Gracie and Haley joined the older women, who gazed into the depths of the secret closet. Haley began sniffing again, snuffling through a few dust bunnies in the corner.

"Is there any other spot in this house that would have a hidden place like this one?" Theresa quizzed Lulu.

"No. I had no idea about this. Very clever of Franny. Art would never have found it, I'm sure."

"Maybe. But it's possible someone did steal it for real. Art has an accomplice or someone who's threatening him about the quilt. He suddenly withdrew his phony promissory note with the quilt as collateral. He was in your garage the night Franny died." Gloria's arms were crossed over her bosom.

"The promissory note was phony?" Theresa asked, her eyes wide.

"Oh yes. It was a pretty good attempt to forge Franny's name, but when the attorney told him a judge was going to personally examine it, he backed off and said he'd made a mistake."

Haley jumped up on the bed and huddled close to the linens and the quilt folded in a pile on the bare mattress.

"Get off, girl. This isn't home," Gracie grumbled at the dog.

Haley looked miffed and reluctantly left the bed, trotting from the room.

"Are you going to look anymore?" Gracie stretched her arms overhead and yawned. "I've got an early day tomorrow."

Gloria shook her head. "No. We've almost killed ourselves hunting through the house. I can't imagine there would be another place to safely store such a valuable heirloom. I really don't have the energy to look in all the same places again."

Lulu's face fell, and her shoulders slumped. "What am I going to do?"

"You're telling the truth. Talk to your attorney and do what he says," Theresa advised.

***

"Do you want me to call the cops?" Art asked, his voice quavering.

"No. We don't need any more attention on the quilt. Keep your mouth shut."

The caller had let him off the hook. He felt relief flow through his aching body. "I will. You can count on it. Are you going to check at Franny's again?"

"Too risky now. We've lost the deal, Art, and that means you can't pay your debt."

"I know, but I'll come up with something."

"I doubt it, but you know it has to be paid and soon. You've missed another deadline. There are consequences for non-payment." The voice was deliberate and frosty.

He massaged his forehead with trembling fingers. "I was sure Lulu had it. Something strange is happening with her."

"She's strange all right. Nothing in her house or garage though, except a passport. Has she told you where she's heading after the settlement? Like Mexico?"

"No. That's what I'm tryin' to tell you. She's up to something."

"Well, she's going nowhere at the moment. Talk to her again. Let her know that the passport can be returned for a fee. Do you get my drift?"

"Yeah. I understand. What do I tell her?"

"Since the buyer has backed out of the original deal, cash will have to cover your obligation. Ask her for that. The next payment deadline is coming right up."

Art fidgeted, trying to find a position where his leg and ribcage didn't hurt, which was impossible.

"All right," he conceded.

"Now, I'll let you rest, Art. You're going to need it."

The phone line went dead. Art shoved the cordless phone into the base that sat on a wobbly TV tray by his chair. He looked at the brown prescription bottle and threw it against the wall, splattering painkillers everywhere.

CHAPTER 36

Pastor Minders sat waiting for Lisa Stederman Kronk to appear with her official claim on the Stederman heirloom. He rubbed the leather armrests of the chair in his attorney's office. Nathan Cook, Esquire, frowned as he dug tobacco out of the bowl of a well-used pipe.

"She's late," he quipped and looked up at the weary pastor.

"Yes. A woman's prerogative." He'd like to have a quarter for every time he'd either heard or said that over the last forty-eight years.

"I thought that was about changing her mind," Nathan groused, packing fresh tobacco into the pipe and sucking on the stem.

"Everything is a woman's prerogative. Haven't you learned that by now?"

"Humph. I guess not. That's why I'm on number three."

"Ah ... Well ...."

"Mrs. Kronk is here," announced a cheery receptionist from the doorway.

"Send her in."

The meeting went exactly as Nathan had laid out earlier with his client. The discovery of the old fabric would be transferred immediately, and the disputed bedcovering would be as well, if it was recovered. The later agreement

234

superseded the original; Franny never really had valid ownership in the first place.

"When did you find this new agreement?" Albert Minders smiled and watched the woman's expression.

"It was found recently in my grandmother's family papers. She has boxes of old letters and newspaper clippings. All sorts of things. You know how it is with older folks." Lisa returned the smile, looking much more at ease than she had at the former meeting. Her defenses had relaxed, by the looks of it.

"I'm surprised your grandmother didn't go after the decedent for the property a long time ago," Nathan remarked, sliding a couple of papers from an accordion file.

"I don't think she realized the importance of the agreement. Once I really read it though ..."

"Here's the receipt and release for the property we're giving you today. Just sign on that bottom line as your grandmother's power of attorney. You do have it with you?" Nathan's shaggy eyebrows rose quizzically at the woman.

She dug into her handbag and drew out the document. "Right here. I brought it, as you requested."

Nathan gave it a cursory glance and pushed the receipt toward her. Lisa hesitated, reading it over before picking up the pen on the desk.

"All right. Here you are."

She handed the paper back to Nathan, who pressed his notary stamp onto the paper and squiggled his name beside it.

"And I'll go out to my car and get that package for you," Albert said.

The pastor exited the office and quickly returned, carrying the oblong storage container.

***

Lulu stood in Art's apartment for the second time in two days. It was no less nerve-wracking than the first time. Art seemed a little more together and was even up and around on the crutches. She stood by the door to guarantee a quick escape.

"So, Lulu. My friend tells me you would probably like your passport back."

Lulu groaned and closed her eyes. She nodded, her underarms suddenly damp, her hands clammy.

"It will cost you, since you haven't cooperated so far."

"I tried to find it. You know I did. It must really be stolen."

"I have some doubts about that now, but I have a feeling this passport is pretty important. If you want it back, you'll need to come up with some serious money." Art splayed his crutches out, balancing himself in front of Lulu.

She could smell his stale breath and sweat. The man needed a shower in the worst way. A toothbrush wouldn't hurt either.

"Of course, I want my passport back. It's my property, and I can report the theft to the police myself."

Two could play the blackmail game.

"Well, it's your word against mine. How could I have it? I'm housebound at the moment. For a fee, you'll get it back. No fuss, no muss."

Here it was. The dollar was always Art's priority. He must be in pretty deep with a bookie or someone worse, who was orchestrating this scenario.

"How much?" She steeled herself for the answer, clutching the doorknob behind her back.

"Thirty thousand." Art said it as if he were talking about the weather.

"Are you kidding?"

"Absolutely not. Thirty K will buy back the passport, and you can be on your way to Mexico."

"You're crazy, Art. I don't have that kind of cash lying around, and I don't intend to be blackmailed ... least of all, by the likes of *you!*" She looked at him as though he were something rancid. "What in the world is the matter with you?"

Art's face crumpled, his bravado fading. "Well ... I ... I need the money. Franny promised me that money before this whole disaster happened." He hobbled to the disheveled sofa and sank into the cushions, sticking his injured leg straight out in front of him.

Lulu shifted her weight uneasily. If she gave him twenty dollars, Art would be back for more. She couldn't lose her mind and offer anything, even if it meant her passport was gone. She couldn't fall for this.

"Sorry. I can't help you. It sounds like you've landed yourself in a fix, and you need to figure it out without my money. I want my passport back by tonight, or *I* will go to the police. They'll, at the very least, interview you and keep tabs on you. I heard you tried to bilk Franny's estate for this amount. The judge might be very interested to know how you've threatened me. Now what do you say?"

Art rubbed his hair and swiped his hand under his nose. "I'll see. No promises."

"Promises or not, the passport needs to be in my hand by this evening. Let's say, six o'clock."

She drew herself up to full height, staring at the man who refused to meet her gaze.

***

Isabelle stood at the island in her kitchen, debating the best way to ask Kevin if he'd stolen her vases. Then there was the matter of Adriana. She and Kevin had known each other in college. Only friends, Kevin had assured her. Adriana had followed a career into the art world. Kevin had followed the money trail to banking. Both appeared to have done well, despite disparate occupations, after their education at Syracuse.

When the Baker house had been tapped as a featured home for historic residences in Western New York, she'd met Adriana and her editor, Tyler Mack. Then Kevin had shown up, and it had become old home week between him and Adriana. She suspected the photo shoot of the house had taken longer because of Kevin.

There was no refined approach. She had the photographic evidence that her French vases disappeared between Adriana's last photo session and Gracie's wedding. Who'd been in her house during that time period other than Kevin? Her cleaning lady, Lilly, was there every week, but Lilly was pure gold. Not in a million years would she rob an employer.

Isabelle swiped her phone screen to look at her calendar. Art Walczak had worked on the yard twice during the time period, and she'd had a cocktail party with a dozen people. Adriana had also been there to prep for Gracie's wedding. Two couples at the cocktail party were recent acquaintances, and they seemed very interested in the antiques in the house. Had she shown them the vases? Of course, there was the wedding team too.

She pinched the bridge of her nose, feeling sick to her stomach. How could she remember all the details? Too many people had access to the cabinet during a three-week period. Confronting Kevin or Adriana was a fool's mission. Besides, things would settle down now that the article was finished. The breezy *faux* redhead wouldn't have a reason to be around Kevin. Maybe.

***

A knock at Lulu's door startled her from her feverish task at the sewing table.

"Hey, Lulu," Butch Novak stood at the front door with his beagle on a leash.

"Hi, Butch. What can I do for you?" She smoothed her rumpled shirt and picked at stray white threads that clung to her sleeve from her sewing.

"I just wanted to give you this," he said, holding out a small brown envelope. "It ended up in our mailbox today, but has your name on it."

She reached for the envelope, mentally crossing her fingers that it contained what she hoped.

"Thanks, Butch. I appreciate that."

"No problem. Well, gotta walk Rocky. He'll drive me crazy if he doesn't get his exercise."

Lulu's grasp went around the center of the envelope. The thickness felt right. She smiled.

"One of these days, I'm gonna get myself a dog," she enthused.

"Some days, I'd give Rocky to a good home." Butch grinned. "Say, what was all the activity at the Walczak house? I saw the cops there the other night."

She took a step back, unsure of how to answer, her free hand on the latch of the screen door, which she held open. "Um ... I think there might have been a break-in."

"Oh. Anything taken?"

"I don't know. You'd have to ask Pastor Minders. He's the executor for the estate."

"Really? I didn't know he was in charge. Seems strange for Franny to do that. I'll bet Art is mad." Butch bent to pat Rocky, who lunged at the taut leash, whining impatiently.

"Art's always been mad," Lulu said, anxious to return to her sewing, but trying to appear sociable. She didn't need any additional interest from the neighbors.

Butch chuckled. "Yeah. That's about right. I saw that you've been cleaning up the garage."

Lulu swallowed hard, wondering about Butch's interest. "That's right. It was time to get rid of a lot of old stuff."

"The wife's been after me to clean out our garage too. Maybe I'll give those guys you had a call."

"They're very good and reasonable," Lulu smiled brightly.

Would he never leave?

"I might want their number sometime. Well, see ya. Come on, Rocky." He gave the leash a tug, and Rocky eagerly shot down the steps.

"Thanks for the mail, Butch."

She waved as the pair took to the sidewalk at a smart clip. Quickly shutting the door, she flipped the lock. She undid the metal clasp on the envelope and dumped out a passport and money onto the small table by the door. Her threat had worked. Checking that the document was indeed hers, she shoved it into her pants pocket. She glanced at the wall clock. It was even on time. Just six now. She went back to the front windows to check the sidewalk. No sign of Butch or Rocky. She contemplated the perfect timing and then shrugged.

CHAPTER 37

Gloria and Theresa were enjoying omelets at Midge's, when Gracie walked into the dining area. Surprised to see the dynamic duo, she waved to catch their attention. Theresa immediately motioned for her daughter to join them.

"You're out early today," Theresa said, putting her fork down.

"Bank run. I saw your car and thought I'd grab a sweet roll." Gracie dragged a chair from an empty table, setting it on the corner of the small table.

"Now that the wedding's behind you, they're safe to eat again," Gloria said, her sharp brown eyes full of humor.

"It's certainly behind me." Gracie patted her backside, grimacing. "If only the groom were actually around."

Gloria gently shook her head. "I know. A very tough way to start."

"Tougher than I thought. But he'll be home this weekend."

"Good. Have you heard from him lately?" Theresa asked, spreading jam on her toast.

"Over this last weekend. He can't wait to be home. The training has been exhausting for both him and Max."

Midge appeared with a mug and a coffee pot.

"Thanks, Midge," Gracie said gratefully.

"No problem. Two sweet rolls left, if you care," the wizened restaurant owner said with a smirk.

"I care. I care. Only one though," Gracie said, laughing.

"Where's your man? I haven't seen him in weeks."

"Training for his new job. I was just telling Mom he'll be home this weekend with Max."

"Oh. Pretty bad timing with getting married and all."

"Yes, it was," Gracie agreed, warming her hands on the thick white mug full of coffee. "I'm afraid I need to get used to an on-again-off-again husband."

Midge made a face. "Now, what's that supposed to mean?"

"This job has a lot of travel. He'll probably be gone a week or more at a time."

"Humphh!" Midge turned and stomped off to the kitchen.

"Hope she remembers the sweet roll," Gracie said.

"Does she ever forget anything?" Theresa returned her attention to the ham and cheese filled omelet.

"Whatever happened with Franny's estate and that lost quilt?" Gracie took a sip of coffee.

"It's still lost, and things finally quieted down after Art's accident in the cellar," Gloria answered.

"How's he doing?"

"Fine. Albert checked on him a few days ago. Art is quite subdued and anxious to be working. They've fitted him with some sort of protective boot."

"Not many lawns to cut now," Theresa commented.

"No, but still lots of leaves to deal with. He cleans gutters and does windows too. Although, I expect he's not up to those jobs yet. He'll plow driveways in the winter though."

"I need my gutters cleaned," Gracie mused, watching Midge carry a plate with the coveted cinnamon roll, dripping with white icing.

"Here you go," Midge said, depositing the plate on the table.

"Thanks." Gracie pulled the gooey roll apart and licked her fingers.

"When's that auction at Franny's going to be?" Midge asked, adjusting the position of the pencil behind her right ear.

"Next week," Gloria answered. "Saturday morning, starting at eight."

"Any good stuff?"

"Depends on your definition," Gloria said with a pained smile. "Nothing very interesting. Household goods."

"What about that antique quilt of hers? I'd think that would bring a pretty penny."

Gracie chewed on the roll, happy to have a mouth full at the moment. Midge was on her predictable fishing expedition.

"That won't be in the auction," Gloria said quickly.

"Oh. Family got it, right?"

"Uh ... well ..."

The sound of Isabelle's sharp voice rescued Gloria. The women turned to see Lulu and Isabelle walk to a table at the other side of the dining area. Midge frowned, chewing the inside of her cheek.

"Here we go again," she grumbled. "I'd better whip out a couple of the real estate mogul specials for her highness."

They all stifled laughs as Midge returned to the grill, her temper worse than ever.

"Must be Lulu's house closing today," Gloria whispered.

"I knew she'd asked Isabelle for an earlier date," Theresa said.

"And has she said where's she's going?" Gracie asked the co-conspirators.

"No. Not a word to anyone. "However, now may be the perfect time," Theresa said, scraping back her chair.

Isabelle and Lulu looked surprised to see Theresa at their table, and Gracie slid into her mother's vacated chair for a better view. Everyone smiled, and all seemed quite pleasant.

Her mother was smooth, when she had to be. Gracie was afraid that smoothness would never be a skill she'd have, especially when it came to conversing with Isabelle. Her mother was masterful with Isabelle. Information gathering and keeping the peace were child's play for her. Minutes later, Theresa gave Gracie the sign to scoot back to her own chair.

"Well, what did she say?" Gloria put her elbows on the table and leaned toward Theresa. Gracie continued her mission to finish the now mini-sized treat.

"She's leaving on an extended trip to see America."

"Not Mexico? She didn't say anything about Mexico or Costa Rica?"

"No." Theresa shook her head and picked up her coffee cup.

"Hmm." Gloria's brow wrinkled as she leaned against the wicker-backed chair. "Will she be back?"

"She's thinking of settling in a warmer climate. Lulu's really tired of winter, or so she says."

"Florida then?"

Gracie washed down the last bit of doughy deliciousness with lukewarm coffee, listening to the women.

"I don't know. One would think. Florida is the logical choice if you want to live where it's warm. Everyone we know is down there for at least a month or two in the winter. There's the Wyoming County picnic in Kissimmee every year."

Gracie rolled her eyes. "Florida isn't the only place it's warm. She's apparently cutting her ties with Deer Creek, and she's not letting you in on her plans or the rest of the county either."

"She's the most frustrating woman I've ever known," Theresa complained. "We just tried to help her. Now I think she's holding a grudge against us."

A waitress scurried to Isabelle's table with two plates laden with quiche and fruit.

***

Gracie's heart was pounding when she saw the private jet touch down on the runway. Minutes later she was in Marc's arms, with Max's front legs on her back. She was the bologna in the sandwich at the moment. Finally disengaging from their 360 embrace, Marc slung his backpack over his shoulder, while Gracie took the restless shepherd's leash.

"You'd better let me handle him," Marc said. "Now that we're official partners, I'm not so sure he'll pay attention to you, after all we've done in the last three weeks."

Gracie handed the leash back to Marc, who gave Max a sharp tug. The dog settled and heeled without any verbal commands.

"Nice work," she said, observing the black-and-tan shepherd's cool demeanor. "He's always been a little much. Must be this was good for him."

"And for me too. I'll have my travel schedule in a couple of weeks. But I'll be around the house for about a week. I can't wait either. Let's go home."

Gracie hadn't heard a better offer in weeks.

***

Isabelle pounded the "For Rent" sign into the leaf-covered lawn. The thin metal rods sank easily into the damp ground. She straightened up and eyed her work, testing the sign's stability with her free hand, a mallet dangling from the other. Now, if she could snag renters for the Cook house before Christmas, she'd be happy. The roll-off next to the garage was full of construction debris from gutting the kitchen and bathrooms. With the renovations almost complete, there was no reason why the right people couldn't be living there before Thanksgiving. Maybe she'd advertise it as "Home for the Holidays." It had a nice ring to it. She wouldn't be so fortunate with the Walczak property. Reverend Minders seemed reluctant to move forward on accepting her offer.

Who else would want the property? He should be pleased as punch with her solid offer.

A Mini Cooper tootled down the street, making a quick stop in front of the Walczak house. Isabelle sucked in a breath. Adriana. What was *she* doing here?

The redhead quickly centered herself on the front lawn, a camera hanging from her neck. She crouched and took multiple shots of the house. Isabelle put the mallet in the cargo area of her SUV and walked across the street.

"Adriana! What a surprise! Another photo shoot? I thought you'd finished in Deer Creek."

The attractive woman stood and swung around to face Isabelle.

"Hi, Isabelle. Not another shoot. I have to finish one that was due last week. The historical magazine in Nunda wanted some outside shots of the old Stederman house to go along with the rest of the photos of the quilt. It's a good thing I took the quilt pictures early, now that it seems to have vanished." She peered down at the digital camera's display, checking her work.

"Stolen is what I hear."

Adriana nodded. "I'm skeptical of that, but I guess we'll never know. It's such a shame that it hasn't been recovered."

"I'm sure. I prefer china and glass myself. Maybe I should have you photograph it for insurance purposes."

Adriana bit her bottom lip and looked away.

"I'm sure you don't need my services for that." Adriana knelt on the ground and took another aspect of the house.

"Maybe not. You do know that this isn't the Stederman house. That's over on Butternut." A breeze ruffled Isabelle's blond hair, which fell into her eyes. Brushing it away, she buttoned up her coat.

"Oh no. I thought this was the place. What's the address?"

After precise directions were given and Adriana had driven off, Isabelle walked up the sidewalk to the front door and squinted through the yellowed lace curtains. The auction company had furniture items grouped and tagged for the sale coming in early November. Nothing of interest, naturally.

She turned to leave and saw Gloria Minder's car rounding the bend in the street. The small sedan parked, and Gloria practically jumped from the car.

"Oh, Isabelle. How are you?" she said breathlessly, as Isabelle went to meet her.

"Just fine. And yourself?"

"Running late. I was supposed to meet some photographer here."

"Adriana?"

"That's it. She took the pictures of Gracie's wedding. She wanted to see the inside of the house today."

"Why would she want to do that?" Isabelle's mouth twitched ever so slightly.

"A friend of hers may be interested in buying the property. She wanted a quick look around to see if it would be the right floorplan."

"Interesting."

"I hope I didn't miss her. Maybe she's behind schedule too." Gloria looked both ways down Oak Street, rubbing her hands together.

"Could be. I have a house to show myself. See you later."

She saw Gloria return to her car in the rearview mirror.

***

Gracie spread cruise brochures across the coffee table. Plunking herself on the sofa next to Marc, she said, "Five days is perfect, if you can get the time off."

"I don't think that'll be a problem, because of this training coming on the heels of our wedding." Marc leaned forward and thumbed through a colorful booklet.

"The Caribbean cruise sounds wonderful. Or we can do the Mexican Riviera one."

"Whatever you want to do is fine with me." Marc's cell jangled loudly, and he dropped the cruise information on the table. He hurried to the kitchen to take the call.

Gracie sighed, drawing her legs onto the leather sofa. He was already back to work after one day at home. Couldn't they have an uninterrupted conversation? She wasn't able to make out his muffled exchange. Although he kept his voice low, she could detect aggravation in his tone. Marc returned, carrying his phone, a scowl on his handsome face.

"Bad news?"

"No. Well, just annoying. I have to go into the office tomorrow to be briefed on the schedule. It shouldn't be all day though."

Gracie frowned, sliding her feet to the floor. He'd been promised a week of R & R.

"You don't need to say anything. I'm not happy about it either, but it's part of the job." Marc placed the iPhone on the coffee table. "Let's talk about cruises." He pulled her closer and kissed her.

"Or not," Gracie whispered, wrapping her arms around his neck.

***

Later they decided on the eastern Caribbean cruise. Gracie made the reservations on her tablet. She and Marc took off with the dogs for the field behind the house. It was fallow this year, with no corn crop to harvest. Haley plunged into the high grass, which was browning now that hard frosts hit every night. Max jumped in right behind her, while Marc and Gracie took their time. The two dogs clearly found the crisp air invigorating. Gracie was glad she'd added a knit cap and gloves with her jacket. Marc ran ahead, urging the dogs to race with him. Max easily pulled ahead of everyone, his tail waving. She laughed, jogging to catch up. Her heart was full. There was nothing like simple pleasures.

***

Kevin slung a dishtowel over his shoulder, jiggling the pan of sautéed onions, mushrooms, and peppers on the gas cooktop. Isabelle tossed a salad. She placed the wooden bowl on the table in the kitchen.

"Almost ready, beautiful," Kevin said, humming a tune.

"Good. I'm starved," Isabelle said, seating herself at the small round, claw-footed table.

"Steak all the way coming up."

The strip steaks, resting on the large cutting board, were swiftly served on white china plates.

Isabelle sliced into her tender steak and chewed thoughtfully, while Kevin poured dressing on his salad.

"Very nice," she commented.

"Thanks."

"I saw Adriana at the Walczak house today."

Kevin stopped mid-bite, dressing dripping from his fork.

"Oh."

"From what I understand, she wanted to see the house because a friend is interested in buying it."

"So?" He cut off a piece of steak and quickly popped it in his mouth.

"I find that odd myself. What friend would be interested in buying the Walczak house? It's not what I would call an exceptional property."

"If it's good enough for you," Kevin said, wiping his chin with a linen napkin, "it's good enough for a friend of Adriana's."

"I'm more interested in why she lied to me about being at the house. Said she was taking pictures for the magazine. Gloria Minders filled me in on the real reason she was there."

"You'd have to ask Adriana about that. I don't have any idea."

"Like you don't have any idea about my vases, which are still missing." Isabelle tossed her napkin on the table.

"I'll replace them. I don't know what happened to them. People are in and out of here all the time. One of your friends might be light-fingered."

"Or one of your friends might be a thief." Isabelle rose and stalked into the living room.

Kevin's expression darkened with anger. He pushed back the chair from the table. "You think Adriana stole the vases? Is that what you're implying?"

"If the shoe fits." Isabelle looked out the large picture window to the back lawn.

"Then ask her. I'll ask her, for that matter."

"Oh no, you don't!" she demurred with heat. "I think you've had way too much interaction with Adriana. The rumors about you and her are all over town."

"Is that right? Well, maybe they're true, and maybe they're not."

Isabelle turned around to face the angry man, her eyes blazing. "I think it's best if you leave. Tonight in fact. I want you out."

Kevin ran a hand through his short brown hair. "Fine."

CHAPTER 38

Isabelle plodded into the kitchen, filled the teakettle with water, and set it on the cooktop. Pulling out the French press, she measured two scoops into the glass container.

Her cell phone twinkled out a bright melody. Someone was texting her already. It had better not be Kevin. She ignored it, opting to wait for the water to boil and to watch the rain pummel the driveway. Rain was never good for open houses, and she had two today. She also wanted to pin down the good reverend on accepting her offer for the Walczak house. The desire to have it in her portfolio had doubled since learning Adriana was interested. She could have no reason other than the missing quilt. Maybe Isabelle would search for it herself. Wouldn't that be something if she discovered Franny Walczak's hiding place? Gracie couldn't top that one.

***

"Have you seen what Isabelle's doing with Lulu's house?" Theresa asked Gracie, holding a brown paper bag as she walked into the kennel office.

"I did. She's really spruced up the landscaping."

"A whole new kitchen and bathrooms. Of course, paint and carpets. Lulu wouldn't recognize it."

Gracie reached for the bag, hoping the contents were warm and sweet. "Is she still buying Franny's house?"

"I think there's a competing offer, from what Gloria says."

"Who would compete for that house?" Gracie had no idea why the shabby Victorian would be a hot property.

"Search me." Theresa poured herself a cup of coffee from the carafe on the table.

"Speaking of Lulu, have you heard anything from her?" Gracie pulled a warm muffin from the bag.

"Not a word. You were right. She intended to cut all ties with Deer Creek. I'm not sure why."

"Must be she's starting over somewhere. Somewhere warm, no doubt," she chuckled.

Theresa grimaced. "And probably not Florida."

Cheryl, the assistant kennel manager, knocked on the doorframe. She was dressed warmly in a turtleneck sweater, with an insulated vest and jeans.

"Did I hear you say that the Cook house has been remodeled?"

"Yes. I think Isabelle has a sign out already."

"Good. My lease is up at the end of year, and I really want to be in Deer Creek and not have to drive so much."

"I'll give you Isabelle's number," Theresa said, pulling her phone from her purse.

Cheryl looked at Gracie. "Would you go with me? I need another opinion, other than that of a teenager. My daughter doesn't want to change schools, but I'd rather have her in the Letchworth district. She has some friends I'd like to see disappear."

"Sure. As long as it's after hours. I'm swamped with grooming today."

***

The house immediately met with Cheryl's approval as well as Gracie's. Isabelle never disappointed ... when it came to renovating houses.

"Everything is really nice, Isabelle. I'd like to take it."

Cheryl was eager, and Isabelle had a pen already in her hand. The lease lay on the kitchen table.

"Let's go over the terms," Isabelle said, settling into a chair.

Gracie decided to take in some night air and slipped out the side door to the yard.

Walking across the grass, she noticed a flicker of light in the Walczak house. Someone was upstairs. She ran back into the house to find her phone.

"What's the matter?" Isabelle said irritably.

"There's someone in the house across the street. I saw a light in the window."

"You're not calling the police, are you?" Isabelle huffed.

"Of course, I am. Someone broke in. This is at least the second time." She dug through her bag, finally fishing out her phone.

"I have keys to the house. Pastor Minders gave them to me today. It's probably teenagers, looking for trouble."

"Isabelle. I wouldn't go over there by yourself. That's—"

"You can come with me."

Cheryl's eyes were wide. "I'm not going with you. I think you should call the police."

"Oh. You shouldn't go," said Isabelle. "Just read over this section of the lease and sign on the line below. I'll take a personal check for the deposit. We'll be right back."

Gracie had to admit Isabelle was cool under pressure. Business first. Marc would have a fit if she went with her cousin. However, if they didn't go in, they'd have to wait for the police. By then, whoever was in there would've probably flown the coop.

"All right. Let's go. Do you have something ... like ... like a weapon?" she stammered.

"I have pepper spray," Isabelle replied. "You never know what will happen when you're showing a house. Here's my extra for you."

She handed Gracie an aerosol tube. "Come on."

The back door of the house was already unlocked. They slipped in on tiptoe. A shuffling sound could be heard above. Isabelle made a shushing sound at Gracie. She nodded at her as they moved forward to the living room, where the stairway was located.

Uneven footsteps descended. Gracie's heart was beating double time. What in the world was she doing?

Isabelle switched on the overhead light. The footsteps stopped and then clumsily scurried back up.

"Whoever is here had better show himself now!" Isabelle demanded.

Her voice made Gracie feel a bit wobbly. Isabelle sounded like a stone cold killer. There was more scuffling, and then the odd-sounding footsteps came back down the stairs.

"Mr. Walczak. What are you doing here?" Isabelle asked coolly.

Art looked like a trapped weasel, lingering on the bottom step with a cane in his hand. He finally shambled into the room. A black walking boot encased his left foot.

"Franny had some of my stuff here. No one's wanted to let me have it, so I had to come off hours." He puffed up his chest, putting a thumb into the waistband of his work pants.

"I think not," Isabelle said. "My guess is that the missing quilt is really what you're after."

"Not a chance. It's gone. I'm here for my personal possessions."

Gracie had to give him credit. He was giving an outstanding performance to persuade Isabelle, but she was pretty sure it wouldn't work. The man had guilt written all over him.

"What possessions are you taking then? I see nothing in your hands."

"Well, I ... I ... I was just going out to get a box."

"From where? I don't see your truck around. And in your condition, I'd think you'd need assistance."

Gracie tried to keep from smiling. She glanced out to the street, which was empty. No vehicle was in the driveway either.

"Hadn't we better call the police now?" Gracie asked. No sense in prolonging the man's agony.

"Please don't call them. Please, I'm begging you!" Art wailed.

"Why shouldn't we call them? You broke in," Gracie stated matter-of-factly.

"No, I didn't. I have a key." With a shaking hand, he took a keyring out of his brown Carhartt coat pocket. "Here it is." The jumble of keys jangled as he held up a silver one.

Isabelle looked at him as though trying to decide how to torture him further. She licked her lips. "Let me see that keyring. Do you have keys to other houses?" Her eyes were narrowed like a cat about to pounce. "Like mine, by any chance?"

***

The floodgates of confession were opened wide for Art during Isabelle's grilling. He was like a gelatinous puddle after that experience. Gracie hated to see a man cry and escaped outside to make the call to the sheriff's department. Once the authorities arrived, Isabelle removed her house key from Art's ring and finished up business with Cheryl. This left Gracie to talk to the deputies.

Investigator Hotchkiss showed up, and after a brief conversation, instructed two deputies to give Art a free ride to the county jail. He'd stolen Isabelle's vases and a few other items of interest from some elderly customers. All the items were long gone. Sold to anonymous buyers, according to Art. He readily admitted his gambling problem, but would not utter one word about his fence or bookie. He also wouldn't say how he'd filched a key to Isabelle's house. His handyman and lawn service business allowed him intimate access to a lot of residences, but he'd been sparing in his thefts. No more than a couple of items per household. She calculated that his twisted altruism kept him under the radar. Pinching Isabelle's vases had given him an unwanted high profile. He'd taken a huge chance and lost.

"Mrs. Stevens," Investigator Hotchkiss said with a smile.

She was trim and professional in gray wool slacks and a white jewel-neck sweater. Her short brown hair, salted with white around her face, was quite becoming.

"Hi, Investigator," Gracie responded, realizing how strange it was to hear Stevens as her surname. Actually she'd kept Andersen to make the business side simple, but she wasn't going to correct the investigator.

"Oh, call me Emily. How's Marc's new job going?"

Gracie's eyebrows rose. This friendly persona of the investigator was a new one to her.

"Well, good. He's been really busy—training and all."

She didn't want to get into the strain of separation and how that would affect their marriage. Her mother was now very concerned about Marc's job.

"Those defense contractors have a pretty mobile work life," the investigator commented.

"I guess that's right. It's different, but I'm sure we'll adjust."

"He always has a job here, as long as I'm sheriff," she said, stepping closer. "If he thinks he's made a mistake."

Gracie felt like the policewoman had a bit of manipulation in mind. Red flags popped up immediately, warning her to stay far away from interfering with her husband's new job. Emily Hotchkiss wasn't sheriff yet. The undersheriff was acting sheriff, according to the newspapers, not her.

"You'd have to talk to him about that." Gracie inched away.

The offer was tempting to promote to Marc. He wouldn't be in foreign countries, trying to locate explosives for the security systems defense contractor.

"Have him give me a call if he wants to talk," the inspector said with a smile, as she took her leave.

***

Theresa and Gloria hustled through the kennel's reception area, making tracks for the office.

"Morning, Cheryl ... Trudy," they said in unison.

"Good morning," Cheryl and Trudy responded, smiling.

Gracie printed off the day's schedule and tossed it onto her desk. "Ladies. You're out and about early. What's up?" she asked, surprised to see them.

"We want to know the real scoop on Art," Theresa replied, pulling up one of the brown plastic chairs near Gracie's desk.

"Yes. All the details," Gloria pressed.

Gracie rubbed her forehead and sighed.

"It was his gambling problem, wasn't it?" Theresa continued. "And he actually had the nerve to steal from Isabelle?"

"Yes. Yes. Hold on. I'll be right back."

She stepped into the wide hallway and gave the schedule to Cheryl and Trudy. She could hear Jim whistling "Sittin' on the Dock of the Bay" down the corridor. A growing chorus of mournful howls joined him as backup.

"All right. I'm back." She sank into her desk chair and swiveled to face the women. "Sounds like you've heard just about everything. I don't think you need me."

"Well, Isabelle called the pastor last night and filled us in," Gloria began. "Then that lady investigator called. Is there anything else? Did he say anything about Lulu or to whom he's been selling those antiques?"

"Not while I was there. It's up to the sheriff's department now to find out what he's been doing. He'll probably lawyer-up ... if he's smart."

Gloria shook her silver head, pearl studs peeking from beneath her short hair. "I don't think he's very smart. More of a bully, in my book."

"He met his match last night." Gracie laughed. "It was downright embarrassing to see him collapse so easily under Isabelle's grilling."

"Serves him right," Theresa growled. "He's done nothing but lie, threaten, and now steal from people that have given him work and ... and ... and... It's no wonder Lulu left town. Maybe it's all because of him."

"All right, Mom. Calm down," Gracie admonished. "Granted, he's not a nice guy. He's cooling his heels in jail. Now, at least, the pastor can finish settling Franny's estate." She switched her gaze to the other militant-looking woman.

"Possibly," Gloria conceded. "Once the auction takes place, everything will be just about finished. My poor Albert. Between that awful cousin of Franny's and Art, it's been a nightmare!"

Gracie nodded in agreement. "I'm really sorry he's had such a mare's nest to handle."

"Well, we'd better go, Gloria," Theresa said, looking at her watch. "It's the sewing circle this afternoon."

The pair whooshed from the room, the scent of floral perfumes lingering in the air.

***

Jim walked with Gracie to the house, Haley leading the way with her ever-wagging tail. No rabbits or birds were present for her to chase.

"It's beef stew tonight and cornbread," she said.

"Sounds good to me. I'm tired of going to Midge's every night."

Gracie giggled. "But your girlfriend will miss you."

Jim grimaced. "She'll manage. Midge is always bringing me seconds. I don't need extra helpings anymore." He patted his stomach. "I'll bet Marc wasn't too happy about your encounter with Art last night."

"Well, he wasn't, but no harm no foul. Art certainly couldn't have done much to us, gimping around with that boot. I was perfectly safe with Isabelle. Her tongue is like a two-edged sword. He was cut to ribbons in seconds. I firmly believe he would have offered her a kidney if the police hadn't shown up when they did."

Marc's truck swung into the driveway, just as Gracie was opening the kitchen door. Max jumped out behind him, racing to see Haley.

"Jim's here for supper," she announced.

"Good."

Marc whistled for the dogs, and they bounded inside.

Jackets and hats were jammed on the coat rack, as noses savored the inviting aroma wafting from the bubbling crockpot of stew. While Marc fed the dogs, Gracie dished up dinner in large shallow bowls and piled a plate with squares of cornbread.

"After the briefings today, I'm ready for something hearty," Marc said.

"Pretty challenging job, by the sounds of it," Jim commented, taking a seat at the kitchen bar.

"It sure is. The weird thing is that Emily Hotchkiss called me today. Did she say anything to you last night about a job?"

Gracie had decided against mentioning the investigator's offer for fear it would seem like she was pressuring him to return to his old workplace.

"She did, but I wasn't going to bring it up. You've only been at DACO a few weeks."

"Yeah." Marc rubbed his jaw with the back of his hand.

"Are you thinking about it?" Gracie slid onto a stool with a butter dish in her hand. His expression was unreadable, his blue eyes staring at the bowl of steaming beef and vegetables.

"They probably really miss you." Jim grabbed a hunk of cornbread, and Gracie slid the butter dish down the counter toward him.

"Maybe," Marc responded absently. He looked up and grinned at Gracie. "Good news for us though. No travel until after the holidays. Just training and briefings in Batavia."

Relief washed over her. Maybe they'd have some normalcy in their schedule—at least for now.

CHAPTER 39

A cold November wind nipped at the crowd standing outside of Franny Walczak's house. A gray sky threatened with snow flurries. There were already a few flakes in the air. The auctioneer stood on a small platform in front of the porch steps, a headset strapped on his face. Theresa stomped her feet to encourage the circulation to her toes. Bob threaded his way through the crowd, a cup of coffee in each hand.

"Here you go," he said, handing her an insulated paper cup.

"It's black," Theresa complained.

"Oh. Sorry. I'll go fix it."

"No. The auction's about to start. This is fine."

She took a tentative sip. It was terrible, but very hot. Just the thing to take the chill off.

The auctioneer wasted no time in moving out the furniture and kitchen gear. The bidding seemed lackluster for the most part, but a small secretary's desk and a primitive sideboard brought a good price.

"Now, we have some linens. Very fine quality—vintage linens," the auctioneer crooned.

A few women pressed forward, positioning themselves for a better look. Theresa moved ahead, but Bob touched her elbow.

"You don't need more of that stuff, do you?"

"Well, maybe."

One of the assistants brought out several quilts and piled them on a table, next to the doilies and table runners.

"I might be interested in a quilt."

She stepped forward, noticing that the beautiful Jacob's ladder quilt Lulu had made was in the stack.

"What are you going to do with another bedspread?" Bob grumbled.

"Use it on a bed." She looked back at her husband and flashed him a determined smile. "I'd like a memento of Franny and of Lulu. It's one of Lulu's nicest quilts, and Franny used it on her own bed."

Bob shrugged in defeat. "Don't spend too much on it."

The bidding was surprisingly brisk on the linen and the quilts. A woman, in a dark green car coat and a black-and-white plaid scarf around her head, practically elbowed her way in front of Theresa. The young woman looked familiar. Theresa edged her way forward again, sneaking a look at the pushy female. She shouldn't have been surprised by the aggressiveness. She was quite sure it was Lisa Kronk, on the prowl for any family heirlooms that might be on the auction block.

Lisa's hand went up numerous times when the quilt bidding began. Two assistants held each one up for inspection. Three went to Lisa, who bid way above Theresa's price point. A couple of other women, seemingly very put out at Lisa's success, faded into the crowd.

Theresa wondered if there was any likelihood of winning the bid on the Jacob's ladder. The price of the quilt had almost reached beyond Theresa's range, when Lisa was distracted by a phone call, which caused a momentary lull in the bidding war.

The auctioneer declared it, "Sold! To the lady in the red coat!"

"Got it!" Theresa cried triumphantly.

She wove through the milling crowd to the cashier. Gathering the prize in her arms, she trudged back to Bob, who relieved her of the coverlet.

"Are you ready now?" he asked in a weary tone.

"I guess. Let's go," she said reluctantly.

The next quilt was pretty too, and the bidding was already underway. One was enough though.

***

The house was extremely quiet. Her children, now officially her adult children, Greg and Anna, wouldn't be back from college for another two weeks. With Kevin out of the house, they'd both agreed to return home for Thanksgiving and Christmas. Isabelle stood looking at the china cabinet, admiring her collection. She was still angry that her vases hadn't been recovered. Who would deal in stolen goods? How did one find out about that secretive marketplace?

She opened the cabinet doors and ran a finger over a pink jade dragon. It was cold to her touch. Everything was cold these days. There was no warmth in the house. No parties, no intimate dinners or gatherings. She hadn't felt like doing anything social. For as deceitful as Kevin had been, he was charming and good looking. He always knew what to say. He drank a little too much once in a while. Everyone has a weakness. Well, almost everyone. She, herself, was quite disciplined.

She missed him terribly. Maybe she would call him. She froze at the thought. He had humiliated her. What was she doing? Closing the door, she went to the foyer for her coat. She'd take a drive somewhere.

Just as she opened the door, the mailman drove up to the mailbox and thrust in a pile of letters and a large manila envelope. Deciding to peruse the mail first, she gathered the load, retreating into the house.

The large envelope was from the *Historic Homes* magazine. Her issue at last! Sliding the glossy periodical from the tattered wrapping, she thumbed the pages and found the article with the photo spread. Although Adriana had proven to be an adversary, Isabelle had to admire the woman's camera skills. The rooms looked magnificent, especially with the lighting and the different perspectives. Turning the page, she looked twice at the full spread photo. Her French vases were arranged on the sofa table with masses of cut flowers and greenery draped over the edge, the rays of the afternoon sun filtering dreamily over the southern side of the living room. It was a gorgeous setting that hadn't been in the galley proofs.

She felt like she'd been slapped. That malicious cow! There was no doubt in her mind with whom Art Walczak had worked.

As she expected, Adriana didn't answer her phone. Kevin, however, did.

"Did you know that Adriana was complicit in taking my vases?"

"Huh? Hello, Isabelle."

"Your cupcake was working with Art Walczak."

"I have no idea what you're talking about." Kevin's voice was gruff. "As you've made quite clear, you and I are no longer together."

"We aren't. Did you give Adriana or Art a key to the house?"

Silence reigned.

Isabelle twisted her mouth in anger before speaking again. "Which one?"

"Adriana needed to get in one afternoon when you weren't available. I gave her the extra one you keep in the kitchen drawer."

Isabelle stalked into the airy kitchen with its white cabinetry, a mix of glass and solid doors. Opening the drawer next to the sink, she found that the extra house key was, indeed, not in its place. It must still be on her keyring when she'd taken it from Art. She had forgotten about that until now.

"And she gave it to Art, who took my vases. Now, why would she do that?"

"I don't know what game you're playing, but count me out," Kevin said sullenly. "I guess I forgot about the key. I had no idea she'd hand it off to the yard guy, if that's true."

"Is she there with you? I want to talk to her."

"She's not."

"Where is she?"

"I have no idea. Haven't heard from her in weeks."

Isabelle ended the call and searched her handbag, which sat on the counter, for Investigator Hotchkiss' business card.

***

Theresa unfolded the quilt on the dining room table, showing the fine stitching to Gracie. Marc and Bob were watching college football. The aroma of homemade pizza filled the house.

"Nice, Mom. I'm glad you won the bidding. Sounds like it was pretty competitive."

"If I'd had to bid two more dollars, I couldn't have saved it from the clutches of the lady in the green coat, who bought three others. I'm pretty sure it was Franny's cousin—the pushy one I told you about, who wanted the Stederman quilt. It was a good thing she got a phone call right before she bid again. I squeaked through because she was distracted. It seemed like she was on a mission to buy all of them."

Gracie fingered the soft material and lifted the corner. "It is very nice. Pretty heavy, isn't it? Which bedroom are you going to use it in?"

"The guest bedroom next to the stairs."

"That'll work."

Gracie turned it over and examined the backing. She'd never have the patience to piece together rectangles and squares of fabric, never mind arranging them in an actual pattern. A loose red thread on one end caught her eye.

"Better trim this, or something will come apart."

She gave the thread a gentle tug.

Theresa put on her reading glasses, which lay on the sideboard. "Oh rats! Let me see."

She examined the long thread, which led her to the edge of the coverlet.

"It's just a whipstitch on this. Lulu would never do that kind of sloppy work."

"Maybe she was just in a hurry." Gracie sniffed. "I think that pizza's done. I'll take it out."

Theresa nodded and looked at the seam again. Something about it struck her as odd.

"What a minute," she whispered, her mind churning. "What if…?"

With a sharp intake of breath, Theresa hurried to the kitchen and grabbed a pair of small scissors from the junk drawer.

"It's done," Gracie called out, setting a rectangular pan on the grates of the stovetop. The thick crust piled with sausage, pepperoni, mushrooms, and peppers made her stomach growl. "Everyone help themselves."

She grabbed the pizza cutter from the counter and began slicing large squares.

"Gracie, get in here!" her mother yelled.

Her urgent tone sent Gracie racing back to the dining room, pizza cutter still in hand.

"What? What's wrong?" she gasped.

Theresa peeled the backing off the quilt and revealed the extraordinarily fragile, but intact Stederman quilt!

***

Investigator Hotchkiss took Isabelle's statement, nodding over her notebook as she wrote.

"Do you have an address for Adriana Reynolds?" she asked.

"It's right here on this card."

Isabelle slid the colorful business card across the granite countertop.

"Geneseo. Oh."

"Is there a problem?"

"Well, yes. She lives in Livingston County, so I'll have to contact the sheriff's office there."

Isabelle sighed impatiently. "As long as someone finds her. I'm sure she was the one working with Art Walczak, as I said on the phone."

She ran her hand over the glossy magazine photo of her living room, still shocked to see her stolen vases on display. Adriana certainly had a twisted and unwelcome sense of humor.

"We'll do our best," the investigator assured her.

She snapped the notebook closed. A startling ring shook her cell phone, which lay on the counter.

"Hello." The woman's brow furrowed as she listened to the call. "A *what*? A quilt?" Her tone was incredulous. "At the Clark residence ... No, I don't need directions. I know where they live ... Okay."

Isabelle's eyes widened, watching her reaction.

"I don't mean to pry, but was that call about the Stederman quilt, by any chance?"

"I really couldn't say, ma'am," Hotchkiss replied, her face a blank. "I'll be in touch as soon as we locate Ms. Reynolds."

The investigator took her leave. Isabelle stared after her, her face thoughtful.

***

Raucous barking made it hard to hear. Gracie shut the office door against the din. Two agitated boarders had taken up a barking contest, egging everyone else on.

"Jeepers creepers, Jim! We need to put those two in separate corridors," Gracie said.

"I know. I'll take Maestro, the coonhound, to the "C" section. The population is low in that one. I think the old basset in there is practically deaf anyway."

Gracie shook her head and chuckled. "Sounds like a good plan."

The door swung open, and Isabelle steamrolled through, a grim smile creasing her airbrushed makeup.

"What a surprise! What brings you out to Milky Way?" Gracie asked, wondering why in the world her cousin would be making an appearance.

"I'm on my way to Geneseo, and I wondered if you knew where your mother is."

"I have no idea. Didn't you call her?"

"Of course, I did. But her phone seems to be turned off, and no one is answering at home."

Jim gave Gracie a miniscule wave and slipped out the door.

"She's probably with Gloria somewhere," Gracie offered, glaring after him. "Why are you so keen to track down Mom?"

"Oh. Well, I was talking with the sheriff's investigator last night, and she took a call ..."

Gracie sat down at her desk, motioning for Isabelle to take a seat.

"I'll stand, thank you," Isabelle said, giving the chair a disgusted glance.

"You want to know about the Stederman deal. Is that it?" Gracie zeroed in on the actual subject of her cousin's prying visit.

Isabelle's face softened. "I was curious, since it appears that Adriana helped Art Walczak steal my French vases."

Gracie was certain Isabelle exaggerated the "ah" for effect. "Did she have something to do with the quilt as well?"

Gracie leaned forward, her hands splayed on the desktop. "Adriana did *what?*" she asked in astonishment.

An exchange of information quickly passed between the cousins. It was quite satisfactory, from Gracie's point of view. She reckoned that focusing on the misdeeds of third parties, rather than on each other, might help the conversation pass amicably ... for once.

"I wondered why Adriana hadn't sent any more wedding photos. I've tried calling her for days. I probably won't see any more if she's on the run."

Isabelle sniffed, finally deciding to sit down on the grungy chair. "Possibly. If the police do their jobs properly, she should be sitting in a cold, lonely cell very soon."

"At least she sent me a good sampling from the wedding."

"My vases will probably never be recovered. You know, they were an anniversary gift. Expensive with a great deal of sentimental value."

Gracie sighed. Back to transmitting on different frequencies. Situation normal, she thought, doing a mental eye-roll at Isabelle's self-centered rant.

There was a scratch at the door. Gracie opened it for Haley, who went straight to Isabelle and laid a wet muzzle on her skirt.

"Get away, you awful dog! You're all wet!" she shrieked.

Isabelle shoved the black Lab away, abruptly standing and brushing at the wet marks on the beige skirt.

"Haley, go to your bed," Gracie commanded.

The dog moped to the green cushion, flopping down with a dejected look. Leave it to Haley to ruin a momentary truce.

"Where does this leave you and Kevin?" Gracie just had to ask, now that their "magic moment" was shot.

"We're working things out," Isabelle said evenly, tightening her grip on her metallic-colored designer handbag. "We're taking a trip next week."

"Really? Any place special?"

Isabelle smiled, smoothing her already perfect coiffure. She tucked a strand of hair behind her ear, revealing sapphire and diamond earrings. A makeup present from Kevin perhaps was Gracie's conjecture.

"Belize."

Gracie's eyebrows shot up. Isabelle had to be crazy to give Kevin another chance. Deciding on the spot not to offer any relationship advice, she instead shared her own plans. They were pretty good ones.

"Marc and I are taking a cruise of the eastern Caribbean in the spring. You know, Aruba, the Bahamas. We have several ports of call."

"Oh, you'll love it. I've taken that cruise several times." Isabelle's tone was imperious.

Truce well and truly kaput. The competition was on again.

***

Gloria and Theresa walked slowly behind Albert to the car. The quilt had been officially transferred to the Stederman family without incident. Gloria felt as if she could breathe again. A rather subdued Lisa Stederman Kronk had actually been polite and even friendly today. Maybe her attorney had given her some pointers.

"I wish Lulu was still around," Theresa said wistfully.

"I know. She would have some closure about that silly quilt."

The woman got into Theresa's small sedan, while Albert drove off to complete his hospital calls. Two parishioners were flat on their backs at Wyoming County Community Hospital. One with pneumonia, the other with an infected toe.

"Shall we go home?" Theresa asked, turning the ignition.

"I'm taking the rest of the day off," Gloria declared. "This estate of Franny's has been nothing but drama. Poor Albert! He hasn't caught a break until now. Hopefully, the worst is over."

"It must be. I just wish I knew where Lulu went. Isn't that the strangest thing?"

CHAPTER 40

The sand was warm under her feet, the foamy azure water receding as she padded down the beach. For the first time in over a year, Lulu was happy. Really happy. Her loose, gauzy beach cover-up blew softly against her skin. If she were in Deer Creek, she'd be bundled up to her chin in clothes. She reached the small table under a yellow-striped umbrella, joining a darkly-tanned man in sunglasses. His gray hair was long and tied back in a ponytail. He stood and kissed her. They both sank into webbed chairs. A waiter appeared almost immediately with tall glasses of sangria.

"I still can't believe I'm here," Lulu said, taking a sip of the fruity drink.

"Believe it, babe. Everything worked out perfectly." The man slid his sunglasses to the top of his head.

"Not everything. Franny would have loved it here."

"That was really unfortunate, but it's in the past. Let's focus on the present, all right?" He leaned forward and took Lulu's hands.

"Right. No looking back."

"We head to Roatan in a couple of days. The house will be ready by then. Honduras is perfect. We can live it up, better than we ever could've in the U. S."

"I can't wait to see it."

"You'll love it. And the best part is that it's all paid for, thanks to your sewing skills and my planning." He flashed a broad grin, taking the straw from the glass and gulping down the drink.

Lulu closed her eyes, remembering the days of gut-wrenching grief after the accident, and the constant fear the subterfuge of stashing rolled-up cash in the quilts for the orphanage would be discovered by her friends, the postal authorities, or the orphanage staff. Piling all that stuff in the house had given her a sense of safety. She couldn't even tell Franny everything. Just that they'd take a trip to Central America when the insurance money had come in for her.

"You were lucky the quilts got there. I'll never figure out how you were able to work at the orphanage."

He batted at the air with a careless hand, a satisfied look on his lean face. "It wasn't hard. I remembered you talking about it when you were helping the place with the church group. I showed up with my new ID and offered to lend a hand. The administrator was buried in work, and I was a volunteer, after all. He gave me a place to lay my head, and I took care of the books. Even the American-run places need free help. I had to learn how to use a seam ripper and sew myself. That was the hard part. Picking up the mail was easy. Setting up our new accounts was easy too. Foreign banks ask a lot fewer questions than American ones."

Lulu bit her lip. "But, Ed, the guy in your truck. I still wonder about his family. You didn't ..."

"It's Rick, Lulu. You can't keep calling me Ed."

"I'm sorry. But it's hard to remember."

"Just focus, Lulu. I didn't kill him. He was already gone when I found him on a trail near the cabin. No ID. There was no vehicle anywhere around other than my truck. He must have been a transient of some kind. He was the answer to my problem. I didn't know what I was going to do, until I stumbled on him."

"But Ed ... Rick, it was terrible for me. When you called me six months after the funeral, I almost had a heart attack myself."

He reached over and stroked her cheek with the back of his hand. The lapping of the ocean steadied her jangled nerves, and she offered Ed a weak smile.

"Oh, babe. I know. I'm so sorry about that. It was the only way. After thirty years of service, the company was going to downsize my position into extinction. Without any consideration for what I'd done for them." His voice grew bitter. "I deserved everything that was coming to me. We got it all. The life insurance, the pension that comes to you now—everything."

It was true. Ed had been shattered when the news had come down from the top that the reorganization would eliminate several executives at the higher end of the pay scale. He'd taken off for an early fishing trip to get his head together. When she'd seen two New York State troopers at her door, she'd known something terrible had happened. She didn't want to ask how Ed had changed his identity to Richard Talbot. He had a full set of identification papers with a U. S. passport. Now they were free. She could continue to collect Ed's pension, and the generous life insurance proceeds had been transferred to an offshore account. Her own retirement accounts, along with house proceeds, would be handled by the island bank as well. No worries. No looking back. They would be comfortable the rest of their lives—in a new life, a tropical one at that, which suited her just fine. There would be no visits to Deer Creek. She was a different person herself. She lifted her glass, a slice of orange sloshing at the rim.

"To new adventures, Rick."

***

Isabelle thought the profiles of the man and woman under the umbrella-shaded table were familiar. The sunglasses and beach clothing gave her pause. The woman's floppy hat hid a portion of her face, but the nose was … was Lulu Cook's. That was impossible. Lulu was touring the United States. At least, that's what she'd said. Was the man her new love interest? He had long hair and seemed quite fit. She looked hard at the man who seemed very interested in the woman facing him. If she didn't know better, she would swear that it was Ed Cook. He was thinner and older than she remembered. It couldn't be, could it? He was dead. Her eyes must be playing tricks on her. Yes. That was it, and maybe one too many drinks today. Her mind was just a little fuzzy.

Kevin blocked her view, bending to hand her an icy mojito.

"Need anything else, beautiful?"

His lips brushed her cheek before she settled back into the low-slung beach chair. The sun was delicious on her skin. Kevin had been so attentive. She didn't need to think about anything remotely related to Deer Creek, especially the Cooks. She sipped the citrusy drink and leaned back, stretching her legs out to catch every tanning opportunity. Gracie would be envious of her golden glow when they were together for Thanksgiving.

Thank you for taking the time to read **Pins & Needles**. If you enjoyed it, please consider telling your friends or posting a short review. Word of mouth is an author's best friend and much appreciated. Thank you. –Laurinda Wallace

ABOUT THE AUTHOR

Laurinda Wallace lives in the beautiful high desert of southeast Arizona where the mountains and fabulous night skies inspire risk taking. A native of Western New York, she loves writing about her hometown region including Letchworth State Park. A lifelong bookworm and writer, she made her foray into the publishing world in 2005. She's contributed to a variety of print and online magazines, and along the way created the Gracie Andersen mysteries, and more.

Visit **www.laurindawallace.com** for more information and be sure to sign up for the Mystery Mavens Society. Subscribers receive free short stories and insider book news. Your email is never shared or sold.

OTHER BOOKS BY LAURINDA WALLACE

Gracie Andersen Mysteries

Family Matters

By the Book

Fly By Night

Washed Up

Pins & Needles

The Mistletoe Murders

True-Crime Memoir

Too Close to Home: The Samantha Zaldivar Case

Inspirational Books

The Time Under Heaven
Gardens of the Heart

Historical Fiction Short Story

The Murder of Alfred Silverheels

Historical Mystery

The Disappearance of Sara Colter

Made in United States
Orlando, FL
04 March 2023

30675725R00152